A Voyage to Pagany

WILLIAM CARLOS WILLIAMS

With an Introduction by Harry Levin

A NEW DIRECTIONS BOOK

Library of Congress Catalog Card Number: 76-122108

Harry T. Levin's Introduction was first published under the title "William
Carlos Williams and The Old World" in *The Yale Review*, Volume LIX,
Summer 1970.

Manufactured in the United States of America
First published clothbound and as New Directions Paperbook 307 in 1970
Published simultaneously in Canada by McClelland & Stewart Ltd.

New Directions Books are published for James Laughlin
by New Directions Publishing Corporation,
333 Sixth Avenue, New York 10014.

To
the first of us all
my old friend
EZRA POUND
this book is affectionately
dedicated

Contents

III. THE RETURN

APPENDIX

Introduction

The Atlantic Ocean has tended to act as a magnetic field for American writers, no two of whom have come to quite the same terms with those cultures on the other side. Critics like to polarize their problems into such dichotomies as High-brow/Lowbrow, Paleface/Redskin, Virgin/Dynamo. But simplification is hazardous because the presence of Europe has so pervaded our background that the stance of every significant writer has been affected by it in some way or other. Whitman's reaction, to be sure, was at odds with Longfellow's response. Yet the strongest testimony has been lodged *a fortiori*, not by professed cosmopolites like Henry Adams or committed expatriates like Henry James but by local colorists like Irving, who celebrated Old Spain and Merry England as fervently as the Hudson River Valley and the western fur trade, or peripatetic regionalists like Cooper, who vainly sought to turn from Leatherstocking to European romances. It was through the grand tour chronicled in *The Innocents Abroad* that Mark Twain emerged as the humorous voice of America. Most of Hemingway's fiction, which the world accepts as the exemplification of a strenuous Americanism, takes place on foreign soil. This transatlantic impetus reached its fullest intensity with the artistic movement that surfaced after the first World War. Its impatient manifesto was a symposium of thirty intellectuals, edited by Harold Stearns and published in 1922 under the heavily ironic title, *Civilization in the United States*. Its inevitable break-up, under the economic and political pressure of the Nineteen-Thirties, was indicated twelve years afterward by Malcolm Cowley in his journalistic memoir, *Exile's Return*.

Meanwhile all sorts and conditions of Americans, dough-boys and playboys, gold-diggers and prophetesses, loners and joiners, businessmen and bums as well as bohemian artists, had been making a continental sojourn, or at least a trip. Merely to list a small handful of titles and dates would be to suggest at how many levels this had become a part of the national experience: *Three Soldiers* (1921), *The Enormous Room* (1922), *Mr. and Mrs. Haddock Abroad* (1924), *Gentlemen Prefer Blondes* (1925), *The Sun Also Rises* (1926), *Dodsworth* (1929), *Eimi* (1933), *The Autobiography of Alice B. Toklas* (1933), *Of Time and the River* (1935), *Nightwood* (1936). The point of convergence for these various pilgrimages would be what was then the world's capital of the arts. Someone has told the hero of the book that lies before us: "You know, dear, all good Americans go to Paris when they die, and we are dead, as far as they over there are concerned." To which his interior monologue frames a reply: "Yes, but are we good?" Having been there twice before, he clearly realizes that its touted frivolity is "America, not France." For the serious artist, if not for the *flaneur* of Montparnasse, Paris looks beyond the pleasure principle—here Freud is echoed in the original German. On the verge of his return, the pilgrim hails France as the "blessed home of all wanderers." But he is not at heart a wanderer, any more than William Carlos Williams himself, who managed to live within a half-mile of his birthplace for nearly all of his eighty years (1883-1963).

A Voyage to Pagany is the fictional reminiscence of a rare interlude during that firmly rooted existence, so much of it devoted to the practice of pediatrics and general medicine in the middle-class community of Rutherford, New Jersey, not far from the dreary industrial town whose epic he composed in *Paterson*. The paradox of his career was strengthened by the mixed strain of his parentage. From his mother, who seems to have exercised the greater influence on him, he inherited both Spanish and French blood. His English father, who had traveled widely in Latin America, never gave up British citizenship. Young Bill spent his fifteenth year in Switzerland, in the school at the Château de Lancy near Lake Geneva that he mentions here. During the following year in Paris he was privately tutored, since his French turned out to be inadequate for the Lycée Condorcet. As a medical student at the University of Pennsylvania, he contracted his lifelong friendship with Ezra Pound, then pursuing his graduate studies in Romance Languages. Theirs was a complementary relationship, sustained on both sides by personal affection and mutual respect, though they would be moving in opposite directions: Pound abroad on his quest for the spirit of romance, Williams homeward to push his own roots deeper into the soil along the Passaic River. It is not hard to read Williams' position between the lines of Pound's letters over the years; even the burlesque Americanese of the expatriate seems to mock the convictions of the nativist. "You'd better come across and broaden your mind (1909)" has its dialectical counterthrust in "I note your invitation to return to my fatherland (1917)."

If there is a touch of asperity in that last remark, it is because Pound, with "the virus . . . of nearly three bleating centuries" in his veins, was haughtily retorting to an American of the first generation. "And America! What the hell do you a bloomin' foreigner know about the place?" Williams has not even been west of the Maunchunk (N.J.) switchback. This letter was quoted in the polemical prologue to *Kora in Hell*, where the London expatriates are consigned to Williams' private inferno and Pound is singled out as "the best enemy United States verse has." In a subsequent letter Pound elaborated his clinical metaphor: Williams has avoided the endemic blood-poisoning because he had "the advantage of arriving in the milieu with a fresh flood of Europe in [his] veins." For his own part, from the first, he had criticized Pound's "unconstrained vagabondism." His correspondent, recoiling from the early constraints of Idaho and Indiana, was heading for the center, was putting himself in touch—indeed in command— of what he would later call "a live tradition." The real eccentric was the "dago immigrant" ("Finest possible specimen of course," Pound genially added), since he chose to stay behind and play the "old village cut-up." Williams, scientifically trained, approached his experimental objectives directly, and feared that those bookish courses which Pound pursued and prescribed would lead back to academic conventionality. In any case, the exile recognized that the hyphenated descent of his friend made him an authentic spokesman for the realities of *Patria Mia,* such as they were. From Paris, in 1922, he wrote to Rutherford:

> *. . . I don't really believe you want to leave the U.S. permanently. I think you are suffering from nerve; that you are really afraid to leave Rutherford. I think you ought to take a year off or a six months' vacation in Europe. I think you are afraid to take it, for fear of destroying some illusions which you think necessary to your illusions. I don't think you ought to leave permanently, your job gives you too real a contact, too valuable to give up.*

Williams took up Pound's challenge, arranging a sabbatical leave from his practice. He was busy writing in New York during the last six months of 1923. Thence he and his wife embarked for Europe on January 9, 1924; they would disembark from their homecoming voyage on the twentieth of the following June. He sums it all up in his *Autobiography* as a "magnificent year," and its European itinerary would furnish the framework for *A Voyage to Pagany.* When the book appeared, it would be loyally dedicated to Pound, "the first of us all"—a vernacular counterpart for Eliot's dedication of *The Waste Land* to "*il miglior fabbro.*" But, significantly, *A Voyage to Pagany* did not appear for four years; the immediate consequence of the journey was the renewed commitment of *In the American Grain.* D.H. Lawrence had recently brought out his seminal *Studies in Classic American Literature,* stimulating American writers and critics in their perennial search for a usable past. There was no flag-waving or eagle-screaming in Williams' rediscoveries among the explorers, the settlers, the founding fathers, and other predecessors. Mencken could not have been sharper in attacking "the inevitable Coolidge platform." Williams sometimes waxes apocalyptic, as he looks beyond the blandness of American life to "its—horrible temper," beyond its technological achievement to its "gross know-nothingism," beyond the puritanical inhibition to the lawless violence. From his six weeks in Paris he recalls a congenial dialogue with Valery Larbaud. Though the French had been much more humane than the English to the Indians, their colonies had failed because of their Latin sense of history. America's strength is its break with the past, Europe's weakness.

The Great American Novel—a parody of the genre, like the preliminary efforts of so many novelists—was written just before Williams' *Wanderjahr*, and is more intransigently nationalistic: "Europe's enemy is the past. Our enemy is Europe." *In the American Grain*, coming subsequently, illustrates with historical *collage* and critical commentary "the battle to establish a European life in the New World." Hence it may be read as a sequel to *A Voyage to Pagany*, wherein a copy of it retrospectively figures as "a keepsake." Its final emphasis, on grounds of immediacy rather than patriotism, is "Here not there." But the interaction would continue, prompting Williams to his brief sortie in the wake of Pound, his own exploration of "there," *là-bas*, Pagany. The collective name that he chose for Europe, though it had scarcely been repeated since the sixteenth century, was appropriate for his purposes. Pagans had originally been dwellers in rural villages; the early Christians used the term at Rome for those who still practised idolatry; more neutrally, a *paganus* was a person who did not share the prevailing beliefs. This relative concept could be reversed, as would be demonstrated in 1930–2 by the publication in Boston of the little magazine, *Pagany: A Native Quarterly*, with Williams as a leading contributor and nativism as its literary program. The novel charts a return, via "old Pagany," to primal forces antedating both Europe and America. The central section, "At the Ancient Springs of Purity and Plenty," seeks to revive a sense of power and beauty through communion with "a resurgent paganism, still untouched." Long obscured by Christianity, and by the Renaissance, the pagan gods survive as stone images in the cathedrals.

In the *Autobiography* Williams speaks of *A Voyage to Pagany* as "my first (limping) novel." Since the junket of a husband and wife would hardly make much of a story, he decided to romanticize his material. In *I Wanted to Write a Poem*, based on a series of interviews with him by Ethel Head, he describes the genesis of the book more fully. It was composed at Rutherford as usual, albeit in the absence of Mrs. Williams and their two sons, who were then attending his old Swiss school. A laconic diary from 1924 served to nudge his memory and tap his imagination. "The protagonist was, of course, myself; his experiences, in a measure mine." Thus Dr. Evans, a forty-year-old physician from "the New Jersey town of P. where he was born," and born of immigrant stock, wants more than anything else to be a writer. "Loaded up with Americana—his love of America," he believes that Europe is "turning pagan." Since he is travelling alone, the actual Floss Williams —devoted companion, "the rock on which I have built," whose German-Norwegian parentage balanced her husband's admixture of bloods—has dropped out of the overt picture. Nonetheless, "the women figures in the story were frequently my conception of my wife," Williams confessed. And even more intimately: "There are other women, women the American might have desired to go to bed with, sometimes a woman whose face had registered in my mind, a woman out of the crowd." One of his unconformable sonnets may epitomize Floss's role:

> *With one woman*
> *I find all the rest . . .*

On the other hand, few writers can have delivered so many babies, or have acquired so special a feeling for the moods and phases of womanhood. Elsewhere, again in the *Autobiography*, he tells us: "Men have given a direction to my life and women have always supplied the energy." In the novel his surrogate has already determined upon a direction, but the women help him to test the alternatives and confirm his resolution with their respective energies—and with his resistance to them. A study of Williams' groping plays, *Many Loves* and *A Dream of Love*, might throw further light on the relation of his marriage to his fantasies.

If Eros does not personally intervene in the narration, which is so susceptible to her sway, it is because she has been deliberately exorcised. The publisher thought that the manuscript was too long, Williams frankly told his interviewer. Accordingly, the author decided to cut out "the best chapter in the book" and to publish it separately as a short story. It is entitled "The Venus," and would have come at the novel's midpoint.* There the goddess is invoked through the painting of Botticelli and the statue from Cyrene; the invocation is heard as a verbal *Leitmotif,* but our Tannhäuser has definitely left this particular Venusberg behind. The tale, when we take it up, proves to be slight and poignant. It involves a beautiful blonde German girl who is staying at the same *pensione* with Evans in Rome, "the little *fräulein,* " "the Cyprian," with whom in the novel he has no chance to speak. In the story there is a conversation between them, little more, while they wander off from an excursion to the antiquities at Frascati. With Teutonic earnestness she raises the question: "What then is it like, America?" How can he explain what he himself, a kind of refugee, has been puzzling over? By contrast, the United States "seems less encumbered with its dead." He can show her a flint arrowhead, and she is momentarily attracted to the notion that Americans are almost savage, "not quite civilized." But the ultimate prospect seems "even more lonesome and frightening . . . than in Germany." Daughter of a Prussian general, resigned to taking her vows and becoming a nun, she too has considered and rejected the alternative world to her own.

Williams returned to the theme in one of his finest poems, "The Birth of Venus," which opens with a nostalgic glimpse of the Parade Grounds at Villefranche—the well remembered vista from his travels that reappears in both the *Autobiography* and *A Voyage to Pagany.* Now it is too late: "we / are not there." The sensory values of love, though reaffirmed, are harrowed by the negations and deprivations of war. Aphrodite, buried or in exile, has played an elusive part in latterday fiction. Exhumed, she takes a stern revenge on a loveless bridal pair in Mérimée's *Vénus d'Ille.* In the guise of the Venus de Medici she fascinated Hawthorne, who evokes her image to symbolize the underground passions of *The Marble Faun.* One might have expected the anti-puritan Williams, in a volume contemporaneous with *Lady Chatterley's Lover,* to

*"The Venus" is added to this edition as an appendix.

have advanced the subject somewhat farther. But if Venus is the personification of that chthonic force which his traveller seeks in Pagany, then it must be said that either she eludes him or else he evades her. She has incarnated the artist's goal: "striving to cut between the show and the fact, . . . undeceiving, living—shedding fig leaves." Williams was once persuaded to hold forth publicly on the novel ("a form I have never respected"). Perhaps his disrespect colored his theories. His appeal to Carlyle's philosophy of clothes was more than metaphorical, since novels have so much to do with external appearances; and, of course, it has been their classic function to expose the actualities beneath. For Williams, however, the novel is little more than "a strip-tease"; only the poem can lay bare the nudity of things.

Figures of speech have their limits, and this one would never do to characterize the works of the major novelists. Yet it might help to distinguish between Williams' poetry, where he plays the realist (his word would be "objectivism" or "contact"), and the present novel, which—as he owned—"turned out to be much more romantic than I'd intended." The novels located on his own terrain, *White Mule* and *In the Money,* like most of his stories, would be unequivocally realistic. In *A Voyage to Pagany* little is made of the novelistic opportunities for characterization, observation of manners, or human relationships. Its burden is reflective and highly subjective, paying less heed to the impressions it gathers than to the impressionist who blends them in with his thoughts—thoughts on art, in the main, and its interconnection with the two hemispheres. "Florence, city of makers," of artists *par excellence,* inspires a meditation on the banks of the Arno, while the river itself, in continuous self-renewal, seems to be the prototype of art. "Reality, romance: it sums up, to make." All novels have combined the two components in varying proportions; the modicum of romance in *A Voyage to Pagany* stands out rather self-consciously because it has been superimposed upon a spontaneous flow of autobiographical reality. Our identification with the problems and preoccupations of Dev (Dr. Evans-Williams) is all but complete. Evans recounts details which Williams remembered specifically from 1924: for

instance, the three smiling Japanese tourists at Notre Dame
or the joyous walk from Eze to Monaco. The get-together
with the *avant-garde* really happened, and the character of
Jack Murry was modelled on the Left Bank impresario, Rob-
ert McAlmon.

Williams did not aspire to be a Baedeker, and his topograph-
ical descriptions are often impressionistic to the point of dis-
tortion. When he calls the Santa Croce a cathedral, he is
confusing it with the Duomo, and the confusion is triply
confounded when he descries within it the tombs of Dante
(buried at Ravenna) and of the Medici (adjoining San
Lorenzo). Poet though he be, Dev is equally the compatriot
of philistines like Sam Dodsworth, Mr. Haddock, and the
excursionists of Mark Twain's *Quaker City.* The Forum leaves
him cold; he is homesick in Venice; and when he tries to visit
Ferney, "old home of the divine philosopher" (Voltaire), the
house is closed and the gates are bolted. Nonetheless, like
Gershwin's *American in Paris,* he responds with a peculiar
zest to whatever comes within his wave-length. His appreciation of a particularly fastidious sequence of French wines is
voiced by an indelibly American exclamation: "Wow!" The
beer in Switzerland makes him worry about Prohibition at
home. It is not surprising that, during his first night in Paris,
he dreams of Walt Whitman. Leaves of grass, he discovers on
a picnic by the Seine, can be symbols here as well as there.
He is immeasurably more concerned with living humanity
than with its historical monuments. At Carcassonne his attention wanders from the uninhabited fortress and its medieval
legends to the modern settlement at its base, which is not so
far removed from New Jersey after all. "People live here!
Good God. And they are happy and they sent soldiers to the
great war." People, with the consistent exception of Jews
encountered on trains, draw out warm sympathies from him
wherever he goes.

This cannot be regarded as a travel book, though it was
apparently mistaken for such by its limited body of first read-
ers. And no wonder; for its basic pattern is geographical,
framed by arrival and departure and by a haunting sense of
the oceanic depths beyond. The succession of settings might

almost be Dantesque in their triplicity. The focus of the first section is on Dev's affair with Lou Martin, which seems to have motivated the whole adventure. Its principal locale is the Riviera, and the idyll seems to be more closely associated with the place than with the girl. Since he feels no deep chagrin, we need not, when she leaves him to marry her English tennis partner. Thereafter his motivation broadens and becomes more general: he is travelling to enlarge his view. The second section, proceeding from France to Italy, is the most scenic part of the book—although, in the absence of the blonde Venus, it sadly lacks a heroine. Instead we are faced with Dev's esthetic reflections; instead of dialogue, with his monologue, or rather with the interplay between his mind and the masterworks that interrogate it. Sightseeing can but excite "his lust to make," even as antiquity confirms his resolve "to make—new." The third section passes from art to science, insofar as it concerns Dev's professional interests. Now the scene is principally Vienna, to which Williams transposes some memories of a postgraduate year spent in pediatric studies at Leipzig University. In his admiration of his medical teachers, he can envisage a reconciliation of the sciences and the arts, of the disinterested pursuit of knowledge and the passionate cult of beauty.

Having rambled among the Italian monuments, the protagonist seats himself in the concert hall or the opera house —or, climactically, the Spanish Riding Academy—to continue his artistic education in Austria. Bach's *Saint Matthew Passion* presents him with the highest model, along with the realization that "Art kills time." Here the long-drawn-out message of Proust is condensed into three terse monosyllables, carrying a latent ambiguity: is art merely a pastime or does it confer immortality? A talk among medical colleagues, reflecting back the less permissive sexual attitudes in the States, recalls the exposure of Viennese puritanism that Shakespeare dramatized in *Measure for Measure*. Dev finds a musical mentor, as well as a mistress, in the American bluestocking, Grace Black. While they stroll along the Danube, it is she who voices the sharpest counterstatement against the homeland: its childish athleticism, its materialistic tech-

nology, the "political flimflam" of its democracy. Since the
lovers are so divided by their cultural allegiances, they have
no choice but to part. Heading for France again, Dev joins his
sister Bess *en route*. We already know, from an earlier discussion, that she hates America even more than Grace does.
Now, as they picnic by the Seine, she too pleads with him to
stay in Europe, to quit his job and study it out. "Like Eliot?"
he asks, and she answers: "Who is Eliot? Like nobody."
Rather than perform his "aesthetic duty to the Stars and
Stripes," she would have him settle down with her and learn
the secrets of life and art from the French. But he has seen the
handwriting on the wall and read his own destiny in it. "Art,"
he has discovered, "is a country by itself."

Williams declared that the episode of the picnic had been
suggested to him by the example of the expatriate brother and
sister, the writer Lawrence Vail and the singer Clotilde. Into
his fictitious account of the situation he has injected a hint of
incest, orchestrated to a theme which re-echoes from a performance of *Die Walküre*, where the Wagnerian siblings join
together in the procreation of Siegfried. *"Brüder! Schwester!"*
This association would seem to imply that it would be a
decadent gesture for Dev to settle down with his "Seine
Sister." But the implication is treated symbolically rather
than psychologically; Williams' characteristic vein is inno-
cence rather than decadence; Dev and Bess would simply be
reverting to their childhood. It was for Thomas Mann to make
the most of the same sinister *Leitmotif* in his "Blood of the
Volsungs." Dev's three American women, then, remain in
Europe. His most appealing heroine, the German Venus, has
escaped from the novel, and the short story about her is a
parable in which there can be no meeting between two minds
or two worlds. The cycle is revivified by the ending, which
is likewise a beginning as with Joyce and Eliot, when Dev
catches sight of the Nantucket Lightship. Behind him lie the
Seine, the Arno, and the Danube; ahead, once more and
forever, the Passaic. It is easy to understand why the author
should testify, while admitting freely its imperfections, that
"A Voyage to Pagany was important to me in my education as
a writer." He has told us something about its only previous

publication in a modest edition by the Macauley Company of Passaic, N.J., with a jacket designed by his architect brother: " 'The Worm' encircling the world."

Williams regretted the neglect of his book, and hoped to see it reprinted some day. He felt it to be the most lyrical and descriptive of his prose writings, possibly because of its—for him—exotic subject-matter. Not that he had been conducting a travelogue or exploiting the picturesqueness of the scenery. The distance he keeps may be gauged by his uncertain handling of foreign names and phrases. This is far less important than the fact that he remains his unaffected self, that he so manifestly wrote to please himself. He was interested not in making an impression but in registering an impact. Though he said that Dr. Evans represented him "as a person—not as a writer," the two are finally inseparable. When he tells us that Evans "was a man who enjoyed writing," he is obviously telling us about Williams. "He wrote because he loved it and he wrote eagerly, to be doing well something which he had a taste for, and for this only did he write." His boyish zest, his wide-eyed openness, and his spontaneous energy made him an especially responsive witness to the American-European encounter. Looking back upon *A Voyage to Pagany*, Williams wondered whether it might conceivably have been influenced by Henry James, who was never one of his favorites. He need not have worried, for we cannot imagine Dev getting into one of those dark entanglements that seduced Roderick Hudson and menaced Christopher Newman. There may be some resemblance to Lambert Strether in the belated curiosity for finding out what one may have missed by living in Woollett rather than Paris. But no Jamesian personage would have made the westward crossing so happily, or found so much that was genuinely poetic in the American scene.

Harry Levin

Outward Bound

Chapter I

Outward Bound

AT ONCE the great sea, never calmed by divine feet, came from astern, a northwest gale that caught the old Rochambeau on her starboard afterquarter in sleet and rain. The wind shrieked as the whipping spray struck the ship's cabins momently all day long for three days; while from the sheltered foredeck the clouds and stars—for the middle sky remained often clear in spite of the storm—and could be seen to circle and zigzag overhead. Evans, standing in whatever shelter he could find, was thrilled by that ferocious might of Nature, the ancient antagonist and begetter, green, protean, slippery, yet pointed and personal as a god, while he thought, watching—lace white, spinning among the waves—of white flowers, bunches of them, yarrow, boneset and of the epithet "privet white."—How apt that is for seafoam.

Leaving New York harbor, January 18th, 1924, during a month known for heavy storms at sea, Dr. Evans had acted fairly upon his wish to see the ocean once again, not as a placid millpond, but as he felt it still to be, home of the wild gods in exile.

Nothing so delightful to Evans as to be immersed in the feelings bred by a ship's strong run against the seas. He gave himself completely to the ship's contesting motions. Wildly at peace, after America, lay himself down in his salt bath the first in the morning, waiting for the steward's tap each day, each gesture of the voyage during the storm or after it quieted his solitary mood the more. The gulls paralleling the ship's course without a move close by the rail held him at stance, a deep peace washing away the strains of his immediate past. At sea he felt secure, nothing more solid than that turmoil. A great shout of exultation was often at his lips—making them smile alone, with a kindly indulgence.

It was, in effect, to him each day as it had happened to the ship one night, a ten foot section of the handrail forward had been torn off and was gone, only the twisted iron stanchions remained; with him the same, each day something of his immediate past the sea struck at and carried away—to his everlasting relief. Some day, my God, let the whole works go. I should never think of the practice of medicine again. Never! And, in all probability, this was so. Evans had practiced medicine all his adult life, so far, up to his present fortieth year, in a continuously surly mood at the overbearing necessity for it —wanting always to do something else: to write! Why? Because then only, when he was stealing time for his machine and paper, did he live. Why? One thing about the man, he never argued with his instincts. Temporize with them he would, saying secretly to them: Wait. Some day I will give myself to you, you whom I love. I should only lose you, myself and the world if I went faster. Meanwhile, he had gone back from college to practice medicine in the New Jersey town of P. where he was born.

But he really loved the irregularity of a suburban practice, rushing out into the weather at any hour; in the spring stopping his car at four a.m. to hear the hylas waken, watching the snow figures on the windswept roadways at night in a blizzard, plunging in his car through impromptu lakes of rainwater with lightning flashing all around him and thunder splitting the sky, dust and mysterious fog banks at sundown, the stars peppering the sky, the new moon coming—and thoughts flinging up words to that accompaniment, words that occasionally would have a bewildering freshness upon them as they rose to his sight, it seemed, from somewhere in the center of his brain. And yet he was a good first line doctor. But at the next breath he was off. Let the sea carry it away, all of it, he should never think of it again. And at that moment, if he had been certain that he was bound for the sea's bottom, nothing could have stopped his enjoyment. A dark, medium-sized, impressionable fellow in very ordinary clothes, he looked at the sea.

In the cabin opposite his own was that excellent young American violinist, Marjorie Kent, about to undertake her first European tour under the chaperonage of her devoted mother. In that heated young imagination Evans found some confirmation for his joy. Marjorie played. He had not yet seen her; it was the music which first came to him. He listened a long time. In the first place, it was extraordinary for any one to want to play hard exercises, scales, arpeggios, and passages of difficult bowing during a storm at sea. Yet there was the music. Its insistence struck him with delight. Once he heard a boyish voice admonishing her.—You'll never be a world beater, why don't you shut up once in a while and give us a rest?—But then came the question. Is this it? Is this the real thing? What is this? He listened fascinated by the problem for two days without seeing the girl. There were moments—yes, there were moments. So he could accept and let the player speak. He let her speak. By moments it was the exultation he felt in the ship's solid pitch and roll, of the determination the Rochambeau was offering to the sea, a naked offering, naïve as a ship at sea, the sweetness of sailing through dark and light.

But when in the night of the third day the storm grew heavier he smiled like a baby. With some pains, but resulting in exquisite comfort, he wedged himself into his bunk and listened to the creaking and groaning of the ship while outside the waves brushed or pounded against the heavy glass of his cabin porthole—so near almost one could touch the gods.

An old woman had fallen during the day and broken her arm. Few were at the tables. Thank God it was not a larger

ship! One could still feel the sea. The ship was rolling heavily
with a steady list to port from the force of the wind which
carried her lower to that side on which his cabin lay. Down,
down she went without a great amount of pitching, but down,
down, down till the trunk near the door squeaked in its lash-
ings and loose objects in the cabin shuttled and slid about the
floor. Then with a slight shudder she rose slowly, leaning
again for a brief moment to windward—and with this motion
and joy in his heart—such a peace as there is not elsewhere
in the world—he slept.

His own parents had come to America in ships. His uncle,
the doctor, had died in a ship and been buried at sea. To him
the sea was the grave of all his cares, the one power hopelessly
subtle and uncontrolled, unbridged, unbeaten.

"I am beginning to think we should have no mercy for
anyone—unless we love him. Get all you can out of the other
fellow before he takes it out of you." Curious bits of conversation he picked up going about from one deck to the other.
"J'étais un homme très vulgaire—j'étais un voleur"—"the twist
of years"—"Truth and Beauty married and the child
was love." *"Deux cognacs s'il vous plait. Je suis polis, moi."*
French once more! His ear drank it in with avidity. *Benedic-
tine* 10¢. *Fine* 10¢. That's something!

Then the wet and cold of the storm passed but the great
waves continued, causing the ship from time to time to give
three or four lurches deeper than the rest. The sky was blue
overhead, the decks sanded. Evans stood by the weather rail
watching the seagulls flying near the ship's side, especially
one, a beautifully marked Mackerel gull, larger than the rest,
which with motionless wings was gliding, keeping pace with
the ship not ten feet from his hand resting on the rail. He
watched its eye watching him—and its head shifting slightly
from time to time.

There was a hailstorm that afternoon. The wind was now
due north, the weather cold and squally.

Then swiftly, the sea, limitless, filling the imagination
roundly on all sides, supporting, buoyant, satisfying—was

damaged. Forward, to the left, a section of it had changed, the whole mind was changed along with it. As if the work of birds flying out from beyond the horizon, the thought of land! land! The seahold upon the imaginations of the ship's company had been broken.

England was there, little as a boat. One felt all England, all one had ever heard or felt of England, from Old Mother Cobb to the last pantings of discomfort in the daily press. There it was, pathetic, an island in the sea, powerless and naïve as the small strength of a lion, or the boom of a big cannon. From the sea one could come to hold it as a god might hold an infant on his arm, for a moment. Later, the twin lights of the Scilly Islands gave an inkling, the only inkling, of the world beyond them, silent under the night sky.

At one a.m. the last night the men in the smoking room went wild, threw bottles, glasses. Captain G. had to summon sailors to put them out.

Sleep. Then, early in the morning Evans was standing once more by the rail watching, eager for the arrival. He went forward and forced his body into the very angle of the ship's prow so that the ship thus, behind him, remained invisible. The mechanism that propelled him was annihilated by his concentrated mood. And now he felt himself advancing over the sea, alone and unaccompanied, from a height. To the south a long, low, smoky strip of land was slipping slowly back. A narrow steam trawler wallowed in the dirty swell; the tricolor was at a masthead. So this is France.

Land!

Fickle, by nature, Evans longed now to be again on shore. In this desire, everything else melted and was lost. Time too went by the board.—On such a day, on such a day in early spring, on such a sloppy, dirty-yellow sea, the first coracles put out from the bottom of the red cliff there (they were now close in to Le Havre)—and the wind blew them over to England. I am among them.—He could feel the anxiety and strain of that adventure. There we go by the prow of this mythical ship, invisible to us just as to them we, too, are invisible. For

there is the land and here is the sea, exactly as then; and this
is I, the same. Now am I come home to old Pagany.

In this mood as the ship was drawing closer to the houses
and he could see people moving about in the grayish sunlight,
standing uncertain along the edge of the dock and waving a
scarf sometimes uncertainly, he was interrupted by the deck-
steward who presented him with a wireless.

> *Greetings. Have reserved room Beausoir.*
> *See you later.*   JACK.

Fine. How in hell did he time that so nicely?

The train for Paris started gently, to a birdlike whistle from
the *facteur,* passing slowly through the back streets of Le
Havre. Like a child, he seated himself at the window and
began to drink in the scene. Everything seemed afire in that
soft-gray morning sun. He was looking, watching. For what?

Of what importance this small garden of some switchman,
a row of sprouts, a cabbage growing almost in the cinders?
Poor, insufficient, it seemed. Along the track little boys ran
barefooted shrieking for pennies. They looked sick, poverty-
stricken, lost. The whole city was as if pillaged.—Where *la
France?* he cried within himself, as if expecting to see some
symbolic image of joy rise from the ground and stride forward carrying flowers in her hand triumphantly beside the
train.

Unhappy beggars! He longed to give them—what? What
had he to give? What could anybody give them? This is
France, that's all. But then a remembrance of the old gods
came upon him as the train gained headway and between
high embankments started into the country; and this poverty,
this loss, he began to blame on the death of the gods.—And
they starve, they starve, not because there is no food but
because there is no one to give it to them any more.

Then he remembered what Kay had been saying: These
people are clean, hard-working, traditional in thrift, fixed as
the months in the year and the hours in the day.

The train was moving rapidly now between farms.

He looked and he began in his mind to see how they are waiting, these people. Waiting. Wise and lost. Lost. Lost—just as he was lost. Foreign. Inaccessible. Nothings. Just cut-outs from a paper unfurling itself from rolls turning outside the car windows. Paper people forever inaccessible. Never to be known.

And now of all times he wanted them, while the train mechanically ticked off the miles. At a bridged street crossing there was a boy in a blue jumper looking up. He was holding a bicycle and turning half around to look at the train. A fat *gendarme* was standing by as if he had just been talking to the boy. Gone.

Gone! Whither? Everything went just like that. Living and dead. Turn the corner and it is gone.

But to his wonder, it being January, the bank of this winter landscape began to burst into yellow bloom, flaming yellow to the tick of the train. Whoo! Whoo! and with a crash the train kept on—to Paris. *À Paris, à Paris, à Paris*—as he heard the comedian imitate the train's talk at the "Olympia" when he had gone there as a boy with his mother and Trufley, in '98.

Magpies were flying, black and white among the bare trees.

And now sober France began to ply out, field after field of winter wheat, neat, regular; fine farms. Cattle turned and looked at the intruder or browsed on indifferent. The walls of the gardens and houses were covered with bare fruit trees, carefully pruned—neat as a hat.—The French are careful, dextrous, they love to arrange petals and twigs.—Sometimes farmyards were hedged with fences, a moat, a ditch, cutting them out from the fields.

And then at Mobray when they were beginning to slow up near the station, he saw a deserted garden, all brown and weather-beaten. It was the garden of an old square brown house which stood in the background. No one was in sight. The ruined flower patches were covered with winter débris; the garden was close to the track, so close that the railroad seemed to desecrate its graceful humor. But in the corner of it by great trees that looked like elms, Evans saw a small mound. All on it were shrubs, leafless but marking the spiral of a path that wound around three times before the summit of the miniature mountain was reached and there there was a tree and under it a stone bench, perfect. All was ruin, there was not a blade of grass to be seen anywhere, but the little mound seemed to Evans' too willing sense an altar to some forgotten household god.

And again the country seemed ravaged, beaten. Each man looked to be feeling his destiny there. Waiting. Encitadeled, waiting. Meanwhile, a garden.

And so going on to Paris, growing night, the train came to the hollow of Rouen with its great gloomy cathedral filling the bottom of the bowl: a great pile of stone, full of death. Evans looked and was chilled as if it had been the angry center of all this country which it was depriving silently, sordidly, of its life; as if it were drawing the life in; stone sitting in state over the green.

But he laughed away his mood, calling himself Antichrist and a fool. He remembered Sister Julien, the Mother Superior, at the French Hospital in 34th Street, with her sly pride and great vigor—and how, as a young man, he had loved her.

Oh yes, this is where Pichat was born. And he wondered what effect all this had had upon the mind of that modern French genius of whom New York had been ecstatically talking just at the outbreak of the war; that fine painter whose pictures had been so admired and ridiculed—and whose influence on several of Evans' painter friends had been so great. Pichat was born in Rouen, so Evans had heard.

What should this produce?—And as the train went on and began to cut the windings of the Seine along its way, he began to propose what this would produce: or what it had produced perhaps in the case of Pichat.—What light does this landscape give upon Pichat? His character? A land, caged, hemmed, embittered—wanting to—a land to which nothing has happened in a long time. A small wet land. Industrious—with the shadow of a great medieval dragon in the center—as in a pit.

"Oh, let's go to Paris. Paris is where one forgets and works and loves."

What does this land produce? What does any land produce?

Jeanne d'Arc—everyone thinks of her—as if expecting something; just because she was a girl. What of it? Jeanne did something in Rouen. Got killed here, I think. English had it in hand then. England over there, still further out, still more needful. Everybody cut off there. Makes them hard, fearful. No use to go in coracles. Jeanne did it her way. Get out. Take a chance. What good? Had to get out. Wanted to get out. Do anything to get out, and by accident do something great, get crowned for it. *Crowned* is right. Did the thing that happened to be handy. But we can't get to it. Can't get to IT—it wants to get out. That's why I'm here.

The train had slowed up almost to a stop. Three girls, crowded into a factory window close to the track, waved quietly and smiled at the "rich" foreigners in the special train, the finest on the Havre-to-Paris line, the boat train. Deep-chested, buxom—naïve, they seemed—with faces of Oreads or field nymphs; one imagined their flesh would smell of hay and animals, sweet. Evans smiled to think what it would really smell like, however.

"You know, dear, all good Americans go to Paris when they die, and we are dead, as far as they over there are concerned."

"Yes, but are we good?"

Every now and again someone bursts out like Pichat with design. And takes the shape of the moment. But America is off the track completely. But here they are resistant, fastened down by a stone—waiting—as if some power had cast a great spell over the land out of which the people look without means to recall the past or to escape. And this power is beneficent, while it holds them, soothing the irremediable hurt. White sisters are running sterilely about stone corridors; pure, arduous in their devotion, gone in spirit; little plowgirls, diverted; girls from near the sea diverted from looking out at the water.

Time will tell, maybe. And art; maybe.

Or is it alive? It is. My stretching mood is all I am thinking of. America. Here is. Here is. Here is. Dressed in a church.

Paris ahead!

Rouen, past now, he still thought of it—the first of those great medieval fortresses of the gospel of which he would see more—built of stone and pageantry, flowers—in stone. All in a spell.

What kind of people? Something somber, profound, resist-ant, dextrous.—Swiftly the train swept it up at a pace and crashed by it all. A few carts and autos going forward went backward on the road while peasants walking slowly moved their legs as if on a cord while they were whirled behind in the dark sunlight.

Chapter II

Paris Again

PARIS! where notable Englishmen come to see their illegitimate daughters.

Paris, a place abandoned and serious. What is its touted frivolity? The froth of serious waves?—In this way, it being now full evening, Evans had been composing apostrophes to Paris for the last twenty minutes of his ride—Paris! Its frivolity, its frantic milling about for pleasure—that's America, not France—*"Jenseits des Lust-prinzips."* These are the evidences of a seriousness foreign to us; this rock sets us spinning as dry land does feet after a ship. From the small cities of the whole world, frivolous from their bedrooms to the ornate corridors of the minds of their—to every little chamber where men and women hide themselves to do business of whatever sort—and no business without first the gesture of hiding—in Paris it bursts out to become serious—

Paris as a serious city, the beloved of men; Paris that releases what there is in men—the frivolity that means a knife cut through self-deception.

He also thought of Paris as a woman watching for a lover. Paris is a stitched-up woman watching the international array that constantly deploys about the Eiffel tower and goes frantically about its streets in the squealing taxis—hunting a lover.

It must be a lover. He must come of machines, he must break through. Nothing will subdue him.

Yes, that is Paris. Nothing will subdue him. Finally he grows serious, finally clear. It expects lovers out of the hearts of machines. Out of the felted chamber of boredom you must come clean. Somehow you must have saved, must have built up a great seriousness.

Good God, Paris—He remembered how he had hated it; just an opportunity to shed the nerves; the cast-off of international malady, like the crutches at Lourdes.

They were passing through the city now. And Evans began to think of the stern morality of certain legendary great French families, the rigid discipline, the cold aloofness from the loose life of Montmartre, bespeaking a solidity of character which permits liberties no other nature could afford. He remembered his mother's stories. And her brother's.

And they are dextrous. To that he added "argus-eyed."

Paris wipes all frivolity aside and stares in. What are you made of? What are you made of? What are you made of? It coincided with the slowing rhythm of the train. Then try it, try it then, try it then.

This is the secret of Paris—and, that if it be a lover, *here* is the reward.

> *Come, you incestuous,*
> *Bald and uxorious.*

In the crowd at the Gare St. Lazare the porter was drunk and started to put up a scene. What! only two francs. What! for the boat train!—Evans gave him five and demanded the two in return. The porter gave them back grumbling, and the dilapidated taxi started out madly into the rain in the disordered whirl about the station front. At his time of life Evans was less inclined to stop the parade to think than formerly. He was always straining out of windows. And now for the third time in Paris he stared and stared into the gloom of the rue du Havre in an excited frame of mind. Had it changed?

Had it changed since as a boy Trufley had taken him to the Catacombs and on the great boulevards fed him *syrop de Groseille* while he himself slowly sipped absinthe and smiled and smiled? Had it changed since that day when, a schoolboy from great America, he had sat playing with others on the third floor of an apartment house on rue la Bruyère, and one of the little devils had tried to push him out of the low French window? *Coup de poing américain!* He smiled. Had it changed since he had come from Germany reading Heine; from London where he had seen the literary world just before the war?

What would Jack be like now? And he was anxious to meet his sister. No one had come to the station. Well, so much the better. He wondered what luck he would have on this trip. And always he kept saying: Perhaps this is the time. Something may happen and I shall not return.

But what to do? and what to do next?

Bess, his sister, was in Paris ostensibly to sing. She had the available cash of the family that their mother had left them when she died. Evans wanted none of it; he could work. Bess was twelve years her brother's junior. They had sided together against the old man. Evans was like his mother. "Bess is like the old man—purged," her brother sometimes said.

Marvelous to be in Paris, the air is different; feel it at once. Even that night he had to go out for a walk—anywhere—to the Boulevards.

You must not be afraid.—But Evans was uncertain—and American—and this and that and careless—and amused and lazy and more than a little critical and no drunkard at any time and—hard to crack, a sparrow in short. He wanted to write —that was all, and not to have written, but to be writing. He got his whisky that way, he got all he ever got from that. To be feeling it in his mind and his fingers as it flowed out. And there in secret he lived.

What a life! But Paris understands that too. It did not seem to Evans that he was afraid; it was that he had to discard so much to get at what he wanted that he never arrived anywhere. The whole world is built to keep it from being said.

And so he walked admiring the fabric of it—the hateful fabric.
—No, he laughed, not hateful, but in the repulsive phase.
Every discovery is only a discovery to hide it deeper.—How
shall I talk to Jack for instance, when I see him?

Chapter III

Looking About

EVANS walked, though very tired, for several hours on the principal streets of the city, up the avenue de l'Opera, etc., seeing the famous dancers on the portico, all verdigris, and dirtied by the birds. Lit dimly from below he saw the lyre of Apollo featured at the peak of the opera façade and remembered the story: When the poet Verlaine had died and from his poverty-stricken room they were bearing his body up the avenue, a state funeral, to bury it, as they approached the Opera, suddenly the great golden lyre was seen to totter in its fastenings and fall!

He looked at the lyre, refastened in its place.

On the boulevard des Italiens, Evans admired the toylike clocks in the windows of several jewelry stores, their tiny pendulums going, visibly, at a great pace back of a hole in the face—something he had not seen before. But he was filled with a strangeness inexplicable—satisfying—by it all. It was, as far as he could gather it, walking. How much one escapes by just being here, how much of lying, how much of stupidity!

He went for supper to a small place next to the Théâtre du Vieux Colombier. There the waiter brought his Chateaubriand, serving him a portion of it from the plate and putting the remainder of the steak aside, on a shelf—which Evans let him do, half-suspecting he was stealing it, which exactly, he was doing, and did.

A crier came in from the theater announcing the last act of the play.

Waking next morning at the Beausoir, Evans looked out of the window as three planes went by slowly overhead in flying goose formation. The sky was clear, the sun was shining. He flung open the window and saw an old fellow in baggy underwear walking about his room across the court.

Paris! He felt ridiculously delighted. He pried into every corner of his room, the small familiar violinshaped *bidet* was there. This made him think of Mme. de Pompadour. He smiled contentedly.

Without ringing he dressed and went out. Brioche and coffee on the sidewalk at the corner. Fresh butter. A woman at the *caisse*, prim, neat, keen-eyed. Snappy.

On the street an old woman was selling mimosa from a bunch in her hand.

There was the usual morning market on the boulevard Raspail. Evans crossed over, watching the orderly line of people waiting for the bus, each pulling his serial ticket from the bunch fastened to the post, each waiting his turn. Orderly and intelligent. He needed some fresh collars. Walked over to the Bon Marché. They were having a white sale.

Collars, he said to a floor walker standing in frock coat and high collar facing the door.

To the right in the rear.

All about the floor were heaps of linen and cotton sheets, pillow cases, etc. Even at this hour the place was crowded with women in shawls, poker-faced housewives, going about from place to place. But the heaps of stuff were on the floor, the floor was dirty. Towels were being trampled, the edges of sheets were black here and there.

A wash cloth.—He had a devil of a time to remember what it was in French. Yes. He found what he wanted and found a girl to take it up for him.

Follow me, she said. He did so—delighted, grinning to himself.

She took him to the *caisse*. There they checked off the purchase, took his money and entered the transaction in longhand in a great ledger. He was amazed.

The boy who sold the collars asked him the size, which Evans could not, of course, give in centimeters—so they guessed at it. You have a neck *a peu près* the same as my own.

You have the damnedest way of selling things in this city, said Evans. I should think you'd pass out with all this running back and forth, to and from the cashier's desk.

Yes, I've heard they do it better in New York. He smiled. I'd like to take that place in.

Why don't you? said Evans.

Some day, perhaps, but what can you do?

He was a good-looking kid in a stiff collar and a frock coat. He certainly was earning his money.

And I suppose they—of course—they were balancing as they went.

What a country!

Then he went out with his collars, a wash cloth, a nail brush and a leather purse that smelled to be of goat's hide, in a bundle in his hand.

Delight was his on this January morning. Everything seemed to function with economy and precision: the eggs in flat baskets in the stores, fruit, the neatly cut and tied bundles of meat, the children with blue jumpers over their clean clothes, going to school.

He stopped in at the Post Office on the rue de Rennes and sent a *pneu* to his siter: he had not—purposely—told her when he would arrive.

Then, going back to the hotel to rid himself of his bundle, he ran directly into his friend Jack, looking a little stouter, a good bit wiser, but dressed with the same engaging nonchalance as ever. The two friends, the older and the younger, greeted each other enthusiastically.

Never had Evans forgotten the balance of spirit, the distin-

guished attack upon life which had charmed him with Jack
Murry from the moment of their first meeting in New York.
The firm, thin-lipped lower face, jaw slightly thrust out, the
cold blue eyes, the long, downward-pointing, slightly-hooked
straight nose, the lithe, straight athletic build. The whole
picture was there—almost intact.

How would it be inside? for they had had great plans together for rescuing life from the thicket where it is caught in
America, the constant pounding on the head. They had
worked hard to get to an expression—and Jack had left—to
marry.

That night at 42nd Street when they had parted and Evans
knew it was all up, tears had stood in their eyes. Jack had
showed him his new clothes, they had spoken of continuing
a scheme for publishing good writing—and Jack had sailed
next day.

Oh well, that's America, Evans had written down in his
mind.

Now here was Jack. They shook hands a long time. Dropping the bundle at the hotel, they set out on foot talking as
they strode.

You must meet—so and so and so. Van Cleve is not in Paris
just now.

They stopped for a moment at the Dome while Evans told
Jack his plans. Then they set out again walking and it was
important. They went past La Closerie des Lilas.—There's
Harland, said Jack. We won't stop now. See him later.

They were no business partners, no members of a cabinet,
not even members of a team. How would they get on? How
do men ever get on without some business together? Brothers
never do. In the same ship, the same regiment—maybe.
There is the Field Marshal, the General, the Major, the Colo-
nel, the Captains, the Sergeants and the privates or it is on a
ship. The order keeps them down. The order kills it all. But,
as Walsh said, you can't even get drunk with a guy any more
without having the name pasted on you.

Evans thought of his English father. How the devil do you

love a man anyway? Either you slop over or fight or else you avoid each other. He had admired his father, in some things; loved him—for a few things. But here in Paris, nothing to do —he felt uneasy with Jack.

To hell with what anybody else says, anyway. Evans loved his friend, as some one who brought over to him a section of life where *he* was weak to get at it, too shy, superstitious, too stately reverential.

He loved his younger friend for the bold style of his look at life. Often, when Jack demolished situations and people with one bark, Evans smiled to himself at the rudeness of it, the ruthlessness with which so much good had been mowed down. But he himself never could have done that. Jack struck at the false and, in the thicket of good where it lay, it perished —along with a number of other things. But when Jack ignorantly had smitten, he Evans freely could breathe.

God bless Jack, he had said to himself a thousand times, I love him. I stand for him.

But when it came to saying anything to Jack about it— nothing doing. They walked in together and through the Luxembourg gardens, down between the lines of chestnut trees toward 12 rue de l'Odéon, to get the mail.

Evans saw the French children of the better classes playing around the basin. He didn't admire their dolled-up appearance. It isn't the lack of births that keeps the French population down, it's that so damned many of them die before they are five years old. The French are the worst people in the world for bringing up kids.

They went on past the gloomy buildings of the Senate.

If we had anything to do together—anything—

Already Jack was getting on his nerves.

Merely to walk and to talk—What?

The modern ideal is the prize ring. Men soaking men on the jaw. A gentlemanly art. That's all.

But if you want to know a man, if you find him excellent, why you've got to have something to do together. You've got to work.

Why do you have to do anything? Why the hell do you have to work anyway?

Jack and Evans, wide apart as to ages, were not so far apart in general appearance. Evans needed Jack. Jack had rescued him in America, rescued him from much stupidity, from dullness, at a certain time when he needed just that. Evans thought he had aided Jack to get going.

What remained of all that now? One can't go on just beating the air. Was it still there after these three years past?

Each knew the other's antecedents pretty well. Perhaps there was nothing left.

Evans had begun to be depressed without knowing why, at first.

There was no mail at the bookshop. Coming out they hopped into a taxi.

What in God's name did I come here for?

My generation has done one thing, Jack started off, it isn't afraid to be called anything. It—they're not going to be frightened into anything either, by a lot of spineless—just tell them to move along when they get too thick.

Evans didn't know.

He was disturbed, avowedly. The connotations of his affection for Jack with nothing he could do about it—nothing to do—the slipping, slipping way the world has of getting out from under a difficulty and presenting the wrong face of an object, while it gives you, yes, perhaps what you ask, distressed him heavily.

They were lounging in the taxi. Evans looked out across the place St. Sulpice at the façade of the great church which had given the square its name.

How get in? Where was Jack? Why else then was he, Evans, a writer? He *would* do something about it, *something* at least.

Being a writer he could at least make it into a book, a poem, a novel. But he didn't want to make it into anything. He wanted Jack and he did not want a makeshift. He wanted to be let in, he wanted to let Jack in.

He grew angry because as he thought, they wanted to make him do what he wasn't even interested in doing, or if he didn't do that, they wouldn't let him speak to Jack.—You might as well pick up a sailor; but you can't find this——

What was it he found in young Murry? What does anybody find in anybody? Something he can't get except through that somebody. The luck of it gave that one the chance to look in and see; to look through.

Evans wanted to be let in.

Was it literature? To hell with literature. Was it to know the details of Jack's life? Evans didn't know he had any. Was it his soul? What the hell is that? It's to get *through* something. To get down to it, or up to it. There wasn't any act, that Evans knew, that would do any good for that. Not that he knew of.

Yes, you shouldn't be afraid, but you shouldn't let them hand you a sack of guts either—or kid you into thinking you want it. Some day, maybe he'd have to come to that but not yet a while, not while there was any chance of getting through whole.

Maybe Jack didn't need him any longer.

A sudden coldness went over Evans. Jack suddenly faded far away. Evans looked at him coldly and asked himself what Jack had ever done to warrant his, Evans', liking—except to be decorative, as he was.

But to get down to what? That was what it amounted to. What to do, not in desperation and whining self-pity but— whole. How are we going to get to know each other again? said he aloud.

What do you mean? said Jack. Then he went on, You've got to see a whole lot of things over here, people first. They all want to know you, they've read your stuff. Like it.

Evans had forgotten where they were going. Oh yes, to the bank. They stopped the taxi. Jack got his cash and they went on to sit for a while at the Café de la Paix.

Then as J. spoke of his plans for publishing, Evans' mood began again to revive.

So it was the desire to get down to some sort of sense about

writing, then, that was the cement for their friendship and
there Evans decided to stop for to-day. Jack had a fresh mind
on paper. He was distinguished—as a writer. It made no
difference to Evans that he hadn't done anything much as yet.
Evans knew better than that he should fail—and that's love.
Yes, he still loved Jack.

That ended that. He got up positively—Let's go. Jack liked
that and they set off. They took another taxi, Evans improvis-
ing to himself on the streets, staring out.

Now they were coming back again to Montparnasse, and
again Evans saw the façade of St. Sulpice with its severe front
and wondered what in God's name it signified. *La Cathédrale
Engloutie*—signified Debussy. He said that. But there, square
stone blocks ornamented with carvings. What? You looked at
it. Devout people were going in at the doors. Devout? What?
Is it a poem? So is the grass. Leaves of Grass: America, because the people are common as grass—and as green; nothing
showy; on the ground. True enough, but what of that? Does
that help?

Love. Everybody talks about love. It's the commonest thing
in the world. There are no two kinds of love. Love is love. The
moralist will tell you that. You love some one, that is all. If you
love a girl, you want to have a baby. If you love a man, you
want to have—what? If you love a girl, you don't want to have
a baby at all. You just have one. You love her and after a while
you have a baby. He thought of Panurge and the lady of Paris
—called her a name.

It's love and how do these medieval church fortresses help?
Love. Where is it on them? I don't see any love. Yes, it's one
kind, a kind of official love, museums of love! That's what
churches are.

This amused him—Museums of love presided over by men
to watch the cases so that you don't take anything precious.
I wonder if the jewels in the Louvre are real and if they still
look as large as ever.—His mind flew off.

He looked out of the windows of the taxi, and wondered

which of these old houses of the Latin Quarter it was in which his uncle had first slept soundly.

He saw the Musée du Luxembourg.—Paris is love, Paris is the living cathedral of the world. But what of to-day? He did not pray for help. He was interested and felt glad he was there.

Chapter IV

Sis

Back in his hotel, Evans felt half sick. If the truth were told, he had fled from Jack. Now he flung himself across the bed, noting as he did so the soft coal smell in the air from the open window and hearing the toylike toot-toot of the taxis faintly beyond the court on the boulevard Raspail, just before he fell into a sleep.—And a dream disturbed him, a dream in which he was dimly aware of the poet Walt Whitman eating at——

With a start he woke to find his beloved sister Bess a few feet off looking at him while the female floor supervisor was standing outside holding the door.

Dev! cried Bess and the woman discreetly closed the door behind her. You darling! And before he could answer or arrange his sleep-ruffled clothes, Dev found himself embraced and shaken and kissed upon his cheeks, his eyes, his nose and finally, swiftly full upon his lips as if it were some fruit it were that Bess was pulling from its twigs by the lips alone.

They fell more than sat upon the edge of the bed. Laughing and a little out of breath, Bess was about to begin it again when Dev caught her arms and held her.

For God's sake, Sis, quit it, he said laughing. But he pressed her hands eagerly and looked long and fondly into her clear gray eyes.

It's a year and a half, Dev, a whole year and a half since I've seen you. And with that she went on to upbraid him with not letting her know the details of his arrival, holding tight to his hands meanwhile and looking long and delightedly into his eyes, brown eyes, in her turn.

Can it be that we are children of the same parents? Dev said to her.

From America expect anything! Bess replied, even a race immune to——

Stand up, Dev commanded her. As she did so, he pushed her away from him to examine her. As she had stood in the doorway, when he had been so rudely awakened, he thought for a moment that this was the most beautiful woman he had ever seen in his life—though he knew his sister, chin, elbows, and ankles from the cradle up.

What is it? he said. Why Bess, what is it? You are transformed, you are beautiful.

It is these clothes, Dev. The clothes fit me for the first time in my life.

No, but your face. Little girl, little girl, he chided her. Something has happened to my little sister.

Bess shook her head. Not yet.—Bess Evans was fairly tall for a woman, straight, almost too straight, with a longish, even countenance and rather pale skin. Dev had never found her especially beautiful before. The high, rather narrow forehead, and the deep-set, clear eyes seemed now somehow to give her an air of unusual distinction. She was her father's daughter while he was of the southern side of his family which was so mixed that no one ever had been quite certain what they were, except that there was a strong Basque strain there associated with the somewhat mythical name of Hurrard.

Nevertheless, differing as the brother and sister did, they had grown up intimately together, almost as one child. They had shared everything with each other, first by little Bess telling her brother all she knew and later by the brother reciprocating when he had grown more and more confirmed in the state of old bachelordom—writing, and living by his profession as a physician. The war had separated them. Bess had come to Paris to stay with her "aunt." And now here they were once more looking into each other's eyes.

The thing which had always kept them together was the total lack of constraint they felt in each other's company—a confidence which had never, so far, been equally shared by them with anyone else. Bess began thumbing through some papers her brother had lying on the table. What in the world is this? The Ground Bean and its Uses—"Among the additional specimens recently installed in the display of Indian foods is that of the ground bean"—and have you still your vest pocket full of Indian arrowheads, silly?

No, I have saved only one perfect one. Come, Sis, continued the brother, let's go and have lunch, then you can tell me what it is all about.

So they went up the boulevard Raspail to the Restaurant l'avenue close to the Gare Montparnasse exchanging all the family news as they walked. There they sat outside for a moment watching the weather—as it seemed as if it were going to rain—while they sipped their Dubonnets under the awning. But, finding it would clear, they went inside and out again into that delightful triangular courtyard so well known at that time to Americans of that quarter, and took a table in the open.

Think of this, in January. Aren't we lucky? And Bess pressed heavily her brother's foot under the table. Her elbows rested on the table top, she bit her lip and looked even now after an hour's reacquaintance thirstily into his eyes.

She had left the meal to him. As he ordered it, consulting her over every item which she ended by selecting with a quiet word, she talked.

Here was indeed a strong contrast in temperaments. If the truth were told, the cause for Bess' excessive pleasure and excitement at her brother's arrival in Paris was not a natural gushiness of temper but quite the reverse. Bess was not an easy person to know. She attracted men but not those who could expect to profit by a nature such as her own. She was cautious and firm. She attracted two kinds of males. Those she impressed by her slight body, clear eyes and fine forehead and who wanted to win that, and those who sought her intensity. Her pleasure in Dev was that of a totally opposite nature to its opposite. She admired his flexibility, his easy access to all kinds of feeling while her own feelings were so stable, so well known to her that she could have told years ahead, almost, what she would do or think on a certain day. But, most of all, her pleasure in Dev was that here, and here alone, she knew a complete breakdown of her reserve. Dev knew her, had known every wish in her heart from the time she first shook with terror and fascination over the fatalism of fairy stories, to the later phases when her wild anger at the political injustices of her country upset her while he smiled and continued his poems.

We shall begin with the hors d'oeuvre and a bottle of Chablis.

Yes, Bess assented.

Then, we will have a broiled lobster between us.

No, said Bess, let's skip that and have a Chateaubriand and the vegetables.

With a good Bordeau.

No, thank you, I want a clear head today.

A half bottle then?

Have it for yourself, Bess answered.

And then?

A little salad and coffee, that's all I want.

Cognac?

I think so, yes.

So they talked.

The trouble with our philosophy, Dev, and the way we differ from the ancients is that *we*, you and I, are not important people as those masters were, while we still think we are so.

No one is to-day. There is no need. It all goes on mechanically like an advance of trained troops. One drops out and another pops in. There is no sense in it. It's a distinction to be nobody and to do as you please.

Oh no, his sister replied. Some day, I am going into politics. Wait and see.

Dev laughed, rather thoughtfully, however, knowing she'd be a damned sight more efficient at it than ever he would be if she once made up her mind to it.

She continued: You think you are attempting something for America and for the world, you and your literary friends —your artistic friends. You rather look down on the politician and us other poor tongue-tied mortals. But, Dev, you're just kidding yourself, you're just out for your own amusement, that is all.

This was a familiar tune to Dev but it worried him for all that. Well, then, so were Homer and Dante.

No, No. One was a subtle historian and the other a great moralist. You're wrong there.

You think we have no moral purpose?

Do you have the nerve to look at me and say that, Dev? Have you a moral purpose?

Oh, I don't know. It seems something of the sort sometimes.

Bess smiled quietly. Evans remembered with misgivings that she was an M.A.—or whatever it is—from one of the American female colleges.

We have no Christian purpose surely, he answered her.

An international non-Christian purpose, she taunted him.

Yes, and also non-political, he said.

And it is, she concluded, to amuse yourselves. Is that not why you are here in France? You say you are going to Vienna to study. Dev, do you want me to believe that?

Dev, sweetheart, she added, seeing she had hit home, I am not finding fault with you, but sometimes, my dear, you do amuse me, especially when you think you are doing something wonderful.

Sis, if I had your cold outlook over the world, I think I should jump off the Eiffel Tower. How you can go on with life, thinking as you do, makes me shiver. Bless your heart,

Sis, what are you made of, anyway? I guess women are the tougher.

I am just the same kind of a fool you are, Dev, in a different way, that's all. And that's why we love each other. Don't we?

Yes, we do.

Only I'm not a poet. Not a writer. I'm jealous of you, Dev, that's all. I wish I could write. It must be a wonderful alleviation.

Lucky for the world you can't. It's lucky it rains water and not chunks of rock. You'd batter the world into a pulp with your devastating hardness. You'd freeze its marrow, little sister.

No, I'd be no realist. I'd just write nice, silly little stories about true love. And now, what are you really doing in Paris?

A voyage to Pagany, Dev replied. I'm not staying long.

No?

No.

Dev, why don't you stay over here permanently?

Finding nothing to say, he passed it off, this time, looking down without a reply. She did not press the point.

I'm going on to Vienna, he continued.

To Vienna? Why there's nothing there now.

Via the Riviera, and perhaps Rome.

And is that all?

Yes, are you coming with me?

Bess looked at him sharply, then smiled. Dev, that isn't fair.

No, it isn't, he answered. I'll tell you the rest if you'll tell me what made you so glad to see me here to-day.

I'm always glad to see you. Oh Dev, why are there not more men like you? You seem to bring the breath of life into me whenever I see you.

You mean, I let it out of you, he corrected. Bess, have you deviated from your clamlike ways at last? What is it? A man?

No, Dev.

Bess, you've changed.

No, Dev, I'm desperate.

You're not old enough.

Dev, I've got to do something, and you've got to help me.
I've got to break myself in. I have never realized how much
I have loved you, dear. Do you understand me? I've been a
child, a baby. There have seldom been a brother and sister so
close as we have been. That's not it exactly. It's inside myself.
I'm an American, you know what I mean, a fool, all tied up,
letting the wrong things out. I've let you represent things to
me, I've written you letters, silly little confessions, newsy
letters—you know what I mean, just to keep the thread
whole. It hasn't been you, yet you've been the only one there,
but something is ready inside me.

Who is it?

It's nobody. Yes, it is. It's somebody. It's a man. I've got to
have him. You understand me. Maybe I'll marry him. I don't
know.

Dev's heart sank. For a minute he looked at his sister as if
she had slapped him.

Don't do that, Dev. Don't do that. You're jealous, that's all.
Madly and furiously jealous and I'm as elated over it as if I
were sixteen and you were my best beau.

Yes, you're right, I guess.

Bless you, dear old Dev.

Don't call me old.

Nobody could do that, dear, except me, she said reaching
over and stroking his brown hair. I've loved you so long.

Dev was pleased in spite of himself.

Tell me what I should do and I'll do it.

Dev laughed.—No, Sis, you wouldn't but you'd do it without me. Come on. Don't let's talk any more about it now.
Let's finish this gallows meal and get out.

What do you mean?

So he paid the check and they went out. Hailing a taxi, they
hopped in and as they passed the Dome, Evans thought he
recognized a girl he had seen on the boat. Bess looked also and
blinked but said nothing.

Is he there?

Yes.

An American.

No.

Young?

Where are you taking me?

To the Louvre.

All right.

The brother and sister sat silent in the taxi, both felt a little flushed and drowsy from the meal and were glad to be silent. Each looked out of the window on his own side. But they clasped the fingers of their adjoining hands as they rode.

Love, eh?

But Dev was not prepared for the reply.

Coolly, his sister turned around and in a positive quiet voice that had always frightened her brother she said, I shall never love anyone as I love you.

On the Seine, swollen with the early spring tide, men were still fishing as he had seen them in the morning. The view of the Louvre; they alighted and, it being Monday, found it closed.

Well, there goes antiquity—with about as much reason as usual, Evans remarked.

Are you leaving Paris so soon?

He did not reply. They had started to walk.

Crossing the graveled court to the north of the palace they wandered up the river bank under the bare plane trees where the book stalls were closed, to the Pont Neuf and from there to Notre Dame which Dev had not entered in ten years.

They looked at the famous cathedral: It is the lack of solution hardened into this form, twin towered, all the paraphernalia of the aisles. We should not be downhearted if we can't solve it pronto, he said to himself. Of what else are all the great liturgies built?—the Egyptian, the tribal, the Greek—to hide the difficulty; the Christian to-day, to hide the difficulty; equal, colored glass before the blinding face of—this the me to you, impossible to communicate, impossible to put over anything important—the truth, as they call it familiarly, the heterosexual truth—just children trying to do it all at once.

Blood in this street. The Church heads it all, the dead stops
of life, everything made static—stopped that is—made into a
form beautiful.—It gave him a chill, that word.

Inside, along the east aisle a funeral was progressing, the
beadle with his staff marching in front. The body left a bad
odor in the place. The brother and sister walked clear around
the nave glancing indifferently at the chapels and standing to
stare at the great colored windows.

Evans was bored by the lack of light. Yet, it frightened him,
too. Such a mass of inexplicable gloom. To what end? It
always got him the same way, primitive, savage, cruel. It was
like his sister, he thought. A kind of northern gloom. But she
was cynical while he was inclined to be impressed. She was
a cold Huguenot. The light in her eyes as she passed the tinsel
altars was not a holy one by any means. She grinned once or
twice in a way that made Evans shiver.

And yet indeed, this dark interior was like his sister. The
tall columns, the floor marked with effigies. The windows.
Everything still, sure, inexplicable. Dev was always cast into
a spirit of awe by cathedrals.

The pagan strength is in them. When the Christian spirit
conquered the world, the pagan gods were turned into these
stone images. Oak leaves, acorns, the faces of the people of the
streets in the forms of devils and angels. Such was it all. It was
the power of those racial stocks that built them, gone to sleep
there—to go on, to go on, undefeated. He thrilled always at
that thought.

It is like a tomb. Here the sun never comes. When they
want to do anything that will last they come here. Or they
used to. They come here to the early gods masquerading in
these stones, for power. Napoleon came here to crown himself. Here the Kings are afraid. The naked spirit has taken this
inexplicable shape right from among fauns and shepherds.
The——

What are you thinking? said Bess.

That you are a curious phase of the American common-
wealth.

I hate America, answered Bess with so much fire, such a cold certainty, that once again he did not answer her.

Are not the windows wonderful? she continued. I could look at them forever.

Come on, let's get out of this damp place.

They went out into the streets.

Let's go up on the tower.—So they began to climb the hundred steps. Dev was surprised that his sister should be frightened when on the winding dizzy steps, as black as if they had both been blind, she called to him frightened not three feet away and made him come behind and rest his hand upon her back before she would go further.

Out of breath at the top they came forth into the sunlight at last. There they saw three smiling Japanese tourists who were climbing around looking with manifest amusement at the devils in stone all about them.

Brother and sister looked at the great bell, Louis the 14th, which it takes eight men to ring. And saw in the distance the *Sacré Coeur,* the modern sanctuary, which Dev thought looked like the Taj Mahal in the mist. The Japs had left. Then sitting down on one of the stones of the cathedral roof, they had their hearts out.

Bess wanted Dev to free her by pretending to take her south with him. Meanwhile, she would go to stay with some friends at Montreux.

Dev's heart sank anew.

Oh Dev, you've got to do it.

All right, Sis, only I could commit murder, God damn it.

Yes, yes, I know. But I can't marry you and I don't want to go home and do the decent thing. I can't and I won't. I'm no fool, dear. Trust me. If I need you, I'll call—I promise that.

Evans looked at his sister and there were tears in his eyes. But she was blazing with heat. Never had she looked so magnificent. Diana, he thought, Diana of the chase, a flat simile, and a wrong one.

But you, Bess, you, of all people.—He felt as though he had lost something of his very life.

Yes, I—of all people. Exactly. Everyone but me is excused. I am *not* excused. Well, now I don't care whether I am or not.

Sin?

Yes, it is a sin and I will commit it. It is the result of your teaching.

I never told you to sin.

Oh Dev, you blessing! You are my liberator. I love you, I wonder if I have ever loved anyone but you, or if I ever shall. Why are there not other men like you, you precious baby?

Lucky for them. You are much the better of us, Bess. Look at my chin and look at yours. You upright Puritan!

Evans was always delighted with his sister's accent. For, though they were but first generation Americans from their small suburb of New York, Bess had gone to school for three years at Sweetbriar in Virginia and the slight Southern drawl she had acquired there had never left her. It amused and tickled her brother.

Virginians, that describes us, Bess. Virginians. A Virginian, that's what I am by selection—not descent, thank God.

He began to tease her: All I am is a ticket to you. You don't care for me at all. It's just that I mean freedom for you from your own miserable conscience—by hanging the blame for what you are going to do on my weak shoulders.

Dev, I want to go the limit. I want to get drunk completely, thoroughly, to forget this sinful world and all its devices.

Do you call it that, Sis?

Yes, sin I insist.—The old fight did not flare up; instead, both laughed.

Would you care, Dev, if I went off? Answer me.—He loved her and was turbulently resentful. He couldn't help thinking of her as little Bunny.

Without answering her directly, Tell me, he said.

Bess watched his face a moment then: Oh you do love me, you do still love me, and she said nothing more. But the brother and sister laughed again together. She threw herself on her knees before him where he sat and embraced him eagerly, kissing him on the eyes, the neck—he held her and was troubled.

And so they went down from the cathedral roof and took a taxi to a small place on the rue du Medicis for dinner, and later to see Aunt K. who had been expecting them for several hours.

Chapter V

The Supper

The third day of his stay in the French capital Evans called, as he would think of it in the following weeks, just Paris. He had had a wildly sleepless night. But in the morning he received a note he had been expecting. It read: Arrived safely. All set. Wednesday evening at the Quai d'Orsay. Signed, Lou.

All right. America to the fore. And with that he put all trouble behind him, arose and went out into the air.

This was the night for which Jack had promised him the literary banquet. At noon he was to lunch with his sister and their aunt. Now he went for a stroll toward the *Champs Elysées.*

As he crossed the river before the *Chambre des Députés* he leaned to watch more closely the fishcatching. The poles were so long, the men so staid-looking, the fish so bright and shiny and so small that he could not but laugh.

Again as he walked he saw men and women greeting each other familiarly with kisses on the street. It was the Paris that charmed him. Just the sense one had of being here—just Paris. But it semed absurd that the greatest thrill he had that morning was when, still early, he stumbled by chance upon the *place François Premier.*

The tiny gray plaza, but a step from the great *Arc de Triomphe*, did for him exactly what he wanted France that day to do. Standing there he found himself all unconsciously addressing the low gray houses, with the small plot of grass around the statue in the center, as if it were a person.—Where did you come from, you beautiful creature "with the cross between your horns"?—Thrills coursed up and down his spine, tears came to his eyes as if he had been a starved man looking upon a fruitful oasis. It seemed ridiculous even to him to be thus standing there crying; he looked around hurriedly to see if there were any from whom he should hide his tears. But the cobbled streets abutting upon the little symmetrical place were all empty.

And still he stood and looked at the low gray houses ranged around in an hexagonal symmetry and, feeling broken down, low, peasant-plain, he put a pear, which he had just bought, again to his lips like a country bumpkin and looked, asking himself what it was all about. Was it just an *asile*, an escape from roar to quietude and symmetry? This did not seem quite enough. As far as he could tell, it said Braque. It linked completely with the modern spirit. It was France, cold, gray, dextrous, multiform, and yet gracious—its smallness, in this case, endeared it to him. It came all pressed up ready to understand, to be understood, to carry away like the bundles they handed you so graciously in the department stores.

He walked thoughtfully on, eating his pear.

But at the bridgehead facing the *École Militaire*, he stopped again at a piece of brilliance unequalled in his experience: there passed a high-powered motor car, a limousine of great size and most immaculate blackness, with two men in staid untrimmed livery on the front seat. But the car shone, the glass flashed brilliantly as if specially polished, and inside Evans saw two boys about twelve and fourteen years of age, blossoms of a stagnant birth rate, males exquisitely finished, sitting in position on the back seat with eyes as brightly burning as the car was brightly polished, but restrained, symmetrical, one like the other: design, intelligence and a cold fire.

At noon he went to keep his engagement with his family, when, with their "Auntie" at the famous *Tour d'Argent,* his sister and he attacked without relish the well-known *canard pressé.* At the same time it must be added that though the duck at the old hostelry was far too bloody a morsel for these two plain-eating Americans, yet the bottle of Corton they had before it Evans remembered as one of those significant minor events which by being perfectly appropriate to the moment remain forever memorable. And here they arranged the trip Bess and he were to take "together"—feeling somewhat subdued and mean about it all.

At four, leaving the others, Evans went to the Dome as agreed the day before. Jack was there with Salter and his lovely wife. Jack at a table next to the open sidewalk beckoned and Dev sat down. The tables were crowded. Jack said little but pinched his·thin lips up once or twice and sipped his whisky. People were jammed in, one on top of another, it being a fine p.m. Three "girls," arm in arm, were talking earnestly together at the curb before the tables: Kiki, Zaza and a little Polish model. Jack began pointing out the celebrities, Russian, English, French and American of various degrees of distinction, success, despondency; rich, starving, lewd or whatever it might be. There was a certain type of international Dome face one might have detected in them all, a sort of wary face, a little on parade. There was little vivacity apparent in anyone. Occasionally some woman would come up and be kissed by a man, her husband watching or not as it might be. She would sit then with a little group, a man here or there moving a few inches to give her place. People got up and wandered off. The waiters moved about with glasses. It was as if each group was more or less in its own rooms. One was walked upon without resentment—unless it suited. Some avoided the eyes of others. Occasionally two would look, whisper and stare. All seemed waiting. Not all, for some, inside the windows, were playing chess in what appeared to be complete absorption. Women wandered about. A man would stand in the door staring off down the street.

How is your baby? asked a wealthy married woman of the little Polish model who had come up to greet her.

Very well, now, and how is *your* baby?

In general, it was a well-dressed crowd. There is Léger. Evans saw this one, that one. Presently George Andrews came up, then Mary Lloyd and her beautiful daughter. All sat and drank, the women painted their lips.

It was fun. Joyce did not come here. But many Evans had known, whose work he had admired, whether in writing, painting, music, sculpture, seemed to be here or had been here or must be coming here soon.

It was decidedly an atmosphere where conversation could take place. It was an atmosphere, liberal, phoenix young or old, like a park or a place in the woods, or it had an air of isolation, indifference, about it that might have been the atmosphere of a wild tribal village—without the danger of attack. A prince here or there, a prominent figure from some last year's show in New York. All came up to the level of the Dome. One left behind all his "side." One was, at least for the sitting at a table and drinking, equal to any other, while no one presumed to believe it so. One came and went and looked or did not look. One talked. Ah, there's so and so.

Let's get out of this, Jack said suddenly in his usual abrupt manner.

They got up and hailed a taxi.

At the Trianon, where Jack had arranged for the supper, the regular patrons of the little restaurant with the strong cellar smell in the entrance corridor, were departing. In the back room six or eight small tables were placed end to end before the upholstered wallbench to one side and in a moment eight or ten of the guests arrived. Others followed—more than were invited for this is the custom, it seems, in Paris. These were mostly English and Americans who Jack thought might be interested in Evans; at least, he wanted to honor Evans by having them meet him. For the few things Dev had contributed now and again to the lesser known literary papers had been frequently admired.

Evans was a man who enjoyed writing. He wrote because he loved it and he wrote eagerly, to be doing well something which he had a taste for, and for this only did he write. As far as wishing to advance his acquaintanceship by his writing, or to advance himself, it never entered his mind. If they liked it, he was entranced; if not, he didn't blame them. So that now he felt uneasy. But none let him be so for long.

With the American cocktails the conversation became general and before many minutes it became uproarious. Evans need not have worried about himself. They asked him for a speech, which he could not make. He said something stupid in his embarrassment, however—something he never forgave himself for saying, and Jack heard it. Something about the honor that is done corpses in Paris—where all men on the street doff their hats when a funeral is passing.

But it was a magnificent dinner, wine flowed fast and expensively. Jack sang Bolliky Bill. Others sang. H. tried vainly to shout a sailor story across the table. Some ate for the week, perhaps. But some were silent and looking.

Evans drank. Some one kissed him. He grasped the arm. He was being swallowed. He playfully nipped the tender skin of his admirer below the elbow with his teeth—Is not this what is required?

But he knew Jack was watching him.

To him it all meant nothing, something that might be for some one else; he drank, he was restless. He was glad it was over.

Back to the Dome went many of the guests, others turning home early. For the former, after several highballs, taxis were chartered when out they all piled at a Negro joint on the other side of the river.

Jack forgot everyone and stood from then on at the bar. He drank.

Evans drank and danced with Delise whom they had picked up at the Dome. He had at once formed a passionate attachment for this sleek-haired American woman. The minute he had looked at her clear eyes, Evans had determined to keep close to her. She was wildly hilarious that night. Before many minutes she was on the table taking off her stockings. One foot at a time she held in the air removing the shoe, then the stocking, then putting back the shoe she repeated the process with the other leg. Dev was jammed in between two others on the cushion side of the table next the wall. Delise jumped down forcing herself next to him and turning at once looked full into his eyes while the others, seeing how things stood, found other interests. They two became oblivious to everyone as he began to kiss her again and again.

No one paid any attention.

Delise jumped to her feet in another instant and seeing Jack at the bar, she ran over and grabbed him by the hand. Out into the middle of the floor she drew him and there they danced —wildly. Several well-groomed men at another table applauded her loudly. She danced like mad, her bare legs flying, Jack followed her as a foil till he was tired and went back to the bar.

Dev, slightly drunk, could not get up and go, he could not. He looked and admired her. One of the gentlemen outside the party got up. Delise accepted his offer. They danced to the Negro jazz all over the place. An American sailor and a French girl now got on the floor; this was the girl Dev knew was going to the tuberculosis sanatorium in the morning.

Delise left the floor and acknowledging the gentleman's bow carelessly she came back to Dev's table, panting, placing her arms out flat on the cold surface and her head over them, panting. Dev stroked her hair.

Dev thoughtfully kissed the back of her neck, tenderly, lovingly—with greatest admiration and tenderness.

What a delightful thing—drunkenness. He grew furious at the damned stupidity of his people. Whose people? Look, he thought, at this beautiful girl, this armed, able woman. Look! compare her with that, that God damned hell hole of a country.—He wanted to be profane. Instead he kissed her arms,

admiringly, tenderly again, with intensity, with peculiar heat
such as he knew, he knew—but who else would understand
it in him? He was a timid fool—not at all; only *he* knew, or
could ever know.

He kissed her drunkenly. But she looked up with an understanding smile and taking him with her they were on the floor
together, nobody watching them.

But Evans was a poor dancer. The fire was not in him for
that. Maybe it was his age. Once he had danced. Delise soon
left him and then all moved out once more to the taxis. It was
three a.m. Where shall we go now? To the Dingo.

There, there was a crowd at the bar. They sat, Dev and
Delise, to themselves in a corner and Dev patted her face
between his hands, the drink bothered him a little but it gave,
it gave much. There was an English woman in the corner
gathering up her man, her man in a dress suit, silly, paralyzed,
helpless, drunk. But Dev shook his own head a little to clear
his vision and—caressed Delise. She was quiet.

Why are there not more men like you, dear? she said. He
looked hard at her clear eyes. You are tender, kind. Nobody
else knows how to be so kind.—Dev only kissed her. She
leaned over the table into his arms; tenderly he held her as if
it were the whole world he were holding. Amazed, puzzled,
wishing nothing else, knowing it was nothing.

Leaning closer she confided to him her jealousy over
Garda. Her feeling that when Maurice smiled at her, at
Garda, that she, Delise, couldn't bear it. Why are you so good,
why are you so good? Why do I tell you this? she kept saying.
You ask for nothing.—She leaned over and nipped the graying hair at his temples with her sharp white teeth. You don't
ask for anything. What is it?

Dev felt—as he always felt: what? And that's all he could
say. What? What? I love you. I love to kiss you, dearest. But
what? What?

Then he drank, drank and slept with his head on his arm.
Delise had gone to another table and was leaning upon another's shoulders. Later, all went out to a little place near the

Gare Montparnasse. They had fried eggs with the laborers who came there for breakfast.

Jack didn't eat. He was drunker than Evans. He was peevish.

They left the others and walked home in the dawn. Jack felt quarrelsome.

The trouble with you, Dev, he said, is that you're a damned fool. Didn't know you were so soft.

Yes.—But it cut deep. The whole thing was clear to Evans. The asinine attempt at a speech, and so forth, and so forth, and so forth. Anyhow, he felt that way. To hell with all of them then.

Why don't you *do* something?—and there were worse things said.

Chapter VI

Carcassonne

Dev was wakened from a heavy sleep next morning by a phone call from Bess wishing him good-by. She was leaving Paris as they had planned and would write to him from wherever she would be—later. That was all.

Immediately after, he was desperately sick and didn't give a damn where she was going or in fact for anything about her. He felt horrible. After a while he flung himself on the bed and managed to go to sleep once more. At about noon he roused himself for the second time. Things began to come back a little. This was the day. He must get up, get washed, catch the train for Toulouse—or wherever it was he was going. He dimly remembered something about Bess. Bess had called. Bess had gone. Hell, he must get up.

By five, he was at the Quai d'Orsay, feeling rather gaunt, but there was Lou, as planned, standing in the midst of her luggage—hat boxes, tennis racquets and all. She had not seen him. He lit a cigarette before going up to her. She *is* beautiful, a blond beauty. Legs a trifle heavy though.

Lou was trying to keep from meeting the eyes of a chap standing by one of the pillars a short distance off. She was very glad to salute Evans with a kiss as he came up.

The thing had been so carefully planned that for the mo-

ment neither felt at all the novelty of the situation. Both were
dead tired.

I'm so tired, Dev, she said, after they had arranged their
bags in the compartment. And so, without further dallying,
he went out for a smoke.

Standing in the corridor smoking as, leaving Paris, the train
began to assume its rapid country pace southward, the
thoughts and events of the day before began slowly to come
back to Evans' mind and it dawned on him that at last blessed
Lou was here with him on the train and that he was going
south and away. At last, he was going away. He was on the
train with Lou, going away.

Jack would like that.

Neither he nor Lou had cared for supper, so that when
Evans thought she had finished her preparations for the night
he went in and sat on the edge of her berth a while, quietly
talking. Finally, kissing the tips of her fingers in a sort of daze,
early as it was, he, too, turned in, in the berth above and both
slept.

It was in the fulfillment of his wish that Evans and Lou were
going to Carcassonne. Now they were sleeping near each
other on the train, neither knowing what the outcome of this
adventure would be.

In the night he woke and looked out at the stars. It was
sparkling moonlight. The stars were big. But on the fields lay
a coating of frost. It was getting damned cold in the compartment. There was no hurry. Cold and starlight; fields and still
villages. Thank God, Paris was behind.

Carcassonne, the medieval city. And blessed Lou: cool,
caring. So he dropped away again half remembering low hills
off to the west covered with frost.

And Lou. It was for Lou that the whole trip to Europe had
been arranged—with the greatest care. Lou Martin was taking a chance with Dev. She didn't know whether she was
engaged to another man or not. Dev, at least, wanted her and
had gone to the greatest trouble in the world for her pleasure.
Dev would take trouble to please.

Carcassonne, Carcassonne, Carcassonne, said the train.

Still the lovers slept like tired man and woman out of whom all passion has been drained.

Carcassonne, Carcassonne. The moon shining outside, Evans dreamed bitterly of his life. He saw them taking what he loved away from him and he could not open his mouth. They were degrading him and he knew they were right. He looked and looked and seemed to be living in his eyes alone. He smiled to himself, in his sleep.

The Statue of Liberty seemed ten miles high to him. He felt small but fascinated by his own fate. It was not so bad as long as he could see. All he wanted was to see Carcassonne.

Suddenly he had the feeling that the train was going in the wrong direction. He was wide awake now. He half sat up feeling the train rushing north, back to Paris with great speed. Great snow mountains, which he knew could not be there, he saw in the region of Chartres. He felt himself rushing through space feet first, instead of head first as they had started from the Quai d'Orsay. Then he realized what had happened, the train had been turned end for end on a siding in the night.

He looked at his watch, holding it up close to his eyes to make out the hands: 4:15. He had a notion to get down and crawl in with Lou. What in the world did it all mean?

He had come to Europe to be going away. He was going away now as hard as he could, but he knew, somewhere in his mind, that he would be coming back. Too often, he, Evans, had been secretly wanting to turn back—this was what he had been hiding from everybody. Yet they saw it plainly anyhow.

Bess saw it. Bess knew him. Others felt things about him, but Bess knew. Wonder what's happening to her now, poor kid? She'll come through though. Leave it to Bess. She'll come through, all right.

Why not want to turn back? What sense is there in going on? There was nothing idle in wanting, not *wanting* but *knowing* he would be getting out of this, somehow. But he hadn't gone into it that way. He'd gone in, fair and square, not knowing the end, just for Lou. But it was cheating to be pretending to be going on and to be certain, inside, that he would be returning and not have gone really at all. And yet that was not all. That is not all: there's more to it than that.

Where was Jack going, anyway? Damned if he knew. He, too, would go, would be freed from his enslavement, if he knew any place to go to or how to begin. He was trying to, now. But he wasn't going to kid himself; there was nothing in it.

Not yet at any rate. He hadn't seen anyone just go who had kept his, Evans', admiration for long. Just go. Why? He couldn't let himself do that. Why not just kill yourself. It's more sensible. And yet, he dreamed to go, madly, as he remembered at twelve he had sometimes done, madly, with no end in view; that day the kids couldn't catch him at hare and hounds, that phenomenally successful day when he had kept them baffled all the afternoon in a certain neighborhood, running, hiding, showing himself, doubling on his tracks, escaping, running again, showing himself and so on, hour after hour, running on. So, desperately scattered, he had remained *still;* whereas they, Jack and the rest, being always collected, could go loose. But if he should go loose, he would die, of this he was convinced, since to go loose to him was to go totally ungoverned, drunken, syphilitic, starved, jailed, murderous: Finis. The rest were pikers really—careful schemers, really. This had been his excuse. Not an excuse. It was the wall over which he could not climb, short of annihilation. This kept him enslaved. He could see himself running, hitting against the bushes madly; bruised charging against Moresco the giant back; going against insuperable odds.—Yet that is the only thing worth going against. He was willing but he couldn't—that was all. If they wanted to be damned fools, all right. Yet, that was what he wanted to be—really; abandoned.

Dearest Lou, how I love you.—But he decided still not to bother her but to let her sleep. The train was going at a rapid charge, charging down on the south. Vineyards, that's what they are. Vineyards. It was growing colder and colder, excessively cold. Looking out of the window just at dawn when he next wakened, Dev this time actually saw the mountains, great icy peaks not so very far off to the southwest. It was the Pyrénées! And beyond them Spain! There they were, covered with pure snow. Dev was amazed, he had not expected these simple wonders. They took him quite out of his doubting mood.

He dressed quietly not to awaken Lou but she turned over and smiled. He lay beside her for a moment, dressed as he was, kissing her tenderly upon her face and breasts. She petted his hair.

Have you seen the mountains? he said.

No, and she was awake in a moment.

Entranced, they looked out of the window while in the foreground the dim vineyards flew past them. The sun was just catching the tops of the Pyrénées. They were speechless with the beauty of it all.

Dev, she cried, Was ever anything so beautiful in this world?

Slowly the rosy tint of the mountains grew brighter. They sparkled, flashed.

What a country, what a country!

Lou had arisen from her bed to stand beside her lover to look out at the mountains. It was very cold. As Dev turned to look at her she shivered. Here, he said, throwing something about her. And he walked quickly out, smiling back and kissing his hand to her at her grateful smile.

See you later.

You bet, she said, laughingly.

Carcassonne, Carcassonne, Carcassonne. Dev was eager to arrive now that the strange character of the place had made itself known to him so powerfully. Lou was with him body and soul, as excited as he. They were like children awaiting a fulfillment of delight.

It was still early in the morning and cold, the sun having just risen, when the train deposited them, almost the only ones to descend from it, at the station of the new city of Carcassonne with its small irregular square, the park, the plane trees and, fortunately, a *fiacre* behind the station—out of the wind.

This they mounted and were soon jogging on their way a mile or so across the new bridge around the grassy outer defenses of the old fortress high above them, past the towers and crenelated walls, ascending by the old road to the barbican beside the Porte Narbonne. The drawbridge was down and the portcullis raised, rusted into place.

At the top of the steep ascent the *fiacre* had made a sharp turn and in a tiny graveled quadrangle before the principal gate, stopped—the inner city remaining inviolate to modern wheels.

A wind was whipping down from the tall battlements like arrows. It was February. There were no tourists.

In the barbican wall to the right, Dev saw the name "Blanche" cut in stone. "Blanche." Who was she? Blanche. He saw women—Blanche, all of them—moving in the streets, women violently contrasted with the stones.

The lovers had not yet breakfasted and they were cold—as it should be with beginning passion—in the narrow windswept channels of the old city streets, so that, gaining the rooms of the ancient castle, seat of the legendary counts, with their heraldry emblazoned all round the walls, they were glad for something to eat and to drink.

Carcassonne. They stood for a while looking out through the modern leaded windows over the new town across the river.—How can we imagine that old life, how rough, how inconvenient it must have been for them! In these stone chambers where they lived how the whiteness of women must have flamed against that coldness. With what a feeling of relief they must have welcomed Christianity, its softness—priceless by contrast. So different it is now to us—us whom it has wasted —so that we look back on their crudeness with pleasure even —and admiration wishing for those virtues and that—flavor.

From the warm castle rooms sallying after a rest, by the tiny garden across the paved courtyard to the fortress church of St. Nazaire, the lovers felt very happy. No one else was

there as they stood in the old church on its pagan stones
contrasting the architectural styles—early and late, mixed,
right and left before them.

Carcassonne, a rock ruined by tears. It had to be rock-
rimmed to give it credence, rock-chapeled. It tapped the rock
and sweet water flew out—a hidden gentleness which had no
certain name, in them without excuse—but like rain on armor. A brief advantage for which they panted. Water! Christ.
Water all within themselves. Themselves. Their defenses
broken, out it comes. Tears. Which have now melted the rock
which conserved it and caused it to run and disappear in the
sand.

The chapel was cold. On the uneven floor they walked
about whispering. Very old it seemed but full of a strange
assurance, because, possibly, they were young and felt no part
in it.

The garden was better, though best was to stand in the
southwest wind that tore at their garments as they went to the
western ramparts and looked out toward the snow mountains
across the valley to the southwest, mounting the archers'
galleries, peering through the slits of the *meurtrières.*

Do you remember anything of the history?

Not a word, never heard of it—

They looked long and silently, muffled from the past, at the
far Pyrénées, hiding themselves as best they could from the
invincible wind.

Boso and Irmingard, brothers of *Richard le Justicier.*

The Arabs. Pippin the Short.

It cannot have been an important place or I should have
come across it in my medieval history.

Hand in hand the two ran in the *lice* between the outer and
inner fortifications and found tiny daisies pressed close to the
ground, as earliest flowers always are, for warmth.

They saw much of the place but their minds became stiff-
ened and their faces, too, with the force of the wind and the
cold. They hid in sunny nooks of the walls, but sunless cor-
ners were desolate and they fled at last, up through a postern,

out again oppressed by the stones and the death of the place
—the cold—hating the obstinacy of the defenses—too strong
—senseless.

God, I've seen enough of that to last me a lifetime.—They
were weary too, with the early rising, the long climbing and
the wind, so they decided that they would walk, walk back to
the station—over the old bridge. At once they went fleeing
away from the icy, towering walls and, if they had had to
retrace their steps which an hour before they had taken with
zeal, with excitement, they would have shuddered and violently pulled back.

Going down to the river, the Aude, they looked back once
more with strange regret at the great northern face of the
inviolate walls, picked out with round slate-roofed towers—
unpeopled, wholly lost—and a feeling of depression made
them turn about again for the last time and run down the hill
—by a tiny hovel where a woman was hanging out clothes.
They seemed a thousand miles from the world, from Paris,
from France—they were drawn together like children running together for shelter from the cold and from a nameless
ague.

Behind them, the walls remained unseen, not to be looked
at again until they were on the train bound for Marseilles
when, covered by its warmth, they could spend their glances
once more—in passing and in comfort—upon that forbidding
masonry and its secrets—the image of a past they could not
imagine: Blanche—Mother of Saint Louis.

But now at the old bridge they stopped, their faces tingling
from the run and, looking over the breastworks, below them
they saw women washing in the stream.

The water must be icy cold, Lou said. Look at their hands.
—They felt that they had intruded upon some long-forgotten
age.

At their feet the women had stoves to keep them warm as,
kneeling in wooden stalls made of a box with one end
knocked out, they pounded the twisted sheets on the flat rock
each had before her with a wooden paddle.

The streets of the new town were desolate. The stores were dark, dead. The lovers looked down one narrow alleyway. It seemed an emanation from some impossible world.

People live here! Good God. And they are happy and they sent soldiers to the great war.

They went along the streets encountering scarcely a soul to observe them or for them to observe. The wind! A great tree leaned bending down over a wall. Two dogs they saw violently at their rut.

Spring, said Dev.

Lou was amused.

The driving wind which lifted the dust of the tiny deserted boulevard in a great cloud carried them also before it, until it drove them to the Café du Commerce by the station, behind whose plate-glass windows they sank at last tired to rest.

What lives they lived, what lives they must have lived, those old terrors of men up there—we are no more than their shadows. How must they have defended themselves, from the weather even?

Let us have an apéritif and eat later on the train—at noon.

There were but two or three old fellows motionlessly reading papers among the silent tables. It was not so warm in the café as one might believe on first entering. Cold currents from some corner assailed the feet. The street door kept opening slightly with every stronger wind blast.

God provide furs and brazier fires for the young countess in the castle to-day!

She will be thinking of her lover, and that will keep her warm. In the church it will be cold. The archbishop will have chillblains. War is a necessity when one is freezing and no help but an open fire.

What of the women washing in the stream?

Most likely they did not feel it, then as now.

Shall we stay over and visit the Cité again more at leisure to-morrow? It may be warmer.

Lou looked incredulously at him.

You said it, he replied. There is a train in forty minutes.
We'll take it. BRRR!—The twelve o'clock train to Marseilles.

Marseilles! I hope it's warm there.

Chapter VII

Marseilles

THE treeless plain about Carcassonne is covered with vineyards; through these the train started at noon to the south. Sticking their tongues out at the old gray fortifications as they went by, Evans and Lou went immediately into the diner.

There is in this part of France, in the neck that connects the peninsula of Spain with the rest of Europe, a constant feeling of the sea, the Atlantic on one side—at some distance—and on the other, the Mediterranean, the ancient Oceanus. As the two sat at lunch they looked curiously at the endless brown of the bare vineyards, in February, itself a rolling sea spread off in waves about them on all sides. It was an earth ocean seeming to break upon the very walls of the little châteaux which occupied the hill crests here and there at varying distances from the railroad in the background.

Lou had on a dark traveling suit of some shaggy material Evans did not recognize, a small black hat in the fashion, flesh-colored stockings, and French shoes decorative in cut and boldly buckled.

At least he did not have to consider her a baby.

He liked her because she was strong—and brave. Here were bravery and desire, misty and unquenchable; and she had the wit to desire what he could give her. Not that she

weighed it, but she knew—how to want, to feel and to get—
as in a game. Of love how much was there in her? But what
did he care, really? He felt that she would not break her heart
over anyone. But he had to add that in spite of the constancy
of types—none knows what will happen when the time
comes. At least, they were on their way. He believed it and
he was happy.

The train was running with few stops through the cold
squally weather. There were miles and yet miles of grape
vines, brown waves, colored like a satyr.—But the soil, Evans
explained, is good for little else than these small bitter grapes,
useless for eating and best where the soil is worst. In a rich
soil the wine-flavor is nothing. It is where there is sun, a height
and the salts which make for flavor that the best grapes are
found. Here and there are rare soils, then a wine will be
famous, and the years will bring special favors from the
weather and again the grapes record it by their flavor and
richer yield. So the secret of the waving soil gathers in the
names of the great châteaux, gathers and is gathered and
solicitously preserved. A race of wine men has grown up
flavoring this country, by the soil, as the soil flavors the grapes:
skillful, dextrous and solicitous.—This was not what he
wanted to say, but everything was burning for him in his
present mood.

Warm again, they sat at table for more than an hour after
the meal had been cleared away and the other diners had gone
back to their compartments.

Shall we talk?

No, no, not just now, dear.

They smoked instead. He had not believed she could be this
way.—So much more credit to her then for the escape. From
what? A fury always made Evans' head swell with blood when
he thought of the U. S. Anyhow, the sudden anger cured him
of his mooning. She was magnificent, her kiddishness would
pass.

Thank God, we're here.

You said it, she replied, We're in no hurry, are we?

Comparatively not, he said, and she looked out of the window quickly.

He laughed a good laugh which made her frown.

Evans studied his companion carefully. She had a round instinctive head, a good complexion, firm chin and a large mouth—he had never quite so looked at her before. Her lips, however, were really sensitive and her eyes blue but somewhat shadowed by her brows so that they showed not brilliance but reserve. The whole face was laughing—best of all, it was young.

How old? Evans guessed twenty-eight. She had never told him. Too old to be beginning this sort of thing—perhaps she is much younger.

More of a child than I thought—and he felt a quick pang of regret. Perhaps she would welch. He looked at her and did not think so. He admired her.

You're a miracle, Lou, he said.

Her reply was that the secret of the Sphinx is that she is shy!

Then for an hour they talked of France, of the grapes, of wheat, and Lou wondered about the wine, as if the French were curious addicts to some rite which kept them idolatrous before the wine drinking, amazed, when if they would but plant their ground to oats or wheat—they would be wiser.

No, the wine is cash, answered Evans, and the cash brings more wheat than would the ground itself. It is the intoxicating savor of the soil itself that's gifted for these things.

Finally, feeling strange and too conscious of each other in the deserted dining car, they returned to their compartment.

Now the vines had ceased. There were swampy meadows to the left, great stretches reaching in the middle distance to the glint of water beside which were shining white mounds of salt—or so Evans judged them to be.

But when in a lift of the tracks they saw, they saw, to the right, a sail, over the edge of a dune and then the blue! a great exultation seized the two companions.

The sea!

Evans saw: Grecian galleys; Africa just there, imminent; the blue, blue water. Then over the dunes, looking out to sea —the granite changelessness of time.

The train is annihilated, what of the window or the speed? It is the salt grass, it is the sand, it is the sea. There has been no change.

No change. The lovers were awed by the sea, giving up its history to the imagination. A richness, without loss, ran beside the train as if it had been a toy. It entered on invisible waves that played about their temples full of pleasure: Greece, Rome, Barbary: to-day the same—the accumulation of all time—perfect.

Especially to Americans does the Mediterranean bring memories—to Americans cut off from its good.

It was a bright interval, for as night came nearer, the train turned north again and a cold rain came with the darkness. It was cold and black by five o'clock.

At six they passed Arles but the determination to descend and spend a day there had faded with the forbidding weather. Across the Rhone the lights were shining at Avignon:

No, let us go on at once to Marseilles.

Marseilles, the city of sailor love!

At the Hôtel de France the steam radiator was ardently hugged. Oh boy! A wash. Marseilles! And they dashed out famished, and down the *Cannebière*—thronged by Algerians, French, Spanish, English, Americans, down to the old harbor to the shipping, feeing one of the many beggars sitting there by the water. This was fine. At a table of the *Restaurant au Port,* they ordered a *bouillabaisse.* A cat, outside the glassed-in porch overlooking the harbor, walked up and down, confused by the glass, smelling the fish and trying to get in.

They talked long over their plates and a bottle of Meursault. Lou told him intimately of herself much that he could not have guessed and had not known before, talking in a low voice. He was interested and forgot himself completely in her.

After a while it began to penetrate to them that they were

being watched: at a table nearby were four drunken Americans—or two American men and two French girls whom they had in tow. Lou was nervous, more scared than Evans had imagined possible. A product of Melrose High, enervated by a lifelong unprofitable contact with boys and men—without issue—she was not taking it as easily as he had believed she would.

He put it down to just nerves and hoped she would get over it later.

A noisy party in the next room, the four at their backs, the masts of all nations in the basin and the cat weaving up and down on the roof of the porch outside the glass—in front of the ships and the lights—before them, they continued to eat, toward the end without saying a word.

Lou was very ill at ease.

But it was only that she was eager to be alone with him away from the ears of the heterogeneous crowd. Back in the hotel, she felt serious, alert, alarmed. Her eyes were round and startled when he came to her after the bath, but she was tender and clung to him quite out of her usual temper, but, as she had been all that day, like a small child.

Chapter VIII

The Riviera

THE next morning, windy, clear and still cold, but with a southern brightness of air. Ready for the trip eastward along the border of the sea, the two were in a mood of extreme exhilaration, more especially Lou whose constant warming glances and eager, simple questions, What's that? and Tell me, Tell me, soon had her companion nearly as alert and curious as was she herself. Oh look! It was her first mimosa tree in blossom.

Like your hair! smiled Dev. But she did not notice. Look, look!

All these things also will be discovered, said he half aloud but she did not hear; she was too busy looking from the train window—in this suddenly acquired south hitherto unsuspected.

Evans constructed a more conscious symbolism as they rode along by the sea.—So this is the new life, he said to himself. What would Bess think of me now?

Look, look, Lou kept saying, now darting to the sea side of the car—they were fortunate to have secured a compartment alone—now to the other. Olive trees and cactus and low palms; the sun caught in the protecting mountains; the pale blue sea—and Lou was all delight.

And still it was cold, but cold and sunny—a clear Mediterranean chill full of a crystallic light. So this is the Riviera! It was bare, as they edged along the sea. Scrub pine and oak clung to the towering gray rocks to the north. Now they would be running close by the sea with jagged gray promontories catching the low surges, then they would strike back into the coastal plain where some peninsula would jut out and near them at the left again they would see the low coastal range, the *Alpes Maritimes*, rugged, bare eminences of stratified gray rock, treeless for the most part—and then there at the peak of one, the tricolor of France. It capped a low concrete dome, the beginning of the fortifications about Toulon. Toulon whence Napoleon set sail for Egypt. Military roads zigzagged up the cliffs. A curious bare country into which the sun beat all day long.

Oh look, look, said Lou. It was an orange tree. How wonderful, and just the day before yesterday we were in Paris. It is miraculous.—At the stations men and women were going about in summer costumes and light top coats. In a little station garden there were flowers whose names they did not know. Tangerines were on the trees.

But again near the mountains a small brown village, startlingly apart from the new town, stood out to a peak on an isolated hill or there was one which clustered up the mountain side, reminiscent of the days of quick attack from the sea and the necessity for a mountain defense. Such was Cagnes—but the great town they first came to was Cannes. Should they get out and remain here for a few days?

At first Lou was for it. The tennis matches would be on, they could put up at some small place and see Lenglen and the rest. Tennis was Lou's great key with which, up to now, she had unlocked nearly every good which life had so far offered her. Through that means she had found her friends, formed her athletic opinions concerning life and built up her small talk. She played well.

Logically enough it was in a mood antithetic to her usual one, during a time of uncertainty, that she had fallen in with

Evans. She wanted to stop and see the matches but as the train
came to a standstill in the station of Cannes—the crowds
waiting, the excitement, even the courts themselves to be
seen from the window—she did not move.

Evans was already on his feet reaching for the luggage.

Well?

No.

Evans sat down. He put his arm about her waist and together they looked out at the jabbering mob rushing back and
forth below them outside the car window: English faces,
American faces, and the rest. It was easy to read in the compartment while the train was stopped; they picked up the map
and located themselves, counting the stations before Villefranche where Dev had said they would get down. Another
half hour.

Then they were in the station at Nice: Nice a smooth
indentation of the coast line, the great hotels backing away
from the town up on the hills, glass and bright towers. It was
all a brilliant confirmation to Lou of her newly awakened
insights into happiness. And then the mountains came close
in and they were just at the sea's edge once more ducking
through tunnels, with cliffs below them fringed by white
foam.

In all crevices in the rocks were small gardens. In places
high retaining walls had been constructed to hold the earth
in place. These plots were planted especially with carnations
against the time of the carnival approaching now. Few of the
flowers were in bloom yet but here and there color would
show.

Then after a moment they arrived at the lonesome little
station on top of the high cliff, Villefranche, and there Dev
bade her alight. Only a few others got down. The privacy, the
light, the mountains, the sea, at once appealed to Lou; then
as she turned she looked out over that narrow bay, far below
her, with the wooded promontory behind which lay Beaulieu
to the left and the old fishing port of Villefranche itself off to
the right. Inaccessible, it seemed at first, approached, as she

saw later, only by a footpath beside high walls stuck with cactus and overhung by flowering vines. It was a land of grave promise, gray rocks and the sea—but packed with brilliant light and a keen air.—No wonder they can play tennis in this country.

Three old men in blue blouses put their things into a small hand-cart and started off up the hill, over the bridge that crosses the railroad track and then up the path and down the path to the village. Lou and Dev came behind with their wraps and lighter grips.

To Lou it all continued an inexpressible joy. The old narrow streets by their quaintness seemed to be unlocking a long unused delight. She wanted to pat on the head the little boys whom they passed and who paid no attention to them. But she took tight hold of Dev's arm instead and kept looking into the small dark windows of shops down three steps below the street and below the natural level of the eye, with strings of onions and peppers—in the Italian style—hanging outside before them. The place was full of smells.

Evans explained that the city had belonged to Italy until modern times. In places the streets were precipitous, paved with flat stones, narrow, with the gutter in the center, and went often down irregular flights of steps, dark and not always sweet smelling—yet it was a delight to Lou.

The men they met wore round blue caps. Many were dressed as sailors, though as the lovers found later this was an affectation—for the most part—since few of them had more concern with boats than with those in which they took tourists for a good price on short rowing trips about the bay in summer.

Following the old men with the luggage they passed the central fountain in a tiny square with a strong smell of wine barrels about it; there were all manner of tiny stores with small windows showing caps, dried figs, and other handy merchandise for sale, but all small, dark. Now it would be a smell of cheese, or they'd come to a baker's shop—or it would be cloth in bolts they'd pass, emerging at last into a diminutive plaza with steps leading up to the right to the church and down to the left again to the wharf and the Hotel Boston by the sea.

Before stopping their march, the two Americans, unused to such a February, walked to the edge of the stone wharf and looked down into the blue clear water, seeing the pebbles and rusty débris below them under the movement of quiet waves.

Oh Dev, how wonderful it is just to be here.—At the back of the hotel were two old men smoking. Boats were fastened to iron rings in the massive stones of the wharf. The two were ever filled anew with the charm of the place, its diminutive self-sufficiency, its antique streets and the near lovely sea.

They ate supper in the quiet, rather English hotel which pleased them—with its family air—not at all, and went off on a ramble in the dark looking for a better lodging.

Finding none at that hour, all the inhabitants it seemed having gone to rest bird-like with the setting sun, they went down beyond the hotel keeping beside the sea on the little dock and there lay back across the still warm stones where the sun had beat an hour before. Phosphorus flashed in the water but from a third story window someone emptied some slops near them. A little sobered, they turned back to the hotel for that night at least. The beacon on the point beyond Beaulieu kept flashing its circular flare across the face of the village every forty seconds. It flashed into their room.

Chapter IX

The Villa St. Denis

IN THE morning, waking refreshed after a good sleep which they had both badly needed, having breakfasted, they set out again determined to find a more congenial lodging. Unused to such a February the two Americans walked again to the edge of the stone wharf just back of the hotel to look down into the clear blue water, seeing once more the pebbles and rusty débris below them under the movement of quiet waves.

An old fellow, in a sailor suit, was leaning from the stern of a rowboat fastened to the wharf, slowly, carefully fishing for sea snails by means of a split stick. And in the sun, leaning their chairs back against the rear wall of the hotel were two men idly smoking. As on the evening before, the lovers were ever filled anew with the Idyllic charm of the place beside this lovely sea.

To Lou especially it seemed a promise fulfilled which she could not fathom. A light, it was, piercing a cloudy northern morning. She had not been at ease in the large city of Marseilles. Here she seemed to have come to rest. They intended to stay here a month at least.

It was a perfect day. They took a path south of the hotel through the square below the town and, keeping to the left on along the edge of the sea, they soon found themselves going close above the water by a narrow paved walk hanging to the face of a great wall. At its feet to the left the sea crashed in noisy rushes among the gray honeycombed rocks. They stopped by the handrail to watch the water brilliantly at play when they became aware of groups of soldiers sauntering toward them and passing to go into the town. Evans recognized the famous blue devils of France, officers and men, the *Chasseurs Alpins,* by their broad berets and dark blue coats, their hobnailed boots clacking and grinding on the creamy, smooth stones of the hanging walk.

At their feet the sea pounding in churned itself to whiteness in the gray honeycombed rocks.

Smell it, said Lou as they passed on above the beating surf. That's not the ocean smell.

No, it is less—less something. It is fresher perhaps. Perhaps it is because there is no tide here.

No tide? said Lou. Isn't that part of the ocean?

No tide. The tideless sea. So there is never any exposed sea bottom, as there would be every day at low tide on the Atlantic, and so, I suppose, that is the reason there is less smell.

Going round a bend of the old fortress wall, a hundred feet further ahead the hanging pathway terminated and the lovers came out upon a new vista—a modern extension of the old town, small villas and gardens, at the foot of the hill on which, higher up, lay the road to Nice.

And two hundred feet further on, close by the water, stood the entrance to the barracks of the *Chasseurs.*

Inside the gate there was a long parade ground at the edge of a deep blue basin formed to seaward by a breakwater with a small circular lighthouse at the near end.

To this they crossed on a footbridge and continued back along its top to the lighthouse, getting a fresh view of the basin, the barracks and the hill back of them over the water from that vantage. Outside, churning waves broke continuously against rough granite blocks buttressing the sea wall. It was a delightful ramble and one they would take many times under varying conditions thereafter. But now they did not delay but turned back in quest of a new lodging.

Emerging from the barracks entrance they found a broad wagon road leading up outside the old fortress, zigzag to the top of the steep hill. In the first elbow of this road lay a garden, all fenced in with a modern woven wire barrier. Inside there was a man in slippers and pajamas, beside small orange and lemon trees in fruit, leaning over some plant beds. Lou and Evans looked at each other and smiled, thinking of the man's pleasure.

The gardener, a stoutish fellow of forty, straightened himself and looked hard at them as they began to walk up the road which turned at the end of his garden and led back climbing toward the hilltop. The entrance to the house was upon this road a little further uphill. There was a ticket on the door. Rooms to rent! It was enough.

The rest of the day passed in transporting and arranging their things and there Dev undressed her when, supper done, they sat until after midnight, the two of them wrapped in a single quilt, the windows wide open, watching the darkness and the lights.

Chapter X

First Days

NEXT morning, the second of February, at six, Dev was awakened by a great fanfare of trumpets. Jumping up he opened the jalousies and looked out on the narrow bay: the water was placid and blue. To the right in the parade ground of the *Chasseurs* the band was marching up and down at drill, blowing by squads, *corps de chasse* carrying the tune at a great clip, then, at the proper moment, the rest would fling up their trumpets, twirl them high overhead with a flash in the sun and redouble the intensity of the clatter with their tara tara. Over and over again they played the same tune. It was stirring. From the narrow balcony Evans saw that it was lovely in the garden. A small tree with eight or ten tangerines among its brilliant green leaves was just beneath the window.

Turning about in the dimly-lit room he looked at Lou, still sleeping, with her arms thrown above her head on the pillow, the loveliest arms he had ever in his life beheld, he thought. She was breathing softly. He sat beside her watching her as she slept. He had never been quite so happy.

Breakfast was served to them in bed by the little Breton maid, coffee and rolls, with fresh butter which she fetched from town every day—walking along the sea wall to get it—and now and again, jam. She was very discreet, very solicitous and very prompt, was Gäite.

69

That first melting week the lovers were ravished merely by each other's presence. Everything they could think of that they wanted to do they did, repeatedly, lovingly under all the moods of day and night. And over all, before which they worshiped together at night, she full of growing certainty and he near her in everything, they discovered the parallel by day in the Mediterranean spring, caught by the gray mountains behind the edge of the sea—a clarity that picked out flowers and fruit and the faces of men—as if they had been preceded by Ariel or an eerie attendant who fulfilled all promises.

Sometimes they would stand talking for an hour at the rail of the hanging walk leading back to town, watching the waves as he watched her about the room, at first faintly diffident in posture—or was it the cold, for it was still cold most times.

There were nights when they lay hand in hand for hours while Dev spoke of—the things he would be doing. Her comments were foreign to the matter but to the point if one changed his perspective and this Dev could do quickly to enjoy her. She melted, melted, melted under his delighted warming love which was an extraordinary south to her—until she was nearly freed from everything that had been America.

Evans now set himself seriously to work writing. Lou did not interfere with this, she was rather glad of it. She walked, played tennis and read by his side. They walked together or she went with friends they soon encountered in the village to play on the courts at Beaulieu. He would wait on the balcony to see her returning down the garden path, which she invariably did, swinging along, head erect, eyes slightly raised as if in contemplation of a world bright and in fact visible. At such moments, he would be filled with the greatest admiration and love, waiting to receive her fresh from her athletic exertions and the bath.

At first her postures were staid. She would sit with her head a little bowed or lie curled up and smile at him. Often he watched her standing fixing her hair with arms raised in classic style.

He followed the smoothness of her back with the straight-

ness of the hips or looked at her turned a third from him. Lou
had had a great deal of petting—a strong taste of love in the
American style as a girl—had been more or less engaged (as
it is said) for a year to a boy of her own age.

They early found it necessary to have a fire burning in the
hearth—a fire of oak roots, dug for the most part from stumps
on the hills, stumps of trees long-felled. But the chief delight
to Dev was in the mere presence of this kind of simple wonder, this curious variant of himself—moving about: A woman
—lovely and young. Let me see, let me see! these were his
constant words. He covered her with admiration all day long.

And, accompanying them always, outside, was the garden.
Narrow paths bordered the little beds where, in a curious
mixture, chrysanthemums, roses and potatoes grew. There
was a grape trellis and chickens, two of them, in a little coop
by the sago palm, and oranges and lemons and tangerines
were in the small trees.

Each day it would be something new to be done or seen.
There were several of the walks, however, they took nearly
every day. The favorite was the one they had first enjoyed
down to the parade ground then out by the tiny drydock to
the breakwater's end where you could see a red light burning
at night. Here, outside the breakwater, an old man would be
fishing sometimes, while inside, in the basin, one could look
down ten, twenty feet to the bottom and see small fish going
about in the green water half way down playing follow the
leader.

One day it was stormy—Lou was afraid. She had been
indolent that night. There was no rain but gray waves filled
the harbor. A small French cruiser squadron had come in and
lay now rocking at anchor off to the left. It was beastly cold.
Looking out over the gray sea, Evans saw the periscope of a
submarine.

Dev, what is to become of us? said Lou at his side.

The submarine made straight in, rising slowly to the surface. Spray dashed from its prow. In the heavy sea, for some
reason, it made a great turn, throwing up a white circle and

headed out again. As it reached the heavier waves outside, it submerged once more till only the periscope could with difficulty be seen slicing the rough water.

It was the end of the first week,—the all-absorbing adoration of the white body was past now. Dev could close his eyes and see her standing, lying, walking, every shadow and movement familiar to his retentive eye.

Chapter XI

Certain Days

I've got to go out.

Threatening as it was, they put on their things and fled down to the walk before the old fortress. The waves were pounding in now so that it was almost impossible to pass. There were three bad places. They watched the water as with a great roar it came in. Crash. The walk was inundated. Milky white the recoil churned in the hollow rocks. They passed and took the tram for Nice. At the entrances to private grounds on the cliffs, blood-red cactus flowers and mimosa and geraniums were blossoming; and in the commercial gardens were pinks and daisies to their right. Restless and dissatisfied in Nice they walked along the boulevard des Anglais—past the great hotels. Wealth, English and French; a savor of undesirable sophistication chilled their mood completely. Overawed by the flood of inanity, or forbidding nonentity, they scarcely knew where to turn.

A few dolled-up old women on the raised hotel emplacements looked curiously at them. Now and then someone would turn to stare at Lou. She was disturbed; they walked rapidly from one end of the esplanade to the other.—Dev, take me out of this. I hate it. But turning into the city, through the public square, she felt somewhat easier. At a little dress shop facing the park Evans insisted on buying her a new blue dress.

Are we like these people? Dev, tell me.

No.

By chance they came upon a restaurant, which seemed to promise delight. It proved the find of their sojourn; to this they returned again and again,—for the Châteaubriand, the curiously crisp onions, the pears. Evans wanted to stay on and drink, but after an hour Lou would have no more of it. They hired a taxi, as it was beginning to rain, to take them back to Villefranche—as to a cloistered spot and, locking themselves in their rooms, Lou embraced her lover with greatest abandon. She sobbed. Dev undressed her in the dark as she lay relaxed unprotesting before him. Her body seemed to give off a soft light lying there as if forgotten by her spirit of anguish.

From now on Lou was changed. She flew gayly about the rooms or went off for walks by herself while he was writing. She even came to Dev with her attentions, playing seriously, free—not noticing her own movements as she had done at first. She began to talk to the Madame in her broken French. On the sunny chairs under the arbor downstairs she would sit while Madame made her practice the words.

Not orange but *oránge.*

Citron. La mer. Un chien. They would laugh. Dev would hear them as he was typing his MSS. or reading or—he would find them there together when he would come back from an errand in the town.

One day they decided to climb the mountain back of the village. So they set out after breakfast through the old town and then the upper town and so up and up, to a path that redoubled on itself, a red dirt path, up, up zigzag until they seemed to be right above the roofs of the houses, with gardens of carnations near them and below them the mossy red-tiled church and far off beside the harbor their own home. The Mediterranean spread out its blue cloth, carrying tiny battleships, little tracings of waves and a V-shaped creeping line moving slowly where a small boat was coming to the shore.

Higher and they were in the midst of oak woods, oak and pine with gardens beside an old house by the wayside, the road passing the front and then crossing higher in the rear above. Old olive trees were there. Goats. A jackass. With a cry of pleasure Lou came upon her first violets. Up, until they were quite beyond the village and out in a rugged wilderness —with the sea shining, less marked by waves, over the tops of scrubby trees which seemed to start from the very rocks. They were exhilarated by the climb.

Still up they went with asphodel by the road and some pink daisies, daisies and violets again, until, quite unexpectedly, they were standing on a concrete road, with a roadhouse beside it and autos passing frequently by. It was the upper Corniche road. Winded and thirsty they went into the musty little inn there, where they drank some bottled beer and the old woman of the place presented Lou—as they were going out—with a bunch of narcissi she had picked in the garden. Dev wanted to pay her but the old woman turned quickly away into the house, bowing her head and smiling at them as they waved their hands and departed.

They decided not to take the auto road but instead crossed it and followed a narrow cartway which seemed to promise more pleasure. As they entered it, there was before them a half broken almond tree in blossom. To the left was Nice. But to the north they saw the pure white snowy caps of the Alps, range on range of jagged points, more and more misty as they disappeared into the distance. But the chief charm was that between the lovers and that mountainous snow field was a deep, deep valley right below them with green fields and a tiny silver river flowing through.

They walked now differently than ever they could have done in their lives before. They seemed to be alone. All that they could do, all that they could say to each other, had been done and said, for sheer necessity and delight. They walked and the movement of walking warmed them against the cutting wind.

Here, almost in fear lest a bandit should assault them, they wandered for two hours, resting and playing, picking almond blossoms, looking below into the valley, over at the snow mountains or up into the honeycombed rocks where asphodel grew thickly among the nameless stubble and low growth— up to the summit of bare rounded rock at the right.

Occasionally there would be diversion, rock-clefts that were dripping and dark, then to the left again a parapet where they would lean and look directly down—like gods—amused or merely curious at some farmhouse below.—Come, Dev, do not lean so far over.

But the fascination of the drop held them both and they would look.—So isolated. Alone. The two.

Then they came out on the main road again at Upper Eze.

It was noon now. Here they found a small outdoor restaurant with sunny tables, no company but a small pup and the proprietor, the most genial in the world. They were tired and flushed, hungry and parched, the food was good but the wine, a bottle of old Pommard, cold perhaps as it should not have been, proved the final dot of perfection to their enjoyment.

After dinner, stiff, sore of foot, they didn't know whether to cut downhill to the sea and so turn back home or to go on. So they began walking, going round behind the inn where a very old man was knocking some kind of fruit from a vine covering a high arbor—and the road was peppered with over-ripe olives fallen from an old tree nearby.

Loosened in joint and in spirit they ended toward five o'clock by reaching the sea-rimmed botanical garden of the Prince of Monaco where in the caves below the museum they saw his delicate collection of submarine flora and small fishes —having covered about twenty miles in the day. Then by train they rode back dreamily along the sea to Villefranche.

Another day they spent the whole morning about the barracks, watching the soldiers at their work and at drill. A machine gun squad was charging down the parade ground under the eye of a superior officer. Each man carried a detached part of the mechanism heavy to carry. They would rush ahead, drop to the gravel at command, and assemble the parts in violent haste as the gunner, with his beret pulled down covering his face, took his position at the breech ready to fire.

Another day they walked out to the immaculate lighthouse at the point of Cap Ferrat, footing the red walks of the former Emperor Franz Joseph of Austria.

Another day it was the chilly *Carnaval* at Beaulieu, the first one of the season thereabouts. And it was for this the little round-faced men had been blowing all those weeks. There they were, assembled all, with bouquets in their coats, ready in the center of the court. Dev remembered with delight the efforts of the drill sergeant to make them perfect in their parts, how he had rushed up to one of them nigh apoplectic from his recent efforts and cried out: *Vous avez joué de la salté aujourd'hui!* and how the man had taken it without the quiver of a muscle. Now the decorated carriages and autos were approaching. Small bunches of fresias, carnations, violets, stocks, mimosa, were flying through the air. One thrifty woman was picking up the best of the fallen missiles, carefully brushing and inspecting them to take them home, perhaps to sell them again in Nice later. It was very cold that day.

Many days, after the first week, Lou would be at Beaulieu playing tennis with an English lady she had met in the village. These visits to Beaulieu became more frequent as time went on.

But most days they would just bask in the sun, in the garden, on the balcony or the rocks, just soaking in the beneficent Riviera sunshine, an all-sufficient plenitude that ripened fruit and drew the sweet up in the trees and the alyssum to cover the rocks everywhere. The moat of the old fortress where the soldiers practiced rifle-fire was not far from the zigzag road to the top of the hill. Its edge was unguarded. The drop was forty feet at least—a sheer drop—to the trampled grass below. Another day they sat in the Casino at Nice, drinking cognac until two a. m. Walking to the beach, half drunk, a wave came up out of the dark and drenched them to the knees.

Another cold rainy day they sat by the oakroot fire in their rooms and Lou slept lying heavily half on the floor, half in his arms until he carried her into bed.

Another day he watched the old men, early in the morning from a boat in the harbor hauling in their net, laboriously, skillfully, dextrously, and catching nothing.

One evening they went to the tiny café just outside the barracks entrance with its bar stuccoed to represent a rock, a submarine picture, where the shrieking, squealing gramophone was playing interminably: Yes, we have no bananas—while the soldiers got up from dominos or cards to fox trot with each other in their heavy shoon. The drinks though were good. Now and then the daughter of the house would dance serious-faced, as if for the ten thousandth time, with one of the men, or more often, with one of the non-commissioned officers who fraternized with the others. It was a very small, very poor room with about eight tables in it, and situated twenty feet beyond the entrance to the barracks gates which were never closed.

In the town one day an agent—at the Crédit Lyonnaise—wanted to sell them a place at Beaulieu for 500,000 francs. Evans smiled.

Then one day in the fourth week Lou came in from tennis, hot and uncommunicative, and waited to prepare herself for the bath. Dev went out to watch the waves.

When later he turned and saw her waving to him from the balcony he stood for a moment, watching her, unable to move —he could not tell why. Then he walked slowly back along the path.

Lou embraced him as usual in the room. Then she told him her story.

She became panicky once the excitement bred by the relation of the new adventure had passed.—Dev, dear Dev! What else could I do? You can't blame us, Dev, if we do marry rich men, can you?—He agreed with her that it was right. She had been proposed to by a man she had met at the courts,—an Englishman—and she had fallen.—He is rich, Dev, rich! Do you know what that means? What do I care, now?

That night he walked late and alone. Lou had gone to Beaulieu to a dance. In the little village of Villefranche whose streets even at this early hour were black, deserted, he stopped before a small inn. There was a great twanging of guitars inside and men's voices singing. He paused to listen. The laughter and the singing continued when suddenly the door burst open and a young man came out. Standing against the wall he let out a great hissing stream accompanied by a prolonged windblast, then suddenly seeing Dev, and laughing as if slightly embarrassed, he called out:

Ça fait du bien au corps, and went in again.

That she should go, he was prepared for that; but for this other—he was not prepared. That she would leave him he had sensed long since; but in this other, his sense had failed him. He had believed that he was going on. He had believed it, lived it for three months past, after all these years.—And nothing had happened.

Now he must go back, he must go back like a beaten dog. But the sheer sense of Lou's loss rose keenest in him for the moment and he was crushed.

When he got back to the rooms, she was not there. He was wild with anger and jealousy. He lay watching the light of Cap Ferrat; an evil eye it flashed back and forth across his window which he did not close. When Lou did come in, an hour later, he started up wildly to see her.

She flung herself into his arms.

Chapter XII

The Last Night at Villefranche

Lou was speaking. Her voice was sure.—I'm not telling you everything I know and have felt, dear. You wouldn't want me to. You have made me know it would be ridiculous. Just say to yourself that I have decided to go it alone. You have been tender with me, you have sprinkled me with love as if I were some delicate flower. I love you for it but I didn't really need it. I shall never forget you. I love you, Dev, in the way I can, more than anything in this world. I'd marry you to-morrow if there would be any sense in it. I'll marry you to-morrow anyway if you want me.

He did not answer.

You see. You do not want me. You know that I could cling to you, if I wanted to. I could marry you, you know I could, I could return and live with you back there and life would be just hell for us both. Wouldn't it? And yet we have been happy as angels here. It is only that this is the end—for us. We have been happy and—that is all. Now I'm going on. So are you.

She did not know what the devil he was thinking.

You see, Dev, she continued; he did not answer but held her close to him; she pushed him gently away—Dev, I am not literary. I don't give a damn about all this talk of art and writing. It's all right for you and it may mean much—I don't know. Perhaps it does, but it's nothing to me. You have taught me enough to know that that doesn't make it good or bad or right or wrong either way—but it is not for me. I can't stand those people. They seem weak, inane, even the best of them seem to be putting on their pained lives—for what? I can't see it. I want to marry someone with more—I'm not afraid to say it. I want to marry a man who has a place. I have to have it. I want money—

Oh, Dev dear, perhaps I'm making excuses, but sometimes you seem—Dev, there's something the matter with you. You don't register. What in the world are you about? What does the world mean to you? You don't seem serious. You frighten me. Really, I don't understand you. I want someone I can understand. You are—You should protest more. You shouldn't lie there and take this. Why don't you do something about it? What is the matter with you?

He got up and looked out at the bay, quiet in the dark.—Blond break-up.

To be young, to be gay, to be clever, and not to know where one is going, nor why, nor how? Very well. Less intoxicating is to go differently.

But he felt lonesome and depressed. He was conscious of a lack of feeling—it was true. His design seemed frivolous beside the warm surge of Lou's realistic impulses.

By marriage you do not do a serious thing but a frivolous one—you shift responsibility back upon a crowd of instinctive, senseless—

Whoa! cautioned Lou.

Yes, you do, you lay off a burden—the necessity of invention.

The next day they left the place, together, for decency's sake.

There were two trains, going in opposite directions, due at the station within ten minutes of each other. No one was there to see them depart. Dev kissed Lou and put her on the train for Marseilles and Paris. She stood at the window look-

ing at him with a wry face and half-laughing, half-tearful eyes.
Then the train moved and was gone, only a whiff of sulphurous smoke coming back from the tunnel's mouth where Lou
had disappeared. When she had said she would marry him
anyway, he had been startled for a moment, thinking, My
God! maybe it's going to happen now after all.

At The Ancient Springs

Of Purity And Of Plenty

Chapter XIII

Through to Italy

As EVANS crossed to the other track to be ready for his own train, he had suddenly a luminous conviction that spring was definitely at hand. Lou! he called after the departing train, but it sounded hollow. She had gone and he was relieved, though he strongly suspected that under this lay something else which would make itself known later. He dared not think of certain days, passing backward forever and yet still close at hand.

He seemed to himself to be standing in the noon sun waiting on the east bound gravel walk at Villefranche for a train that was to take him to Italy.—Well, so he was. What of it? He had not known he would be so utterly indifferent to his loss. Lou, he said again, and it meant—almost nothing. He looked down at the bay, rippling below the cliff, and unexpectedly wished to God he could drop through the air into it and never breathe again, yet the thought seemed pleasant.

But out of the tunnel burst with a great clatter the engine of his own train. In another few moments comfortably seated he was moving beside the same old road which they had taken several times during the weeks just past to Monte Carlo—but this time he was going through!

Good-by, Villefranche. He strained to look back to see if he could see the Villa St. Denis. When he succeeded, then truly he felt a hard stab of pain. But it merely made him set his jaw a little and turn away.

It is impossible to live, that is all. What could we have done more?

There for the last time he saw it, the same small red-roofed village at the bottom of the bay protected by the old fortress, tufted with straggly palm trees, and finally—as if they had broken through the confinements of the old town, as they had —the few modern villas stretching out at the foot of the rocky cliff beyond the fort by the blue, blue water. It was a swiftly fleeting view which disappeared rapidly as the train gained speed. Already they were at Beaulieu. A beautiful day. Three girls were walking slowly along a street leading from the station out toward the Cape. They did not even turn around as the train pulled in and came to a stop.

Impossible to live, impossible to live, impossible to live.— But impossible; therefore the arts have authenticity. All attempts at directness end in stupidity. Just to go, that's all— to turn into a steam engine with eyes. While, deeper down— Italy is there, where once men lived, not like me. What can I have done? Insane to lose her, insane to keep her. But the jog of the train was growing more and more restful, working a drugging power to take him from his mood into its own.

The train having passed Beaulieu ran close to the water with the fortified gray hills always to the north. Evans knew every foot of the way—and with happiest recollections to move him to emotion. But by now he had sallied out from his body where it sat slumped in the corner of the compartment, numbed to rest, while, in imagination at least, he enjoyed a freedom to come and go as he would, even in the running train, a sense split off from feeling.

Gardens came up to the tracks like wild deer in wonder of the passing train.

There was a hotel at B—with a blackish cliff behind it, hollowed out.

At the station at Monte Carlo there was fashion; English

faces, long, assertive, bored, puerile, excited, demanding service; Americans, less noisy, more alert, getting to the right place at once without noise. There were French idlers in caps, porters looking up and down blandly or smiling at the foreigner—at Monte Carlo where they shoot captive doves over the sea, and old, brass-faced women and men like galvanized corpses sit by the gambling tables the night long. Exotic, fat-leaved plants grow in beds before the Casino.

Mentone! where Lou and he had gone one day with her delightful English lady friend and another. What a day! Snow up there. They had driven the whole way to Sospel in a taxi, stopping just a moment for a rest at the abandoned hilltop town of Castillon, a wild, inaccessible place, just grass and falling walls.

Sospel! Do you remember the cats under the tables right in broad daylight?

Then the hike back, the taxi following us, snow and asphodel again, and the old olive trees—marking the road with dropped fruit as if they had been old goats tethered there.

She gave Lou a great bunch of cornflowers, stopped the taxi in Mentone to buy them on the way back, a great armful of cornflowers.

That was a humane gesture; if one understood that fully, life would be pushed ahead two hundred years, no doubt. Two thousand more likely. Sospel, high up like a bell ringing in the mountains, holding time back, telling: stupidity breeds fast. We go ahead and leave the best back of us.—High up there, cold in the sun.

Impossible to live. From Sospel, we walked back to Castillon, we four, two by two, half a mile between us, alone on the road, the taxi following. That's sense, plain sense. We were tired. We talked. Impossible to make such things last. Only stupidity breeds. Sospel, like a bell, the bell of the asphodel, green, odorless—flower of Hades, flower of the dead.

So he heard himself talking pleasantly, without feeling, watching the words fall.

She was frightened the way that damned fool taxi guy took

the upcurves cutting out near the edge of the precipice! Why in hell was she the one of us to be frightened? Lou just didn't notice it. Damned risky business though.

Hour after hour the train clicked on, hour after hour lulling him, wheedling him—away. The sea was always at his right all the afternoon, cold looking, flecked with light; the shore was pebbly and yellow.—The sunless sea gives up out of its body, fish.

He forgot the train; he himself slid forward—he alone, trainless—he, the train itself—alone. The sea, a fusion of metals, the xanthochromic sea.—Now, never dropping back to feeling, he was all eyes. The world existed in his eyes, recognized itself ecstatically there. This then was real: all he saw—but not in man. Therefore never could he look long into the eyes of anyone: that, neither they nor he could stand. Elsewhere, everywhere he saw reality, split, creviced, multiplied. The brilliant hardness of the world, clear, full of color and outline, depth, shadow, reaffirming light, filled him with security and contentment. The seasons were to him like four fruits: one of glass, one of wood, one of the most luscious flesh and one of snow. He could see them clearly, plucked upon a board, in a dish—only one of them perhaps to be eaten and that incidentally, quite by accident. Toward them one did not extend the hand.

All along the shore the train ran looking at the sea out of one eye—and by the sea whole families of fishermen, French perhaps or Italians, were pulling in the red nets in the lowering sun, pulling them up, children, women and men, all together, up upon the yellow pebbles, miles of pebbly coast about them. Why just here?

A presence there is, a thing that lives here always, always unaffected by man, always wild. A god be damned. That was a Greek affectation because they were fools like the rest of us —but a presence there is hears the waves rattle upon the stones.

Ino. Who the devil was Ino? Ino weaving strands of seaweed or something like that, on the polymorphic pebbles.

Palemon, shaker of bright seastaff: like glass, a green glassy spear with the sun shining through it, emerald green—

He saw at Ventimiglia, the first stop over the border, Italian troops entraining. He saw prominent among them a stalwart and very much excited young man. His helmet was circled with a garland of leaves and flowers. On either side of him was a younger man, his brothers perhaps. One was embracing him excitedly, kissing him again and again, crying and hugging him and being hugged in return. All about the station it was going on, but this group was the cap of it all.

Leaving Ventimiglia, in Italy now, he saw on the gray hills low hovels of gray stone. He could hear in his mind the rasping voices of the old women, he could smell it, tell it all, every detail known, the dirt in the wrinkles, the pisswet nether clothes of the brats, the tan and grime wrestling, the hair stuck together at the ends, growing from the scaly scalps, from poor soil—

Ç'est lui, l'homme qui ne tue pas les moustiques!

He fell asleep finally.

At Genoa it was near midnight when he awoke with a start to realize that the train was dead in the dark station. The people were leaving it, dragging all their belongings with them. He hurried and got out also.

Chapter XIV

Night

GENOA. The name sounded hollow, depressing as the coldly sulphurous gallery through which he was passing, baggage in hand, to the wicket. He had not wanted to stop here. It annoyed him not to have foreseen this compulsory arrest. He felt stiff of limb, stripped of all pleasure, bewildered.

No, I do not want a hotel. I want to check this stuff.

He knew no Italian. The porter shrugged and walked away. Evans wandered around aimlessly until he found the check room. 12:05 to Florence. Thank God. Only two hours to kill.

The waiting room was gloomy, deserted. He walked out into the fresh air. Two drunks exaggerated in size by their shadows were doing a slow motion wrestling match among the heavy columns of the station portico. Evans began to stray off in the dark into the space of the great *piazza* before the station. The whole neighborhood seemed desolate. He had no idea in what direction he was going. He feared he might get lost if he went too far.

The harbor, he said to himself walking on. It was the only thing about Genoa that stuck in his memory to attract him.

To the left the houses seemed to rise, one above the other in an endless embankment. He could not see the tops. They passed up into the murk. The stores near at hand were all

The Return

Chapter XXI

Vienna

WHEN Evans arrived in the Austrian capital on the last day of March, 1924, six years after Versailles, he found Vienna still showing marked traces of a reduced condition. From being one of the world's greatest capitals, inhabited by a brilliant court, it had become no more than a socialist stronghold, chief city still, it is true, but of a small bankrupt nation, its richest provinces stripped from it to make up Czechoslovakia and the rest of them to the south. The public buildings looked neglected, smoke stained; the stone work on the Rathaus had crumbled incredibly in the ten years since the war began— not a stroke of maintenance having been done upon it during that time. Just now workmen were beginning to repair cornices, ledges and window sills; blocks of new stone stood on the cobbles waiting to be hoisted into place, but very few laborers were on the job. Obviously there was no money.

But there was more than that of neglect about the city. Few motor cars were running, the stores were empty—the people themselves seemed subdued, impoverished. Taxis were scarce. Everyone rode upon the street cars and most who rode were of the laboring class. There was no flash, no aristocratic flash anywhere, no jauntiness. It was perhaps more the lack

of this than anything else that impressed Evans so un-
favorably.

Of course the Hofburg, the Imperial palace, looked like a
tomb. People, very few of them, went haphazard across the
great cobbled courts. There were no guards. Everything
seemed let down. True, the grass was coming up and the trees
were trimmed but that was all. There were blackbirds on the
lawns.

Evans had never been in Vienna before, so that he could not
estimate how much of the depression he saw was due to the
cold spring weather and how much to national misfortune,
but walking idly that morning on the Ring he was impressed
by a feeling of desolation.

He looked at the people whom he passed, rather finely built
people, heavy but with a good mien, even handsome, people
of the office type and city laborers. Yes, he thought, Vienna
is theirs all right.

On the inside of the Ring back of the Hoftheatre, he
stopped a moment at the sound of bagpipes. A double file of
men and women clad in peasant costume and led by a fellow
who was doing a few dance steps now and then and playing
vigorously on a bagpipe, was coming along the sidewalk opposite him. Nothing else happened. The little procession in
costume, fifteen or twenty in all, walked solemnly on. A
wedding, he concluded, as he watched them pass.

For himself he felt gloomy and alone. Perhaps it was the
new Vienna. Seeking the *Allgemeine Credit Anstalt* where he
hoped to get some letters—perhaps one from his sister—and
to cash a check, he cut in through the business streets striving
to interest himself in what was going on about him. There he
passed a delicatessen store, apparently a very prominent one,
before which he saw more life than in any other place. The
window was packed with foodstuffs among which he saw
three whole roast chickens at 50,000 K. each. There were fish
of several sorts pickled in tubs, hams, roasts of beef and veal,
cheeses, and all kinds of bread, dried fruit, preserves, sausages,
and potted stuffs of many kinds.

People were standing looking in through the windows.
Evans stood watching for a short time. Some simply looked.
It was perfectly apparent that they were satisfying their appe-
tites by the sight alone. It struck him at once that Vienna,
even now, was not eating all it should. And of course it is not
the laboring class who are suffering—but the people like myself, the artisans, the professional men, the schoolmen, the
people of independent fortune. In front of this store their
want was clearly written in their faces.

He paused again before an optical instrument shop and
admired the array of photographic and laboratory material—
at stupendous prices, but when converted into dollars, quite
cheap. Book stores, he looked into, with formally bound
volumes; he even saw a translation of Upton Sinclair's works.
Good God, Socialism!

Old women were selling chestnuts on the corner of the
Brühl and rising opposite was the Stephan Church. There was
small business anywhere however. The only places that were
surely packed were the pastry shops, marvels of their kind,
the delicatessen places and the coffee houses.

Evans had heard of the Viennese coffee house, comparable
to the Parisian café. Everywhere he went he saw these places,
informal clubs with men and women—women sitting alone
—reading the papers (free there) and sipping whatever it was
they had before them. There they seemed to be sitting as if
never intending to move.

There were no letters at Cook's.

He crossed the street and, through a transept door, entered
the Stephan Church, Vienna's oldest place of worship. Inside
it was at first as black as night so that nothing could be seen.
It was cold too. They had laid boards upon the stones to
protect the knees of the worshipers—that they might not die
of rheumatism or pneumonia perhaps. After a few moments
to accustom his eyes to the dark, Evans became conscious of
the altar, guarded by a high iron fence; then, in the aisle quite
close to him, he noticed a tiny shrine to the Virgin, covered
with devout candles, before which many vague figures were

kneeling. Passing closer he could hear them mumbling as they bowed low in the silence and induced night. This was terrifying to him. The gloom was excessive. He made his way quickly out of the old church and went with a hollow heart further upon his way, oppressed, out into the comparative brightness of the streets. The failure to get news from his sister or the few friends he might have heard from, Lou or Jack—coupled with the gloom of the city itself and the tomb-like atmosphere of the old church—crushed him completely.

The bank, however, when he came to it, rather footsore from the rambling walk on the cobbles and pavements, was another matter. Here things were still alive. The building itself was modern, extensive, and seemed not quite so beaten as the rest of the city. It seemed to have had better days, as did everything in Vienna, but money moved in it, worthless as the money might be, moved and had thus a value. Dev sat on one of the great leather lounges in the alcove reserved for the tourist business, and looked about him trying to right himself, and to rest his feet, after the depressing hours just preceding.

To his inexpressible delight there was the girl from the train, sitting on the other end of the lounge, reading a letter. He still had his hat on. As he removed it, she glanced up. She looked at him for a moment and then went on with her letter.

I've got to say hello to you, Evans broke in smiling. Do you mind? We met on the train this morning.

She looked up.

Have you been in Vienna before? he continued.

Yes.

Speak the language?

Yes.

Seems a mighty depressing place to me.

Yes, in many ways.

But Evans felt desperate. No use batting the air any longer. —I wonder if you'd take lunch with me—somewhere, he said.

She looked at him for a moment, then smiled and said, Why, yes, if he wished, she would be pleased to do so.

Fine!

He hurried with his business at the cashier's window, while she waited. Then they went out together, boarded a tram car, at the lady's suggestion, and rode to the Opera Ring.

There she introduced him to an excellent eating place, *Am Weissen Hirsch*, a narrow room with freshly covered tables and expert service—the food being to Dev a surprise after his sense of the poverty of the city in general.

For a full hour they sat, eating in a leisurely manner, speaking politely of Vienna, of the war, of this and that, the trip up from Venice and then—with a few words of thanks—she bade him adieu.

As Evans had told his companion at table, he had come to Vienna, as do so many doctors from the States, to observe new methods, to check up on his diagnostic technique, and to prepare himself for new adventures in his profession, for time and cash and renewed interest in his work. He did not delay now.

The great hospital of the Lazarette Gasse, with its cluster of buildings around the courtyard of the oldtime monastery and all the adjoining institutes of anatomy, pathology and the various specialties, formed the hub for many similar hospitals in the city, the external evidence of a high degree of scientific perfection and world renowned research in medical matters, which the world had had foremost in its mind for generations —great names which it had seen in textbooks and heard attached to various phenomena, discovered and catalogued in Vienna.

Toward this veritable city of the sick—rich in the knowledge of its chief men as it is overflowing with clinical material, Evans went after lunch, past the lower class coffee houses of the S. Strasse, the postage stamps advertised for sale in small shops, the surgical instrument houses, past the long low wall of the old hospital—having a vague idea of the location of the Kinderclinic where he hoped to see Von Knobloch and to get started at once on what he had planned as a month of concentrated scientific effort to be the apex of his tour. And then Switzerland—a flying trip—Paris again and back to the old grind once more.

The Children's Hospital was among a great modern brick group inside a formal entry with portals and a triple gateway that could be closed at night. Up a long walk, rather badly paved, Evans went, as he had been instructed to do at the entry, to the group of buildings on the right, decorative brick. He read the notices on the door and walked in. It was an empty tiled corridor where an old woman was going over the pavement with a moist mop.

There was no one else about; the immaculate hallways opening off the main corridor were empty. There seemed to be no reason why he should not look about a little so he asked the scrubwoman, Dr. Von Knobloch? to which she replied by pointing toward the doors at his left.

Evans walked through what seemed to be an outpatient department, with empty benches standing in rows upon the scrubbed tiles, and so into the passageway beyond. A young doctor in a white gown went by, but said nothing. Evans continued in the corridor, looking into the various wards, marvelously well kept and, strange to say, with few children in them. On certain doors he saw doctors' names until by chance he came upon the one he wanted. He knocked but there was no answer.

Then, greatly impressed by the quiet, the exquisite cleanliness, lack of bustle, the serenity of this world-renowned pavilion, he walked out again—back through those corridors, all unmolested. Here he would, for a brief month, touch again with wakening interest his profession—a profession which had begun to fade in his imagination through its money exigencies, till he hated it at times—he would touch again that sheer beauty cast upon it by the Teutonic mind; a spell which drew men and women from all parts of the world to worship. Already he felt it, not an odor of food, of medicine—just clean.

Going out into the street again, Evans saw on a café entry the sign, *The American Medical Association of Vienna,* and stepped into this fifth class coffee house to see what he could see. There was a grimy door opening off the café proper into the suite of two rooms occupied by the Association. A few people were sitting around eating sandwiches or sipping cups of coffee brought from the public room next door. They were all doctors, women and men, regular American professional types. Evans wandered aimlessly among them until he came upon the bulletin boards where the courses offered were posted, and picked up a few pointers from a rather decent looking chap there.

Now he went back to his room. It was a cold evening. Rosa, the maid, lit the fire and brought in a few slices of meat, bread and some jelly. As he ate, Evans could hear a rattle of dishes outside and Rosa giggling—a man's voice—her husband's he found out later. But it made him angry as he lay thinking of —something else.

What a day! He undressed and went to bed. It was as dark as if it had been midnight. Watching the fire in the cracks of the tile stove he thought to lay out his course for the next few weeks, but hearing the giggles and talk in the closet, the clink of dishes and the rattle, once or twice, of a dumbwaiter, it was not long before he began to think of the girl, his companion of that morning. Decidedly he was attracted. What was it? Of course, the first thing was that she was young enough, straight enough, and willing enough. But the thing that caused him to recollect her with most serious interest was the inevitable one, that she was like no one else he had ever in his life seen before, yet he seemed always to have known her. There was not one flashy thing about her. Her conversation was extremely limited,—in fact, he was not a little startled to recollect how much he had told her of himself and how little he had learned of her in return.

She was reticent, then. Marvelous!

She had on another black dress, different from the one she wore in the train. But Dev could not remember the fashion of it to save his life. He remembered her arms, firm, well muscled, but slender; strong useful hands without the least affectation about them. One small ring she wore on her right hand; might have been an old one, a group of small dark stones.

Rather a small face she had. All he could say finally was that she was quiet, dark, reticent, about middle height for a woman, slightly but well built, with firmly rounded lips, an expression friendly enough by moments but, still, for the most part, rather definitely depressed. But her smile was extraordinary.

Several times she had looked up at him, when he was telling her of his life in the United States, with a smile that seemed to come from deep inside, long, slow and full, suffusing her whole face with understanding and interest. Then he could see it begin to fade and gradually disappear when the nervous depressed look would come again. Dev had never seen such an opening and closing, an opening to intense brilliance and a closing to absolute night.

Queer type.

So he grew sleepier—hearing her short replies to his conversation—seeing the deep flash in her dark eyes, looking at her neck, her arms, her shoulders, her breasts—when she would be glancing down and touching her plate with her fork.

Are you alone in Vienna, she had asked him.

Yes.

Dev told her then that he was here for the first time, that he was a physician interested in children—infants, nutrition.

You are here to study with Knobloch then.—She knew something.—I am here for the music—and because I enjoy Vienna.

She had been in Europe four years, in France, Italy, Austria —especially Austria.

Was she rich then?

Evans kicked himself, lying in bed, for his awkwardness at the end of the meal. At the restaurant door she had merely said, Good-by and thank you. It has been a pleasure. Then walked off. Left thus abruptly he remained standing stupidly for a moment watching her walk away, then he turned in the opposite direction, toward the left, around the Ring—Well, that's that, he had said—feeling a little irritated but—that was all. Damned good dinner. Must remember this place.

Chapter XXII

The Doctors

HE was up at six and out at seven next day. The rooms of the Medical Association were rank with stale air and the stench of cigarette stubs, and when he went to the toilet in the rear, it was enough to knock one down. He turned again to the main rooms and began to look over the courses posted on the bulletin board. It was the Easter recess at the University— something he had not bargained for—so that several of the good lecturers were away. Some courses were already half completed; some were being made up; others were for him unattractive. But Dev noted and got his name down tentatively for several clinical lectures and demonstrations by Knobloch's assistants; differential diagnosis of diseases of the osseous system, with X-ray demonstrations; a course by Auchmuller on diseases of the ear in infancy and childhood; practical demonstrations, on the cadaver, of the pathology of childhood by Waldheim; skin by Hahn, etc., etc.,—coming at different hours of the day, different days in the week—at so much a course. He was absorbed in planning a possible curriculum when a plump young Jew from Los Angeles, Tieman by name, seeing him write down his name on the list of a certain course, accosted him.—Glad to see another children's

man around, it's been hard to make up the courses, just about
seven of us here, needs ten for most of the classes before
they'll begin. What are you doing now?—Nothing. Waiting
to see Knobloch.—Come on then with the bunch to Kern.—
But—Oh, that's all right, you are allowed to visit any of the
lectures once without paying.

Tieman introduced Evans to three or four other fellows of
the bunch, mostly under forty. All caught a tramcar and beat
it out in a drizzle to the C. hospital on the outskirts of the
town, a military-camp-like affair which had in fact served as
hospital-barracks during the war.

Evans detested his profession in the herd; he had no inti-
mates among its members. Enough that he had to be classed
among them to do his work; when he was not working he
never wished to see a doctor, barring one or two the mood
and perfection of whose work he admired with singular en-
thusiasm. As for the political "lights" of the clan he had no use
for them whatever—and so likewise for the rank and file who
emulated their leaders. He had already seen the officious officers of the *American Medical Association of Vienna*—loud-
mouthed about the rooms in Lazarette Gasse.—Come here to
feed, to fill up in order to disgorge at a stiff price later; at their
best, good only to acquire some skill which, as they turn it
into cash, they do something of value with it, or at least keep
themselves from doing harm. But which among them is in-
tent to be clear, to straighten out the muddles of misapprehen-
sion which enfold them, to have it straight, clean; to know, to
have a light cast over the whole? What is American medicine?
A hodge-podge of procedure, kindly enough but no head nor
tail to it, no wish to seek clarity in that mass—

What then was he himself here for? To perfect. He moved
away from the smoking, story-swapping crew beside him;
blatant ignoramuses. What a life! To them cash for cures. He
remembered the agitant pathologist secretary of his own
County Medical Society remarking,—What, not a member!
Why, Evans, don't you know that no matter how fine a physi-

cian you may be, you have no standing whatever in your profession unless you are a member of your county and state societies?—He felt nauseated at the thought. He remembered his name in little print instead of heavy print in the Directory of the American Medical Association. And he had seen the lack—the pretense and the lack—which always gave him the feeling of hopelessness that he felt before any successful cult, the horrible emptiness—the impossibility of instilling sense into men with piecemeal minds—gut minds—without thought of the limits of knowledge.

Why, then, had he come here? to enlarge his view, as an excuse for getting away from the grind for a year—to forget.

It was wet, the hospital streets were slushy, it was about as desolate a place as one could wish to see. Following he bunch, picking his footing, swapping bits of information—one of the men coughing and blowing his nose—they ducked out of the cold rain into one of the sheds where in a low room several chairs had been drawn up in a rough semi-circle. There was a nurse hanging around the room whom a couple of the fellows looked at and commented upon.—Wouldn't touch that bird with a ten foot pole.—A skinny young woman she was, puffing now and then on a cigarette and meanwhile eyeing the men with a disdainful half-defiant smile—which Dev could not help but admire, as much as to say: Some cheap bunch.—But she looked miserable just the same. Several of the men seemed to know her, mentioned syphilis—but she disappeared suddenly as soon as the professor came into the room.

At once, he impatiently called for cases—he was late—and began to lay them open in lucid German—but Dev was not particularly interested in the subject just then and began to look at the specimens more humanely as the nurses trotted them out. This must have been some poorer kind of hospital, for the people were the most miserable, the most dejected he had ever beheld.

Dirt, squalor, poverty, despair—the skin shows it all. Glibly

Kern ran over the different features of the appearances, possibilities of this, that, and the other—and came at last inevitably as if by the pull of gravity, to a case of tuberculosis, which with dirt, neglect, lack of bath, was actually creeping over the surface of this woman like a fungus.

Hustling back with the same crowd Evans found himself drawn at nine into a steep lecture room with eight or ten men of various curious descriptions waiting for a demonstration of diseases of the nervous system by one Gross—who, presently entering, they brought in two cases, in ill-fitting hospital garb, which he began to lay out for the students, two middle-aged men—the well known picture of General Paresis—the slurring speech, mixed ideas.

One poor fellow, an ex-delicatessen keeper, had suddenly conceived the idea that he would be a violin virtuoso: What is so foolish about that? he said. But you are fifty-five, it takes time, money.—That's all right, he said.

His wife had noticed he had begun to neglect his business. She was distressed. He wanted to go to Chicago to study. A portly old Austrian he was. Very serious.

The other fellow was smiling, more used to the clinics—and he was somewhat better off. Here Gross paused to tell the treatment they were using: During the war when they could not be too particular whom they drafted into the ranks, they had drawn in some old syphilitics along with the rest. A certain percentage of these developed General Paresis; but living in the trenches, exposed as they were to infection and disease of all sorts, some of them had been seized with malaria; chill followed chill, but, to the amazement of the doctors, as the malaria progressed, the symptoms of G. P. subsided, in some instances, so that men hopelessly insane it seemed, were able to resume their soldiering and even to return to useful occupations afterward.

Thus the treatment they had now instituted at the hospital was discovered: to give malaria to these patients, let them have four or five chills then administer quinine and cure them:

the G. P. would be improved. This was spectacular and amus-
ing, but Dev felt more than this the old lust he had had for
following the complicated course of pathology of the nervous
system—

From there he went to see von Knobloch. Coming out of
the Gross clinic, Dev had just time to get across the courtyard
of the hospital to the Children's Pavilion with his letter of
introduction in his pocket when Knobloch arrived. Here he
would learn to know this man whom in 1910 he had heard old
Curschmann in Leipzig raving against in a jealous rage because of his—Knobloch's—discovery or invention of the simple skin test for tuberculosis known now the world over by
his name.

This is Dr. Evans? Dev nodded. Knobloch read the letter.
What do you want to do? A general survey, feeding, etc.
Come along, then. I'll introduce you to my assistants, they
can fix something up. Would you like to make rounds to-day?
Yes.

They went upstairs rapidly, the tall Knobloch in the lead.
Taking out a key, he opened the door of his office, went into
the inner room a moment and, coming out in a white gown,
started toward the end of the corridor where a small group
was waiting.

There was a Jap, two men who spoke no German but who
looked like Turks, a big blather-mouthed fellow from Chicago
or thereabouts, the various white-coated assistants and some
others. As the group came into the wards, the children if not
too sick, would call out in unison, *Grüss Gott*, very happily,
or as happily as they could. Dr. K. moved rapidly on, com-
menting on the cases, looking at a chart here, a peculiar skin
eruption there, asking questions.

But it was especially on the roof where they went last that
Knobloch became most animated. Here were the cases of
frank, outstanding consumption—children all, whom they
were treating by air and food. The beds were in sheds and out
before them the children able to be up were ready with their

games for the good father of them all, Dr. K. Go on! he called out to the nurse in charge, and they began to play their simple games. He fondled two or three of the youngsters. Others stood beside him with respectful but tender looks in their eyes.

Tuberculosis, the Viennese disease. At once Dev began to get that sense of beauty in arrangement, that fervor which the continental scientific method, built upon their aristocratic thought, had engendered, to go far through the world. The children tested by the test Knobloch had invented, sorted right and left, every child in the hospital divided first into positive and negative groups by that test.

Light! these were the light bringers.

And all this demonstrated on the cadaver, in carefully preserved specimens—for the sake of beauty.

For beauty was the leader, he felt it at once, a clarity. Evans had always known that in the chaos of pedagogy the greatest genius of the future would be he who would give in ten words, ten illuminating words the limits of knowledge—permitting classification.

Knobloch here was great. Surely it was a great love that shone in his countenance. One could understand how he had wanted to leave Vienna at the offer in cash from the University of Michigan or whichever it was, and how being in the United States a few months he could not stand it but had to flee back to Vienna—and the children's hospital where he lived.—We do not keep them in bed for slight fevers, he told Dev, but let them get up and join the rest.

They looked at X-rays of some of the children, compared pictures taken months before, noted enormous gains in weight from the heavy milk diet and then looked at the child. One they were especially proud of, an unfortunate, butter tub of a girl of ten whose lungs were apparently in the last stages of destruction, and yet this was the one K. picked out as she who showed the best effect of what was being done in the hospital. It did not seem possible that she should live.

The rounds over, they went downstairs. There was a lame Englishman among them for whom K. was constantly halting his rapid, almost running gait.—Are you coming round tomorrow? said this fellow to Evans.

Why yes, aren't you?

You know you can't pay for this, and you can't get much out of it unless you're right on top of him, and I think it makes an awful clatter in the wards for us all to be tagging on behind him this way. I understand K. has kept it going almost entirely out of his own pocket these years. They say they may have to close down any time for lack of funds, since the war.

Dev and the Englishman went back to the Association rooms, where after some backing and filling and talk with the harassed secretary (who had an awful cold) Dev made up his card for the month—more or less—and paid for it. As he had nothing to do for the rest of the day, he went back to his room —cutting in through the great Krankenhaus, the yard marked with convalescents, shielded by its walls, who were sitting on the benches resting. Especially interesting were two small boys in blue hospital wear running round with shaven heads bright yellow from what looked like iodine painted upon them.

Chapter XXIII

Routine

AND the next morning he took his place in the little group of doctors with whom, more or less, he was to share his hours of instruction during the month to come—at one of Wagner's clinical demonstrations. There were Tieman; a middle-aged woman who had taken up medicine late in life to be with her cousin, a surgeon in Tacoma; a recent graduate from Chicago, a cadaverous young Jew; the Englishman and one or two others, one from Jamaica, Long Island, and another from the middle west.

So the week went by. There was Auchmuller handling his great *papier maché* models of the inner and middle ear, driving home the points—a world in which he lived. Never had Dev understood so clearly the ear in childhood. Never had he so lived in those spacious halls of pleasure, the cochlea, the semi-circular canals, the tympanic cavity—never so heard it magnified—into a life.

And now it was the criminal child, with a flat-faced stumpy doctor at the head—curious perversions, suicidal, homicidal manias.

And always the little group of Americans were being conducted in this inferno by these devoted men: It got on Dev's emotions. Never had he seen anything like it. Kern, a fat butcher-like man transformed into a thing of beauty by his talk.

There was a strong sense of the priest in all these men, a priest presiding over a world of the maimed, living in the hospital, pondering and dreaming—a great sense of beauty over this sordid world.

Tuberculosis again. A bang on the elbow, a stroke on the back of the hand—the disease gets in. Lupus, scrofula—carefully Kern would take up the thread and unwind the same beauty of discourse, dwelling on every detail with care.

The patients became devotees of a great cult—and as the week went on, more and more it grew certain why men came to Vienna, to Europe to study—and what it was they came for.

There was no feeling but the presence of the truth. It hurt an American. Old, deformed, or young and unfortunate, they came there and were stripped to be inspected. The gross nose of Cyrano, the girl with the warty face, the peasant with deep ringworm of his beard. One especially Evans was fascinated to see—a girl, barely fifteen—with the pock. Poor child, she was brought in cowering, the tears streaming down her face from anguish and shame, her body marked all over with recent syphilis. Kern patted her, but there she stood and was turned and inspected—studied while she cried and bit her lips. It seemed pitiless, but there it was. She was taken out to be cured.

Tongues were projected, men were turned upside down, women were exposed in minutest detail to the last recess, eyes, nose, mouth, fingers, toes; ulcerated, blistered and stained. Pocked and eaten, swollen and bleeding—nothing remained that was not seen, described and—a clarity put upon it.

Nothing remained. In spite of himself Dev was caught by this wonder of abandon to the pursuit of knowledge. The beauty of it took him again and again.

Sometimes the strange inhuman art of curing which possessed these men, so differently from Americans, seemed to reflect too harshly the difference between them and his own soft western kind. Service, use—for what?

Here was the answer. For beauty.

In America we save men, without too much curiosity. Here they are lustful for knowledge, for completeness of living. These priests of beauty save men, but keep aloof. That was it. Dev remembered in Philadelphia when Trendelenburg had given a clinic at the University he had been invited to operate on a gall-bladder case. T. was one of the world's greatest and he had made an incision Z-shaped, from the pubis to the edge of the ribs, till the very surgeons gasped and commented afterward—on living autopsies.

Once Auchmuller had asked the class to wait if they wanted to see a mastoid operation, downstairs in the old Policlinic. It was cold, no heat—since the war. The patient was an oldish laborer, who was standing around cowed by the doctors, joking and elbowing him as they swapped lies in the dressing room: Dev had never seen anything so crude, so informal—so heartless. Finally the fellow was stripped, in front of everyone, who paid not the least attention. They let the old man lie on a cold metal table for nearly half an hour, covered only by a sheet. Finally fat old A. was ready. The assistant socked the chloroform to the patient. He turned nearly black. After a while, however, he breathed again and A. standing over the ear, nonchalantly took up a chisel and a mallet and with one mighty whang was in the middle of the bone soon gnawing away with his rongeur like a beaver.

Evans gasped thinking of the nice, timid, immaculate methods at home. He had never seen anything like it.—Never again, said the woman from Tacoma. My God, what are these people made of? Why, my cousin says she sees one hundred and fifty cases of tuberculosis of the larynx in one morning—something we do not see ten of in a year at home.

"An American experiment," these men would say of some

of our tentative prematurely advertised work at home, and smile.

These things filled Evans with admiration, wonder, amazement. The clarity and thoroughness of the teaching filtered into his mind and his emotions. What American will understand this? Not surely the washed-out soul of his own country.

But nowhere was he so overcome by this overwhelming mood of science as in the course on pathology of children—by Waldheim, that tall kindly man, curious god of flesh, carefully, carefully taking apart the unhappy bodies of dead children and unwinding out of them the secret stories of rickets, of tuberculosis, of syphilis and the gland deficiencies.

Dev's nerves had never permitted him to get fully past the smells, the unsightly acts of pathology, the great science of unhappy flesh. He shuddered now and would have turned back, had he not been so eager to know more, as he entered this building, inevitably foul, though never so scrubbed and clean, with the flesh of generations of the hospital dead—over whom the great spirit of W. and his confreres had presided so many years.

At the very beginning, the trays of specimens, passing in the hall made Dev turn away. He was not a pathologist—he could not overcome his aversion. But when, seated around the autopsy table with the professor speaking his perfect German, carefully, lucidly demonstrating point by point, everything else was forgotten.

Fascinated, Dev saw the intricacies of tuberculosis disclosed, the lung invasion, the scattering, the tiny gray points all over the body. Each part W. would take in his hands like the maker taking apart his model that had failed. This day he had been searching through the miserable remains of some child whom they had seen alive in the wards just the day before,—until the fascination of that clarity was so great everyone in the group had forgotten when the hour was ended.

They arose to go. The boy from Chicago, lean-faced and

despondent, was beside Dev. He, to Dev's amazement began
to speak of the pleasure of it all.—I must go home and write
to my sister about this, he said. It is amazing. I hardly take a
breath from the moment the man begins until he finishes, so
beautiful are his demonstrations. I would as soon think of
taking notes at a symphony concert.

So the first week had gone. One day in the Association
rooms Dev ran into an Austrian who spoke English and who
was selling instruments to a group of fellows. The discussion
turned to morality. The lady doctor from Tacoma was there,
it was among doctors and it was a frank talk.

The Austrian was maintaining that if it were true, as the
American said, that fifty per cent of American young men
grew to manhood virtuous, then fifty per cent of American
young men were little better than perverts.

That raised a row. He said that every Austrian male who
reached the age of twenty-one and had not known that, had
something the matter with him. He maintained that if you
wanted to do something and didn't do it that such a stand was
perverse and in the end pathologic. When you want to go to
sleep you do, don't you? If you want to eat, you eat. Well, then
it is the same with that.

Hold on, hold on, cried an American, If you are in a company at midnight, and you want to go to sleep of course you
don't go to sleep. You take a couple of good cups of coffee and
stay up.

There is no such thing as anything natural. We do what we
want to do.

Nonsense, cried the Austrian—But it was lunch and Dev
walked on with the lady doctor who said she had been court
examiner for a year in Tacoma examining delinquent girls
who had been brought to justice for various social offenses in
that district. And very few indeed of them, she said, had a
venereal disease. But her dentist in Nice had told her that
thirty-three per cent of the girls of France were syphilitic.
What are we coming to? Dev did not know.—We've *got* to

be restrained. I think American men are so far to be praised for their abstinence that I wouldn't look at an Austrian knowing what I know now. It is horrible. Why in Tacoma mind you, these were all court cases, not five per cent of them were infected. But unless we guard ourselves by some kind of abstinence, we'll be not better than these people in another twenty years.—

The problem was too much for Dev. America. He shuddered at the sickening recollection of his own morbid youth.

And the women! But the terrible ravages of disease in Vienna made him recollect his *Measure for Measure*—Better to geld the youths of Vienna.—It was all tied up. He thought of his favorite theme: the abandon of life and the—check; what it does to life in America to ruin it. *Ils déraillent*, Brancusi had said. America never will do anything. Raw, not primitive. Afraid.

Syphilis or none, he could not see but that Europe was in the van—

It seemed a beastly morbid problem. The syphilitic right on one side, and a caponized athlete on the other. It seemed hopeless. He left the lady doctor at her door and went home. Saturday.

Chapter XXIV

First Week

During the week he was certain he had seen Miss Black—and that she had seen him—when he had gone to the Opera Cassa Tuesday morning. As he was coming down the M. Gasse she was just leaving in the opposite direction, but she failed to stop. He watched her go down the street as he stood at the door to see if she would by chance turn, but she kept right on. All right, lady, if you don't want to, I should worry.

Sunday morning he decided to walk out to the Danube, to see if it were blue. A few people were about. It was cold, windy—as usual. He turned to the left about the Ring and gradually, walking briskly, came out on the canal in which lay the market fishboats, their tanks clamped down. He was leaning over the wall looking down at them listlessly when someone came beside him. It was she.

They walked together toward the Danube.

She said: I shall never return to the United States. Here, little as there is for me, there, there is nothing. Here it is terrible: but there it is empty. Democracy, she shuddered. It takes away from the top to feed the—maggots. Here it is sick, but it *is.* I shall never go back to that. But I am an American.

Dev said merely that he was going back.

America, or the United States, we should say, not Mexico or the English to the north, casts a veil, a pallor rather, on everything. Music, how shall they understand it? Jazz! That *is* their music. But the quality of music, what it *is*, not what it sounds like, what it *is*, they do not understand.

Music was one thing Dev never said very much about. He pricked up his ears now.

They do not need music or poetry.—But poetry, again, he knew.

Their dreadful, dreadful colleges with no inkling of where knowledge begins nor where it ends, actually teaching, thinking they can teach the young—the hopeless young, deceived as to history, their own history, misled as to their governors —never an inkling of actuality, but to gather up a hod of small facts of "general information"—looking for day with a candle. All they know is to wall off, to stop—to injure. The stultification of youth, that is all it is, and not of youth alone, of men, dragging their lives out to escape leisure—to escape the horrible fact that they are alive and ugly and maimed and helpless. Never will they wake up save in a company, *geduldige Schäfe:* frightened—or forced.

And women—but it is no worse than life anywhere—except that here they have an inkling that it is not to be a hog or a dog kept for the bench—or—to think you are right because you are packed in a case with one hundred million others.

The surface is all they see there. Can't they see why the Negro is the only product of the country that is anything? Can't they see that they can't be—that their silly salvations are puerile, their prohibitions sordid, their minds blank? That sick as it is here, a culture exists among a few who can smile at the gross absurdities of life and who can at least have art, or your science.—That one can exist and *something* of it flow over into the common effigies even in such a place as England, in Germany, in France.

But in America they are stupid, they only know how to

maim, there where truly one rich man or woman with intelligence might finance a useful purpose in the world, even in America, not to fetter us to the crawling inanities which they think is education, that dreadful myth, to inflict on us their amputations which they think is morality but to break through that surface to—show us the childishness of our hopes; humanity, beauty—

What damage is being done by our laziness, our hysteria to all that is penetrant, deep. Instead they give us airplanes, radio, and philosophies to accompany them, instead of to show the pettiness of our politics or religions—just so many things, puffed up with wind, just small playthings, useful as rattles for children—and the fury about them: just disheartening, cruel, sordid—distracting mistakes. Can't they see, just to open the eyes and to look is enough. Every child can see. But he gets to the point where he knows and falls upon a dreadful initiation, barbaric, maddening, defiling—like Fabre; late in life dragging themselves out of the slime, out of the pitch. American young! Slimed down into a flashy happiness. All smeared over with success, with athletics—and hysteria to oppose it. Olympic champions, they do not know what it means to see, even. But, to see!

They come over here. I hate the sight of them. How can they know Europe? Yes, it is sordid—well. How can they know? Or if there is a class of them that knows anything where are they? Americans tell me I am wrong. I am a fanatic. That there are Americans who know that all the political flimflam they believe in as a horde is baseless, without foundation.—But they never emerge. I have never seen one.

Dev did not answer. He did not feel himself a hero. He thought she was a little excited. Maybe insane.

They walked on in silence, out the long uninteresting street to the bridge. The wind by now had come up in great violence and was exceedingly cold. But they kept on.

So that is the Danube. The water was a dull river-water-green. Toward the city there were docks with river craft tied to them, coal barges and the like. But on the other side the bank was just a great greening meadow.

America, she continued, the only hope they have is to give up their democracy, if they can, their primitive pact to bind them up like cattle all together to keep the wolves out; to forget their fear and to generate, not by consent but by any means, an aristocracy, a small haven not of brains but of understanding, some few who understand, who do not postpone and hope.

Then they can have music—

An anachronistic government, pretty enough to paste up a kind of union when every Tom, Dick and Harry had to be flattered into thinking he was the head—but used up.

But what? Dev was about to say when she interrupted.

Can't they see the perfectly plain truth that it doesn't matter in the least one way or the other all this turmoil of belief or no belief, their democracy, royalty, fascism, soviet, anarchy —that it is just a great kindergarten diversion—useful enough, serious enough when it is ringed (the object of understanding) and that it must be seen and abandoned.—Some few, some gist, must be able to be quiet above it and to live —be, conscious and ruling somehow—ruling enough to get a minimum of sense into the situations which concern us, and powerful enough, devoted enough, to see to it that some light continues from antiquity. And they mustn't slip, and that in America there is nothing of this—that all this clap-trap of seriousness is just the buffoonery of nitwits. Just by opening the eyes—She weakened off and gradually stopped talking; morose a moment, looking at her feet, then gradually brightening she turned and smiled.

Along the eastern grassy bank of the river were anchored at intervals of fifty yards or so, ten or more flat scows one behind the other stretching off into the distance, round a bend upstream. Dev and the lady stood on the bridge watching the river rushing by with a tremendous tide when he became conscious of these scows. At the back of each was a long pole

pivoted near its middle on an upright piece, the far end projecting over the stern downstream. As he looked at the boat
nearest them, he saw this pole being drawn down inboard,
forcing a great square net rapidly up out of the water astern.
The bagging net hung poised there a moment dripping and
was then lowered again into the river. Come on, he said, I
want to see that.

They trotted amused to the far side of the bridge where
they discovered a winding stair in the eastern stanchion
which led down, in a lot of filth, to the flats below. It had
begun to drizzle lightly but Miss Black was game. Not a soul
but they was on this great stretch of what seemed to be
filled-in land along the river bank. Evans was elated, after the
travel and the winter and his tourist life, to be setting foot
once more on unhedged green turf; he sprinted forward to
catch Miss Black who had gone ahead for a moment, then he
shouted a bar of some tune, he did not himself know what, but
it turned out to be the first eight notes of the clown's song
from Pagliacci. Miss Black turned and snickered insolently at
him, then laughed outright.

What's the matter? he cried a little out of breath.

Look, she cried, in response catching his arm to hold him.
There comes the net.

Sure enough, the men in the tiny cabin of the second boat
were plying a windlass, Dev and his companion could hear
the squeak and grind, while swiftly—slowly the quadrangular
net came up and was scanned. Empty it was released and sank
again into the water. Almost at once the net from the first boat
was coming up again. Again they watched. Something was
flapping in the water. Both started to run. Yes, shouted Dev.

It was a big eel which a man, coming from the little caboose
on the scow, scooped up with a long handnet. The cable was
then released and once more the great net dropped into the
water.

From far up the flats came two girls crying out at intervals
as if they had lost a child or a dog. Seeing the man and

woman, the children made a detour around them through the wet grass and continued calling out but giggling and whispering together as they looked at the two standing there in that great meadow.

Now the walkers went slowly back to the bridge, the same fine drizzle still falling. Back to the city with the wet wind behind them, they walked. There Evans asked her if she would lunch with him.

Thank you. I have promised my friends. Won't you join us, though, at one o'clock in the Rathskeller. I'm sure you'll be interested.

Chapter XXV

Old Vienna

It was strange that Evans could be in Vienna a week and not have discovered the Rathskeller which was in fact no more than two blocks from his room. To be sure, he had seen the entrance to the place on the north side of the Rathaus but it looked so unattractive, so few seemed to frequent it that he —feeling disinclined to drink those days—had passed it up.

Now, having gone home to change and wash up a bit, he found himself going down the broad stairs leading under the Rathaus foundations to this cellarway. It amused him to be there on Sunday, in the City Hall, going down to a drinking place. Superhuman intelligence these people have, he said, while he tried to read the legends painted on the walls, wine, wine, wine, and man, ill off for the lack of it, raised to exultation by its magic. There were the usual frescoes in the German style, vine stems and grape clusters, with figures caught in them, monks straddling hogsheads, cavaliers and buxom girls with glasses and steins; while in the panels so entwined, were legends, in colored German script—from Goethe, from the Bible and common legend—praising the virtues of drink and the wisdom of the drinker. Dev paused here and there on the steps to read but a delicious odor of cooking came up to meet him—and he was ravenously hungry after the morning's walk.

What an idea to keep the wine in such a place—but he had not realized, until Miss Black had intimated such a thing that there was a restaurant there. High prices? Good? Bad? He wondered as he pushed upon the swinging door at the bottom of the steps and looked around.

Waiters were going by in rapid succession but in the room into which he had come no one was being served. It was a large room spaced for generous boardtop tables, by columns like those in the dungeon of the Château de Chillon. At the tables men, women and children were sitting eating bread and cheese, drinking wine or beer or doing whatever they pleased. The simple wine list was posted on cards hung about upon the stone work, wine of the country sold by the glass, white and red.

The mood of the place was decidedly familial, informal and inviting. It might have been in the mountains at a village tavern. Dev liked it well with its stone walls, floor and arched gothic ceiling. A couple of waiters walked around in a leisurely manner with tall glasses of the favorite greenish white wine on trays; or mopped up the wooden tables as a party would get up and go.

But there was another room. Into it the waiters with laden trays were passing through glass doors. Evans looked in. This room was high, columnless, and filled with tables, with white cloths on them, at which perhaps two hundred people were noisily at dinner.

Hardly had Evans seen than he heard Miss Black beside him and he was meeting her elderly companions. Her immediate friend Frau Von Linden was a small, nervous woman with a fine, intelligent, narrow face, who spoke English beautifully; while with her was another woman, older, much more vivacious, a face of true humor and full of spirit, the Baroness De Groff who spoke French and German only. But

Evans saw at once that these were people of the world—
whom the war had injured. He held open the door for the
delightful Baroness who went in first, followed immediately
by the others. A table had been reserved for them far over in
one corner.

All the tables were close packed and everyone was taken.
There were people waiting at the doors. As they were being
seated, Dev took a quick look around. The usual restaurant
crowd, it was. In the middle of the room was a large group
of fat men, fat and skinny, just finishing their repast, the table
was littered with plates, bottles and the miscellaneous débris
of a heavy meal finished. There were the usual quiet couples
at the wall tables, young people leaning over and talking
intimately to each other; the usual vicious-looking cyanotic
men of fifty, each with a young woman companion; and the
family groups—children lolling about and their parents talking bloatedly. The guests were of all classes, serious men,
middle-aged, impressive faces, eating alone, seeming to be in
the confidence of the waiters, scanning the bill of fare; while
quite near them was another family group, apparently Americans, two small kids, with the character of their bright young
country written all over them, in free confidence making a
good-natured waiter show them how he held a paper bill
between two fingers at the same time flipping it with a third
so that it gave forth a loud smack.

But from that time on Evans was absorbed in his own
immediate friends. The meal was delicious. None of the ladies
drank wine so Dev abstained also. To begin with, they had an
excellent omelette with greens, cooked to a lightness and
fluffy texture such as he had not seen bettered. So it progressed. Everything they had was good and the bill was extremely moderate. Frau Von Linden who was the hostess
would not permit Evans to take her bill. It was she who
suggested that they go to her apartment after, for coffee and
cigarettes.

So there they went—the Baroness and Miss Black in the

lead and Dev and Frau Von Linden coming behind. The conversation had been animated, Dev had explained his mission in Vienna. They had apologized lightly for their city— wherein Dev could read their pride and their sorrow in the present condition.

At dinner it had come out. The war. Frau Von Linden, a widow, had been wealthy. An assured income from English gold bonds had allowed her to partake of the life about her: Italy, Semmering, Salzburg and the rest of it. She had her apartment, all furnished with finest appurtenances, three servants, in fact a woman who knew the best people in the city; while her friend, the Baroness, a member of the outer court circles, had lived in her modestly fashionable house surrounded, quickened, enlivened by the heat of the great court, for to her its affairs, its gossips, its fashions, its manners, were the bread of life.

And now—the little party arrived at the entrance to the apartment with its formal, broad corridors and took the lift to the fourth floor. They were admitted by the simple-minded old serving maid who still kept up the appearance of old times there—though Frau Von Linden admitted that she was more a care than a help. She had to have her, however, to keep the Socialist City Council from requisitioning half her rooms to house—anybody in.

She had had a battle to prevent it, the requisitioning of her rooms, a heart-breaking battle but by acquaintance, persistence, and in the face of insults and doubt to the end, she had managed to keep her great dark chambers for herself— stripped of their richness it is true—but still unbreached by the new order.

Here the little company sat down to coffee, Miss Black taking charge for her friend.

Inevitably the conversation drifted off again to the old Vienna, the war and the havoc left after it. Dev started it by telling how, the day before, he had gone looking for the Museum where he had heard there was an exhibition of pic-

tures by Brueghel, and that in passing a large building on the
Ring and seeing a man sitting in a chair at a small side entrance beside the great formal one he had asked him, *Dies ist
der Museum?*

Nein, said the man, This is no museum, this is the Parliament!

Thereat, the old Baroness on her corner of the sofa rocked
herself back and forth in her glee, holding her napkin to her
face to hide the gap in her teeth, laughing, laughing, uncon-
trolledly.

That's right, she said, that's right. It *is* the Museum, with
all those socialist nincompoops there. Yes, yes, it *is* the museum, and she was mightily pleased.

The conversation was in French.

Coffee was served with brandy from a decorated flask, each
of the older ladies putting her dram into the dark fluid and
sugar too.

It is terrible, terrible, said Frau Von Linden what has happened to poor Vienna. It was not so before. The people on the
street cars, the peasants, the common people elbow you aside,
they push, they take everything to themselves. It was not so
before. There were good manners in everyone. Now all that
is past.

In the opera! said the Baroness whom Dev liked immensely
for her half-closed wrinkly eyes and enormous amusement at
the tragedy that had befallen her and her people. There it is
wonderful! The *Shiebers* took all the boxes. You could not
hear the music for their talking, they had to imitate everything without knowing anything. They brought their supper
and ate it in the boxes; beer steins they sat on the railing and
food was all over the floor until the place was so full of rats
you could not go there any more. But they are better now,
the newspapers made so much fun of them.

It was awful during the revolution. It was not safe. An
American, a friend of ours, was in the streets, in afternoon
dress you know, with gloves on. A mob gathered around him.

They knocked him down, they smashed his hat. I tell you we were frightened. We did not have enough food but we dared not leave the house. You could hear the firing all at once. Some American friends came to bring us enough to eat. One Englishman was wise. They broke into the hotel. He had much money and jewelry so he rushed out into the hall, without shirt, just his pants, and yelled to the mob, Here, here! and he burst into his own room and began to steal his own things, as much as he could get, leading the others, so that he got almost all. If he had fought them, they would have taken it away from him, but he joined them.

But the funniest is a delicatessen dealer I know, said the Baroness—who confessed to making a fair living teaching *hoi polloi* a few rudiments of good manners. I had not seen her for three years. Once some years ago, just after the war, her daughter had come to me for piano lessons. So now she asked me if I would come to her house, she would send her carriage. No, I could not do that. What! ride in the carriage of a delicatessen dealer.—The old baroness here laughed so she could not speak. What do you think? The house was magnificent! Furnished with everything, everything and, in the hall, armor! What is that? I said to her. Oh we have to have that, we bought it at the store. Think of it! Armor! and they bought it at the store! and the old Baroness was again convulsed with laughter.

But to me, said Frau Von Linden one of the saddest, most maddening things I know was when after Charles was beaten and the Empress had to leave the city, we had to give her, the Empress, imagine, enough clothes, a few things we could get together, for her to travel in. Nothing would they let her take. And all that priceless linen, the laces, the bedclothes of the palace, the finest, most beautiful—one of the socialist deputies had it given to his daughter when she was married, all of it. —It was terrible; stolen, and given to nobody, gone—ruined.

Yes, that was very hard, said the Baroness, but it was worse in those times of war. We had no fat and no meat. We all got

sick, we did not know we were sick at first but it was terrible.
—When I began to eat meat after we could get some, said
Frau Von M., I was made ill.

But the lack of fat was worst of all. The people at the
delicatessen stores were pitiful. But I was lucky, said the
Baroness. One day a little Jew, a boy from Budapest, came to
me to buy furniture, so smart were they. I told him no. But
he came and he came and he was a nice boy. So he asked me
if I could tell him some friend who had furniture to sell. I told
him of a lady, Princess J., who I knew was in very great
trouble and would sell some things. The little Jew went to her
and bought many things. He came back to thank me and said
he would send me some wine from Budapest. He did too.
He brought me a bottle and, when I opened it, it was
full of goose-grease. It saved me and when it was eaten very
slowly, he brought me another bottle. Now he has the finest
store of old furniture in the city just near the Stephan
Church.

It was the better classes who suffered most and the people
in the city, said Frau Von Linden. The peasants were not so
badly off. It is strange how the peasants are wise in these
things. Why when the war began, I was in the country with
my niece. *That very day* when we heard there was a war and
everybody was saying it would be quickly over, I went with
my niece to a peasant to buy some things to take back to
Vienna. Do you think he would take paper money? Not at all,
so wise they are; but the very day the war began. Coin, that
was all. Or later, when there was none, they would take a
piece of linen, or jewelry or what we had in exchange for
butter or eggs or a cabbage.

And then Baroness de Groff who was working on some
embroidery, told of the decay of manners. Imagine. Love! she
said. What it is now. Why when we were girls—but I heard
of a young woman, like Grace—and she looked at Grace,—
about her age. She was alone and would walk in the park
sometimes and so she gradually became acquainted with a

man, a very nice fellow it seems who fell in love with her. She liked him too and they would meet in the park in the evening and sit there. But then one day he told her he was in love. But, he says, I am a poor man—Imagine that! at such a time, to say, I am a poor man—and would she come with him to his aunt's house—and the old Baroness rocked with mirth once more— And that is love! I am a poor man! what is that? To talk of love and to say, I am a poor man and would she go with him to his aunt's house!

Dev was amazed at this old fire. She had few teeth and as she spoke, she could not control her spittle well. But her vitality was brilliant. There was no money for a dentist so that was that. She lived as she could, embroidery, lessons in etiquette, etc.

At the door Dev asked Miss Black if he might see her again soon.—They are singing Bach's *Mattäuspassion* on Thursday, said she. Let's have supper together and go after. But they start early you know, at six. All right, see you later, said Evans and he ran down the stairs.

Chapter XXVI

Bach

DEV wrote regularly these days: every evening not otherwise engaged, he would spend in writing. It was his diversion. He made notes. Auchmuller at 7:30. Waldheim at 10:00.

Dark spring days they were—full of rain. He bought tickets at the Opera Kasse, walked, and went to this place and that —the Hofburg's sad relic. But in his mind, like a somber flower, stuck Thursday and Miss Black. Occasionally he would drop in at the rooms of the Medical Association. Fräulein M. at the desk still had her terrible cold. She accepted his money for the lectures. One day especially she was exasperated. Some American was quarreling with her, on principle, about a half cent's worth of American change. She was angry and down-hearted.—You'd think men who come all the way from America for this would not be so small. Yes? Dev answered.—They borrow and do not pay back.—Cheer up, said Dev, the money isn't worth much, but he felt sorry for her.

When he called that night, Miss Black was dressed as usual in dark colors; she was moody and had at first little to say.

The Baroness is a wonder, isn't she? Dev volunteered after

they had been walking for several minutes toward the Rathaus Park.

Poor soul, what a life she leads. I don't think you realize, even now, what these people have been through, the better classes, I mean. Frau Von Linden has had her English bonds taken away by the Socialists and worthless Austrian ones of a similar value substituted, while they steal her interest as fast as it is made, and no redress if you don't want worse. Is your sister here in Vienna?

No.

Tell me about her.

Shall we not have a bite first?

No let us walk.—So they turned back along the Ring making their way on foot toward the concert house. Do you enjoy music?

Yes, but it is a mystery to me, replied Evans. I enjoy it, sometimes, though I do not know why. It escapes me entirely.

You are bored sometimes?

Yes, even with what they tell me is good music.

That is good. What do you enjoy?

I have not heard much. I have enjoyed certain performers, Pablo Casals, some harpist whose name I cannot remember —I remember once, in Leipzig, it was not a very great ensemble, but they had for a visitor a singer called Sohmer, who sang the part of Wotan in Götterdämmerung. That I enjoyed.

Yes, but what sort of music?

Music where I can follow the design a little, the older men. Händel?

Yes, when it is something I can understand. I think I am more swallowed by Bach than any other—but I have never heard enough, it is too hard—

Yes, one must live in it. That is my life.—Dev wanted to ask her about her life but she did not seem to invite the question.

I never know exactly what to think about music, he con-

tinued. Sometimes it seems the most perfect escape for—
Not that please, not escape.

Sometimes the most perfect, the most designed and sometimes the vaguest of all the arts. Literature seems to have
firmer values, more thought; it is less primitive, less instinctive, less a matter of feeling, but it gains by its solidity.

Nothing could be more lucid nor more firm in thought than
the statements of music, beginning with the earlier melodies
and coming down through César Franck, let us say, to the
crudities of Stravinsky. To me literature is bare, skeletal even
at its best, compared to the refinements of musical statement
which sensitively enters where literature is wholly barred by
its lumpy words which cannot be made to flow but always
seem either frozen or sticky. I think that the moderns are
improving the medium, however,—I have seen some recent
work of James Joyce that resembles music most intimately.

What, said Dev, do you know about the modern writers?

I know them very well, for one not literary.—Evans did not
press the point just then.

Music, he said, then changed and finished the sentence—
Bach has been my greatest curiosity in music for many years.

Fortunate, and here you will perhaps hear him for the first
time. Music is a presence which you feel occasionally during
the playing. A whole season of opera, of symphonies, of concerts, may go by and there be no music. It occurs here more
frequently than elsewhere that I know of. Therefore, I come
here.

Evans was thrilled by her statement and did not answer but
kept repeating it that he might not forget her exact words:
Music is a presence which you feel occasionally during the
playing.

Music is—

But I am extremely interested in the modern phases also.
The only place that is hopeless is America. Jazz is very amus-
ing. It makes me laugh. That is good. The percussive element
in it is the most interesting; that and the newer voices quite

as much as the syncopation, the street sounds—but they are very silly if they think they can ignore a complete mastery of musical form. They copy the phrases of excellence, a bit of Schubert, a phrase from Rimsky-Korsakof, but not yet with the ability to advance them further.

But it is anchored, said Dev eagerly. It is extremely local.

Yes, you mean like peasant themes in European music.

Somewhat that, but——

No, all of it is pure trash. Music is something else. Percussion is too limited, syncopation is much livelier in Brahms. Yet, jazz is extremely interesting if for no other reason than that it paralyzes the modern sentimentalists: it kills off the great mass of drivel and shows some reason for the masters. Music is the youngest of the arts—

No, the oldest, Dev interposed.

The oldest instinct and the youngest art.

Are you a performer?

No, she said, I play enough to work out the details of that which I wish to understand, but that is all.

You compose?

Yes, nothing of moment.

And they were at the Concert Hall. At the same moment it began to rain. A regular downpour.

To Evans, inside the Concert Hall, the great chorus, male and female, the choir boys way up in the loft back of the proscenium arch, raising hell, far off, leaning over their balcony, it all seemed a little exotic. Below and in front sat the grave Philharmonic Orchestra with the soloists, three men, Christ, Peter, Judas, and the woman Mary, in their chairs before them; while the early audience, gathering around, was reading, staring, eating sandwiches—and there was one woman in front of them in whose disheveled hair there were head lice.

Miss Black was extremely serious and silent, absorbed, probably recollecting the themes, practicing the listening, Evans thought. But he, knowing nothing of what was about to happen, was curious in his usual way, wanting to see everything about him.

Not that Dev was not acquainted with Bach—but, that was all; the interest was purely inspirational, pure music-aesthetic. He hated the word.

And now the show was on, the chorus was beginning. Evans knew no more until with eyes almost popping out, his heart wrung, and his mind flooded with the presentation, he was walking out after that black fleeting figure, through the crowds in the lobby.

Never before had an opera affected him with this sense of its reality. He had heard Christ speaking, he had heard the wail of the voice. His hair stood up; the crowd, the insistence of the voices—Crucify him! The tragedy, blowing like a wind into his very blood, had been fused with an art never before nor since equaled; the very monotony; the piping children! No scenery, no strutting!

Miss Black said nothing; nor did he, except to remark, No performance has ever affected me so deeply.—None ever will, was her reply.

They walked back on the Ring toward the Rathaus, slowly, without succeeding in starting any conversation of interest. Dev was sure he had heard the Christ speaking, but not repeating a rôle. It was present, the agony and the compassion, the whole range of the feeling was there, invented by the little organist from Leipzig who almost didn't get the job for lack of Latin.

Must have had a servant to pump, or did they have a mechanical arrangement—springs, weights, his spirit rocking and soaring perilously. No, must have had a man up there. Forget him. I'll bet he sweated sometimes. Just press on the keys and hold them down—fill the church with a roar. Never knew what it would be to us—scarcely an element was there which we see to-day—not even his organ, all different now.

Let's see who were alive then? The Empress Maria Theresa, yes, we remember her. The mayor, the bosses, the vestrymen—Mammas of the boys in the Choir, all dead, forgotten. In United States—China—prime ministers. All dead, forgotten. Professors, princes—But this fellow gets himself remembered. What is it to remember? Good to nobody but the fellow who remembers. It pulls us up together, old and new, together.

Bach eating.

So that is music, he said. He had seen it, felt it, passed through that experience; so that is music. I saw him, my God! He wasn't there; just those singers. The music didn't chase him away. It made him come right there, in power, and say —not sing, there was no singing. He was *there* suffering and we heard him.

What kind of an experience is that?—

It had stopped raining. Evans took Miss Black's arm at a crossing. The pavement was full of shallow puddles. The street was glistening with splotches of velvet black and streaks of crooked yellow light. They crossed the Ring and continued walking together without a word.

Bach! Dev began to call to mind the few things he knew about the composer. Strange to bring up the sight of a man against his music.—He recalled the statues and the lithographs.—Lived across the street from the church, middle class. Back and forth. Sat in the loft, must have been cold sometimes. Lamps, tapers; maybe no light at all, teaching them to sing. Damned choir brats. All dead. He was a singer himself, violin, organ, had to make it up, had to make up something or other, so he did. Had a time getting the job. Rival had Latin—he didn't have much.

Two wives, about twenty children, taught them music too, made 'em sing in his choir I bet, maybe whaled hell out of them if they didn't know their lessons. Christ, there letting them put him up on the wood.

Art's a funny thing, doesn't seem to have any connection with our lives, just gets itself made—and when it is good there's no time in it at all. Kills time, that's art. Brings up a lot of old ideas we thought were dead. Not dead at all. Time can't kill anything, says art. Art kills time.

Funny old figure he must have been going across the street

having generated another child in the night. Over to the old organ loft. Something uncanny about it.—Dev was concerned. A light—coming, I saw him, I heard him and not like a man on the street. I heard him agonizing. I saw him *inside*, not cold but he *lived* and I was possessed by his passion.

Chapter XXVII

A New Place to Meet

THE classes at the University were fascinating, fascinating. Waldheim especially continued to absorb Dev's interest and attention. His studies were all of children. Pitiful and patient, he saw and analytically dissected these sad bits of humanity in all stages of illness, recovery and dissolution. Meanwhile, he looked into street windows; the bookshops interested him marvelously. *Das Buch des Kussens*—with poorly drawn figures on the cover. *Jenseits des Lustüprinzips* and a list of Freud's pamphlets, an amazing list, and all perhaps soon to be refuted, he said to himself uninterestedly.

He wandered much—and alone.

But at last in his walks up and down he began to realize what he was looking for. It was a coffee house, of the right class, secluded, warm and light—not filled with cigarette smoking mobs—not like the Europäische Hof, or any of the ones he had so far visited, but—one where he could sit and talk with Miss Black as he wanted to.

And such a one he found, not far from the flower market on the N. Strasse in a triangular court back of the Scotch Gymnasium. It was not late enough in the season for them to have the tables in the open air, the space was there and the chairs upside down were more or less in place, but the business of the café was conducted in a kind of pastry shop to the south. When he found this place, he rested, went to writing his notes again.

Sparrows were singing on the window sill when he awoke one morning after a restless, dreaming night thinking of money and poetry, and wishing for he knew not what. He looked out of the window and saw a hawk flying over the city. He was restless, though it was but six, and unable to stay in bed. This was the day on which they had planned to take a trip into the country. His mouth was dry, he felt weary without reason.

She was at the tram station waiting.

It was early in the year, few were out, but the day was exquisite. At the end of the tram line they began to climb the worn paths at once, noting with mounting spirits the advancing season. Hepaticas! Violets! as if it had been a novel creation—with petals made after an original design of their mood —growing brighter with the day. They grew hot with the ascent, delightedly treading the grass again, with its springy resilience.

Hardly a thought passed through their minds. They were all among the flowers that day, for no sooner had they reached the summit of the first ascent—overlooking the city from the north—than they ran into a profusion of flowers such as Dev had not expected here.

Oh, look at those violets, and she ran off to lie flat on her belly, fondling the thick white clusters beside a thicket and under it.

You could not walk for violets white and blue on the bright grass under the chestnut trees. Children were about plucking and flinging down the flowers. The two went farther, Grace insisting on gathering a fistful of the blossoms to take back to the city.

Dev took several photographs of her and she of him, then they went up into the woods—quite alone and away from the rest—where the ground under the beech trees was starred on every side with pale lilac hepaticas, thick, thick up the steep banks—millions and millions of flowerlets, in the midst of impassable thickets, edging the paths or rolling up the clear spaces under the trees.

In America the hepatica is a shy flower. But look at this— What can be the meaning of such a difference.

But Grace did not know.

Yellow cuckoo flowers and purple bethany.—A strained day for Dev, full of foreboding in which he had seen Grace as a disembodied spirit flying before him, while he had gone alone walking through flowers—alone.

They were home by one p.m., where she left him. After an hour he met her again when they walked around the Ring, a beautiful day, to his new coffee house.

She liked it. The coffee was excellent. They felt deliciously tired of limb.

It was now that Evans definitely acknowledged to himself that Grace might do as she pleased with him. When he looked at her now his glance came definitely to a point for the first time in the center of her eye. For a moment she looked down smiling. When she looked up again, he was not certain. At least, she had not rebuffed him.

There she told him that her mother was partly French and partly Indian, a Canadian, who had come to live in Maine, on the upper Kennebec, and so forth, and so forth.

Here Evans would meet her afternoons after his work in the hospital. She would tell him of the music, plan their concerts; they would sip their coffee and cream, read, talk of Vienna, of the frowsy, at-home-looking people about them, watch for the papers and magazines and so grew to know each other, and to be indispensable one to the other until the acquaintanceship seemed to be settling down into a still pool of talk—one thing only continuing to strike a flame whenever mention would be made of it: America—and all that word so differently signified for them.

From now on they saw each other more and more, music together and a habit of meeting at the café at about four or five, and sitting for long talks about America and—their lives. They went to concerts. Piccaver. Schelling. A Brückner Symphony.

But Grace relaxed in this mood. She grew careless and sweet in the warmth of Dev's devoted attendance. A bitterness, which had become habitual and which she no longer thought of as anything but the gray walls of life itself, melted in his subtle sun of endless devices for living which was working its way in through every crevice of her uncertainty, prying apart the stones like a lawyer's tongue between the sentences of the law—till she felt on these days, in this hot baker's room, actually happy. She would run there as fast as he. They waited for each other, one as eagerly as the other. Grace was changed, and Dev, sensing that here was a rich ground, a profound rootage, had strange thoughts come into his head,—they were like children playing around the back steps.

Here she told him more of her mother.

A deformity of the legs and hands—those lovely hands shrunken, twisted—Arthritis—you doctors don't seem to be able to do anything about it.

Oh, Father, he's breaking his heart over me—perhaps—I guess not.

But I can't stand him—that is all—I have what I need separately.

Here they stumbled on the *Querschnitt* in which he read of the *Spanische Reitschule.* He mentioned to Grace that they must get admissions. Strange to say, she had heard of it but with no great interest. And they secured tickets for the *Meistersinger* the week following.

But if they would talk of America—instantly the new quietness would disappear and she was stirred to a viciousness which Dev would sometimes incite with malicious amusement—

But she was too quick for him. It's not America. What do I care for that? It's life itself. How tempting it is to men to be spiritualists—as if more life could solve anything when life itself—any kind, anywhere—"that scintillating inheritance which we share with the animals, the insects and the plants." . . . What is Europe, a little more tolerable—that is all.

There is not another country on the face of the earth whose best spirits have run from it as do its artists from the United States of America.

And so they talked—they went to the museum together, to *Gräfin Maritza*—etc.

One day, after a long week in which Dev had grown more and more silent, amazed at his distress—not daring to say what he was thinking—he had made up his mind definitely to ask Grace to be his wife—But the nearer he came to speaking of it the more panic seized him, and the more he desired her to be his wife and go back with him, back to—

Chapter XXVIII

Schönbrunn

AND so one morning, it was Good Friday, April the 18th, Evans noted with alarm on turning the page of his diary that the month was past the middle and beginning to wane. On this day they had planned to go to Schönbrunn, the former half-wild royal estate of the Hapsburgs, situated about three miles outside the city to the southwest.

It was a clear, hard spring morning, but still somewhat cold. Two women were talking French volubly in loud coarse voices toward the front of the tram about a man who had offended one of them.

At Schönbrunn the two Americans walked with scarcely a word uttered, on along the smooth paths under the bare trees of this great park, thinking. The place was lovely, but the sense of departed royalty was everywhere over the ground.

On they went at random over the rolling parkland of the approach, coming out of the woods finally upon the more formal portions of the great estate near the palace. The day did not grow warmer. The spring seemed reluctant. There was still the hard wind blowing—even more chilly there in the open than in the forest.

Men on tall ladders thirty feet high or more were trimming the old plane trees, clipping them into formal twiggy walls that would be leaves later.

Glad they were, the two strollers, because of the wind, to enter the glassed-in Gloriette on the high ground above the palace where Maria Theresa would sit with her famous Frenchman and, talking earnestly, look out over Vienna and the country to the right, to the left, and beyond.

As the two came out again into the cold wind, there were four brightly colored swallows sitting on a low wire near the path, huddled quite close together and swaying back and forth, with the wire's swing. Two small boys and a man were staring up open-mouthed at them.

Crocuses and large dark-colored anemones were coming up on the parterres.

Grace especially was in a still, though friendly, mood.— How quietly beauty goes to sleep, this garden. It is illuminating to be here alone in the garden of the Empress, now before the summer mobs have come, and to be enjoying, because of her, that which she seldom looked at we suppose.

But it's cold, answered Evans, the trees are only half out; that's what one gets, mostly, for being too early.

From the hill back of the palace they saw Vienna and the hills at its back and the plain with the Danube in it to eastward. Unfortunately the palace was stuccoed a dirty yellow.

They passed several hours in walking, sitting in the glass pavilion and watching the birds. Some old men were cleaning about under the bushes, their backs and legs, feet and heads, moving here and there beside great wicker leaf-baskets.

Returning to Vienna at noon, Grace and Evans sat in the Rathaus Park half an hour before separating to go home. The same saturnine anemones they had noticed at Schönbrunn, too dark for flowers, soiled, empurpled—made a curious impression on Evans, startling and stirring him savagely, the unwashed half of him seeming at their sight to stifle him with a mad insistence.

Shall we meet at the coffee house later?

No.

She looked at him, surprised at his rough voice.

We'll have supper together in the Rathskeller.

Very well.

He did not reply nor look up to see her going. Presently he began to walk.

In the evening he met her, having made up his mind. They went to their old table. Grace was still in the dreamy mood of the morning. But still as she had been, she had clung to him this day as if he had been a buffer between herself and the world.

They ate quietly, Grace placid, contented, Dev stewing and sullen, unable to say what was in his mind.

And so he began. They had finished their slight meal and were sitting waiting—for what?—It is past the middle of the month. In another week, I shall be preparing to go—

Grace seemed suddenly to awaken, startled. She grasped his hand as it lay on the table. But letting go again, she gathered her coat about her shoulders. Then she got up. When Dev had paid the waiter, he followed and found her already in the street. She was violently disturbed.—Oh, what stupidity it is, she said. We do not even know each other when we are face to face.—And she turned from him as if to walk away.

What is it dear? Let us sit down in the park awhile.

No. You must take me with you. It is too stupid to stop any longer.

Let us be married. Come back with me to America.—He had not understood her.

Don't talk of that now, but take me somewhere, at once; take me to your room, can't you? or anywhere.

He kissed her hands and they walked back around the Rathaus where he let himself in at his pension without being observed. Grace followed him quietly. Through sheer folly they had gone direct to his room, and by merest chance reached it without an eye being wasted upon them.

But—there were no buts at all.—Do not think of me, I am satisfied, ecstatically so—more than I ever imagined I should be. It is you. Go on.

She had a faintly coppery body, excellently moulded, the breasts small and firm—unusually so for a modern woman of her age.

After, they went out as quietly as they had come in. She would not stay. They walked about the Ring seeing the street cars, the people mounting and alighting, the façade of the Parliament beyond the globular balls of light flanking its grandiose staircase, and sculptured groups of men mastering wild horses. It was a dark spring night. They could sit a short while in the park without feeling cold. They talked.

We must—you must find a new room, dearest, she had said. Somewhere for us to be together without question, at ease.

Let us go to a hotel—

No. You must find a room of our own, at once, tomorrow morning. In the evening I will come to you again.

In the morning—

No. In the morning you will find our place. Some pleasant corner facing to the south so that the sun will come in. Not too far away from this quarter. Good night—she kissed him —dear. Please let me go alone.

He remained sitting a while, letting her go, as was his custom. Later he waked the old concierge who grumbled at the door as usual, letting him in. Evans doubled the usual fee.

In his room he seemed to be sinking back through imprisoning circles of dark light as through the center of a flower, back to some dimly remembered past, Indian games—mad escapades. Back, back to a lost grace—his own early instincts, perfect and beautiful. Scale after scale dropped from him— more than he had known it to happen under any previous condition in his life before. He never felt less voluptuous, but

clarified through and through, not the mind, not the spirit—
but the whole body—clear, clear, clear as if he were made of
some fine material strong yet permeable to every sense—
opening, loosening, letting in the light.

Chapter XXIX

The New Room

In the morning it was a wild scramble. Frau D. was surprised at Dr. Evans' sudden departure. Rosa was disturbed. She insisted on talking.

Dev had to wait for them to make up the bill; he offered to pay the full time. Rosa had a bad cold. He decided he might as well drink his coffee and eat his rolls there.

He talked to Rosa (his German was improving). She was feeling quite ill. Go to the Clinic? Never, she said. I never went there but once. Treat you like a *"Tier"*—an animal. *"Kein Wunder Oesterreich zum grunde geht."* She went on to say she wanted *"weisse Zähne,"* porcelain teeth, not gold ones. The dentist wants 1,500,000 krone for four.—Evans went over his accounts. Not much left.

Then he rushed out and began his search, looking for a pleasant street, then scanning the windows for signs of a room to rent—and finally, just before noon, he located the very place he wanted, a southern window, no hindrances, a clean chamber in an old house not three blocks from the Rathaus. There he went, leaving his traveling case, his books—slinging them on the floor, anywhere. Then he ran from this strangeness, failing to connect it with Grace as yet anywhere. In fact, he began now to doubt that—

Having retained the taxi, he motored over to the city to return the typewriter he had rented. No use for that now.

Now the afternoon lay before him, seeming a year. He could eat little, he could not rest. He walked the streets and began to distrust his own senses.

Now he knew he would never see Grace again. Why else had she thrown him off? Why had she not come with him to find the room?

He doubted everything, while the cold hours seemed like stones which he was pushing aside that he might go on.

Fool. You should have clung to her. Now he began to reënact the whole scene of the night before. He saw her from the first moment, when she had entered his room and looked about wonderingly, surprised to have come upon these walls and the bed—the bed, the chairs so familiar to him, so strange to her. He saw her half nude. He could feel her mind, subdued by her desire. There was no modesty, no hesitation—no amusement. They had been very still. Every sensation, every word he recalled. He felt again the startled wonder he had experienced at finding her body so perfect. He had not, somehow, expected that. It did something to him which he recognized but found rare in his mind—like a note struck fairly and true, like a bell ringing perfectly in tune and time. He had sought a defect, he could remember none. Now he sought a weakness to it all in his mind and still he could find none. The whole episode had passed as if it had been the rolling of a glass sphere. Perfect. Never before in his life had he known anything perfect.

With dread he reinspected his own bearing. Strange that he had not been strained, self-conscious, slow. His whole being had moved like the body of a performer, a perfectly trained artist for the thousandth time repeating the plotted gesture. But he had been alive, going forward for the first time into a virgin continent and he had behaved—perfectly. What had become of his usual distress?

Now he was sure he had lost her. Damned fool, not to have held on. He was certain that it was an impulse, that she had thrown herself away. What?

She had given way to a flood of emotion. To-day she will regret. She will not come.

Several times he found himself looking into windows, the old familiar optical instrument shop on the Brühl. Walking, he would awake and see things in the windows and wonder where he was. Then he would rouse. He felt cold. He walked on among the people in the street.

To-morrow will be Easter. He bought some roasted chestnuts from an old woman and ate one or two of them, keeping them in his pocket to warm one of his hands. It was cold. Only three o'clock.

Why should she come?

Get a room. Not at a hotel. Some place with a sunny window. A home for us. Our own. I will come to you in the evening.

Then he began again to rehearse everything that had been said and done the night before, hunting for a clew to what would happen to-day. From that he began again to see her nude, after; standing with her arms thrown above her head a moment as if she were about to sing—there in the darkened room. He strove to recall the features of her face.

Walking so, Evans wakened to find himself in a dense crowd before Cook's offices across from the Stephan Church. People were lined along the curb, while behind them the crowd was pushing slowly ahead toward the cathedral doors.

He went along with the rest, wondering, and making the turn at the bottom of the blind way which aproached the nave on the south side he stopped at the door of the cathedral. Pushing forward, he made a place for himself on the curb between two women. There he waited with the rest.

The great cobbled square before the church as well as the narrow part of it at the side where he stood was walled off by the crowds around it. A few police were walking back and forth in the cleared space keeping the onlookers in position. A dog ran out and looked self-consciously about. Time passed. The situation was an exposed one. Evans' feet were cold, his heart was like lead. He waited with the rest, he did not know for what. Overhead three aeroplanes hummed by in formation.

Then after an hour, an hour, another hour gone by! he felt a stir about him. Over to his left, he did not see whence they had come, but presumably it was from the great portals of the church, around the other side, the poor procession had started. There were boys in ordinary dark street dress, singing to the blowing of a few horns. This past, there came men in silk hats, repeating a response at a slow walk, just a few. Then behind them walked a fat old man, the archbishop, old and gray and bareheaded, under a canopy held by four boys; an old man, walking on the cobbles, dirty-looking in his white laces and crimson tunic, bareheaded in that biting air. He was unconscious of the crowd which kneeled on the stones at his approach—some of them. His hands were held in the attitude of prayer and his fat lips were mumbling while his bleared eyes seemed those of a man half dead.

Evans stared and wondered. The significance of the ceremony escaped him completely. Poor old gink! And before ever he was by, Evans' mind began to wander to the evening; the nude figure of Grace was in his mind once more.

Furious jealousies overcame him. But what in the world have *I* to be jealous of, from her?

Sore of foot, he must have sat down soon, even upon the curb, to prevent fainting if he should have continued longer in his obstinate wandering, waiting for the evening. After a rest and a cup of coffee at their rendezvous, he sat about for two hours longer—realizing what a Viennese coffee house is for—since no one so much as noticed his presence and there were several there who had come in before himself and who were still there when Grace arrived.

To him her arrival was like the rising of the sun. Fresh, even gay, she came hurrying in through the door. But in a moment he had her out into the street again, hustling along, kissing her hand until she laughed, protesting, a little out of breath, and stood stock still for a moment.—Wait a minute!

Oh, come, dear, he cried, to our room.

They took a taxi.

From then on, they spent all the time they could together in their new home. She came to him when she was able, which was every day, for as much of the time as it was possible for her to spend there. He would return from his classes to find her reading, putting neatness in his few belongings, even sewing a little.

—I am like a bird that has built a nest, she said. Already I have almost forgotten how to fly. It is beyond belief.

They had planned some time before to take a country trip to Neuwaldegg when the weather should be warmer, but now Dev wanted to spend all day in their new room, to talk and to play. No, Grace remonstrated, we shall do everything just as before planned. To-morrow the walk; Sunday, the *Reitschüle*.

Her mouth was like honey to him. He had never realized the fact of such a statement till this time.

Chapter XXX

Reitschüle

SUNDAY: the day of the *Spanische Reitschüle*, four days before
he would be leaving and Grace had not yet permitted him to
speak his mind to her concerning marriage. A weak idiot he
called himself from time to time. She must. It was uncomfort-
ably cold this day with wind and a little dash of rain now and
then darkening the streets.

He went to her friend's to fetch her. At 11 a.m. they were
taking their places in the gallery at the south end of the late
Imperial Riding Academy, the famous *Spanische Reitschüle*,
among the other guests, leaning forward over the broad railing above the tanbark arena to witness this most aristocratic
spectacle of horses, one of the chiefest pieces of living beauty
left in the world, the exercising of the Imperial Arabs trained
in the Spanish manner, for which even "the Museum" still
granted funds sufficient to maintain it.

As the fanfare of horns sounded outside and as with the
swinging back of the doors directly under them the eager
Arabs bounded forward four abreast down the center of the
tanbark, tears of happiness sprang into the eyes of the two
Americans. They clutched each other's hands like little children, holding their breaths with admiration, knowing that

196

here was the thing, the great impossible perfection of the
world, without let or hindrance, "without fault," without sin,
that had drawn them together, the one reason for their love,
a parade of horses by grace of the Arabs—inventors of math-
ematics—and trained in the Spanish mode.

Grace's nails were dug deep into the back of Dev's left
hand, so generously did she squeeze him. All they could say
was, Look, Oh look.

At the first glance, Evans realized the gross subversion of
the circus to a cruder taste, lovely as he had always thought
it; the crowd, bred of vulgarity; the blatant claptrap; the un-
truth of it to the finest traits of the animals.

All the first horses were white, abreast they marched forward and abreast faced the Imperial box, saluting the Emperor—in memory. Then, to a fanfare of trumpets, the riding
began. First, they went through their paces gently, com-
posedly, each animal an individual, each distinguished in the
perfection of neck and fetlock.

Neither of the lovers was a rider. It was not necessary in
them for a rapt appreciation of the scene.

The grooms in hunting dress, blue and buff, carried frail
natural birch twigs which they brushed from time to time
against the beasts' sides. Right and left went the horses, walk,
trot, canter, gallop; gracefully, restrainedly, passing each
other without confusion at the sides of the arena.

As the horses left the oval to a great round of applause, Dev
and Grace relaxed the stare of their watching and sat back
exaggerating their limpness. A feeling of futility, of the passage of greatness, the end of desire, passed over them.

Then again the beasts, a great chestnut stallion this time
among them, were in the ring, waltzing now, now turning,
now clipping the ring through the middle, sidestepping, momently breaking pace to catch it again instantly. And one, the
name was on the program, hitched between two posts in the
center, did her steps unmounted, at a word.

During the intermission, wishing it might never end,

Grace who had been leaning with her head on the railing, on her crossed arms, looked up at Evans. He saw that she was about to say something of importance. No one was just near them at the time.

We are leaving each other the day after to-morrow.

He made as if to answer but said nothing.

Is it not miraculous that everything that we have felt for each other, animal, perfect, aristocratic, so strange to our country and training; that thing that makes us indispensable to each other, that no one but an American can understand as we understand it, with that same longing that we have had, you and I, what we call "love," has been evoked here before us now, by these glorious beasts; everything that we are not, that I hate.—She smiled. And we shall always have it, when we think of this perfect, untarnished, foreign master, the horn blasts, the stallions and mares. I think few people have had their happiness pictured so perfectly to their eye as we have had it done for us to-day. Here we have reached the climax of our minute. Now it ends. Good-by.

Evans did not at once grasp her meaning.

Dearest, she continued, there is a thing that I want to tell you. It is that you are a thousand times more worthy than you have ever dared to give yourself credit for being. It is amazing to me.

How—?

You understand perfectly, everything, but you will not let it enter your mind. You know; I see it in you but you refuse to accept it. You keep off the bare truths. I shall probably never see you again after to-morrow.

So it would not be to-day; he clung to the hope.

It is perfect that it should be so—but you still fight it though you know better. You see, do you not, how futile it would be for us to marry?

He was straining to keep from accepting her words.

Good, she cried, squeezing his hand, it is your honesty and your fear to accept the truth that makes me love you, dearest;

you are as timid as a horse. Accept it, like the aristocrat you
are at heart, beaten by that despicable country, our country,
dragged in the dirt, hated.—But she shook herself away from
that by an effort of the will. Accept it, right or wrong, and
stop.

He wanted to, but he could not. He looked at her and he
wanted to kill her—to take her. For a moment something evil
flashed in his eyes—soon dimmed.

But she was like lightning.

No good, Dev, it's always the savage that is too civilized by
civilization. Dearest! And she looked at him with drooping,
morbid eyes, a look that he had never before seen in her—as
if she were narcotized for the flash of a second.

Now the horses were out once more, but his mind could
not follow them, yet he looked, studying each feature of the
exquisite beasts. The spectators had been cleared from the
Imperial box; the Emperor defers to the animal. Dev wondered if the Emperor actually came down, allowing the horses
precedence. How magnificent! He did not believe that anyone on earth had the understanding to do that. The horses
walked in through the box over the wooden floor which re-
sounded with their hoofs to accustom them to treading on
hollow bottoms, and out again into the soft arena.

But now he turned deliberately to fill himself with Grace's
firm profile, the nose, the round chin, the eyes, fastened with
unusual brilliance and sharp attention upon the scene before
her. But the sudden change from hardness almost to appeal
in her eyes brought him back with a start. She rested her hand
above his knee, idly. He did not place his own upon hers but
remained leaning on the rail.

The quadrille. Then the curvet, the capriole, the four jumps
taken standing on the hind legs alone. Then all the horses at
once performed to the maximum of their bent, the high notes
of their cultured accomplishment—so that Dev saw them in
his fancy caparisoned before a great assemblage—and their
riders riding them proudly.

At noon the company filed out into the wet courtyard, how changed since that first day when he had walked by it—now wringing his heart, almost as it must have done the imperiled owners to leave it—Grace had her arm in his. Neither mentioned their conversation of the morning. Neither spoke.

Grace left him, inside the portico of her aunt's apartment, with a kiss, patted his cheek, made him smile—said she must rest. He did not want her to go but looked suspiciously at her —almost a stranger already in his eyes.

Think of your gods, she bantered. It is written.

Chapter XXXI

Walküre

Evans spent the afternoon miserably; slept. Thought he
might go out to see the Carpentier-Townley boxing match.
But it drizzled. He began to write to his sister but had not the
heart. For several days, as a fact, he had been carrying a letter
from her unopened in his pocket. Now he found and opened
it, just a note:

> *Dearest boy: Will meet you Hotel du Lac,*
> *Geneva, May 9. Room reserved. Don't fail.*
> Bess

Dashed into the middle of his intense preoccupation with
Miss Black, it came like water in the face, leaving him startled,
ill at ease. For a moment Grace was pushed far away, a
stranger, the companion of a month, and Bess, old Bess, came
up close—for a moment; then she was gone again in the
intensity of his reaction, quickened by fear of loss, toward the
newer attachment.

By mid-afternoon he could not bear to remain in the
room longer but walked out to drive his uneasiness from him,
going to their rendezvous behind the Scotch Gymnasium
where he knew she would be coming to join him presently.

201

They had tickets that night for *Die Walküre.*

He had jammed Bess' letter back into his pocket. Very little had he ever said to Grace of his sister.

After a restless hour Grace came. Dull as he had been, Evans was quickened instantly as always by her presence. She, too, seemed content to have found him again. So they were going to begin once more. For a moment he thought all his fears were groundless.

Putting his hand into his pocket he felt the letter and drawing it out placed it on the table.

Grace took it in her hand.

Read it, he said.

She turned the paper over curiously, then read what was written. She seemed to be studying the writing. Having turned the page over and back two or three times she laid it on the table once more without a word. Evans took it, folded it and put it into his breast pocket. Grace was looking down at her own hands resting on the table.

What time is it?

They went out. As they walked along, side by side toward the opera, they said scarcely a word. It was Jeritza's homecoming from New York. They had good seats in the center of the first balcony. As they took their places and looked around at the gradually filling auditorium, Evans felt singularly cold to his companion. Bess' letter had opened the world to him again. The fiddle strings were being scraped discordantly in the orchestra pit.

Tell me about your sister, Grace turned to him.

Oh, Bess is a good kid.

Is she young?

Yes, about your age.

Pretty?

Yes, he said.

Tall?

He nodded his head. About medium.

Do you know Walküre, she went on.

No, barely.

It is a brother and sister against the world.

Really. Damn her, he added to himself, what's she up to? I'd like a libretto.

What for?

I'd like to read it.

He left his seat and went into the foyer where he managed to pick up what he wanted.

He came back, took his seat and began to read the libretto.

After a moment he saw she had turned and was looking at him.

Do you know the music? Foolish to ask, I suppose.

No, just the Brünhilde bit where the War Maidens came in. Though the pumping of the horns has always seemed to me ridiculously heavy—or no one knows how to make them seem less so—at any rate.

She laughed. Why in the world do you go to Grand Opera?

He saw she was irritated and thought he'd give her more if she wanted it.—I go for the show I suppose, like any other, to see the story played and hear it set to a tune.

She turned her head away without smiling.

Why shouldn't I? Isn't it interesting, or shouldn't it be so to a musical ignoramus like myself? It's a show, isn't it? I want to know what's going on, what the meaning of it is anyway. What good is it if you can't understand what they're saying?

It's music, music. Nothing else.

All right. But I want to know what it is about.—He felt rotten.

Do you know enough German?

To hell with the music, if I want it to be that way, but he didn't say this aloud.

He had not read far in the first act when the lights began to go out. He had arrived at the place where the brother and sister were become definitely lovers in the forest lodge and Sigmund was about to attempt the sword—to draw it from the tree. Then the overture started.

Evans dimly knew the story, but for once he felt that he would like to get the thing well in mind before the singing began. He was excited and determined. The orchestra was now in full career.

Unable to read further in the dim light, he reached instinctively for his physician's pocket flash which he carried always in his vest pocket. The sudden flash of the light on the page startled Grace who had been intently absorbed listening.

She turned and gave him a quick look curiously in the eye. To hell with her.

It was Jeritza's homecoming from New York, Siglinde, that great, nightgowned woman, amorous, tragic, eager to please her people.

Still Evans kept the libretto in his hand but now he was following the music. Sigmund had come from the woods entering the heavy door of the great forest abode. In the center stood the huge oak with the haft of the sword sticking from one side of it. The two, Sigmund and Siglinde, unrecognizing, filled the foreboding scene. All around, Evans felt the depth of the forest wilderness. Before Rome, he said to himself.

The music rose and fell in unctuous waves about him—as his mind wandered to Bess—then back to the story he had just been reading. Once or twice he glanced quickly at the page of the libretto to see where they were. He had heard Walküre before but idly—not with the words in his mind as this time. They increased his enchantment. The music seemed to him to be enforcing the speech.

He could see it now, a prehistoric passion, destiny drawing up the inevitable misfortune; love like a glowing metal now invisibly—of the gods—drawing the brother and sister from their own breasts and making of them one—the husks to lie discarded presently.

The music was enormous, too big; one could pass by that. That was Wagner's idea of it. Bess. What the hell, I don't know.

The music raised the words, Which are after all, very bad, he said, the music piles up the feeling on the words, a feeling which isn't there in them.

On the stage, Jeritza was lying with her head in her brother's lap. Now the music had gone over completely. Couldn't put that into words. Words just a blank outline. They'd suppress that if it were in words. Think it's fine, hearing the music. Because it's just excited sound; clear, in words, that would have to be good writing to get by. It ought to be said clear though. The music says it with too much excitement; ought to be clear. Maybe we couldn't stand it. Proust, I suppose that would be. Music is sloppy. Can't write Wagner any more. Music should be clear now. That explains perennial interest in Mozart—Händel. Most music is always muzzy.

But he was carried away by the great surges of sound, and by the story in his mind, when the music would again fade.

Music! a kind of stupidity it requires, a kind of German thickness—light through trees, misty. No good to get all excited this way. I suppose there's a clear logic though, she gets. —He looked a little at Grace who was leaning over absorbed as was her manner when music was being played.

Now, in the face of destiny, the brother and his sister had been united in each other's arms, the sword was drawn, and the first act had come to a close.

For a while the two waited for the aura of the music to fade. Both had been absorbed by the perfection of Weingartner's performance—here in Vienna, a technical perfection which in itself Evans had never seen equaled.

Is it not superb? ventured Grace more to herself than to Evans—in sheer generosity of spirit after the exaltation of her mood.

Yes, I have never realized the full meaning of great conducting before. The *piano* passages, the wonderfully managed crescendos, and the lack of offense in the matter of time and the clarity of the orchestra and other voices.

Grace was pleased that he spoke as he did. She was still

absorbed in her pleasure with listening. Now she had forgotten all else in her admiration for the great beauty of the work that she had just heard. But with the lights in the auditorium lit once more, Evans wanted to get on with his reading.

An amazing story, this is, when you think of it, this brother and sister. Do you remember the scene in Sanine where he sees his sister coming through the garden and he admires her breasts—of course you couldn't write a libretto to an opera and have it mean anything. The music saps the sense out of the words.

Yes, of course.

And without improving them. That is, good writing seems to me far superior to good music; a much finer instrument.

It depends on your ability to listen.

But you *can't* put into music the brother and the sister of this. You don't hear it at all, it isn't there. They're just lovers.

That's why we can listen to it.

All right.—He wanted to read.

Lovers are all brothers and sisters—like you and your little Bess, she added.

Evans wanted to read the second act. So he went on, realizing a little as he read, some of the meanings of Grace's last remark.

Before other words between them, the second act had begun—a colloquy of the gods over the fate of the lovers, then the ride of the Walküre, the battle of Sigmund and his sister's husband, and the magic sword, no good at all, just a sell! struck up by Wotan, and Sigmund wounded,—left to die in his sister's arms.

Sigmund, Siglinde; *Brüder, Schwester.* In the excitement Evans wanted to see the words. Out came his light as he began thumbing the pages.

In the midst of the music, his mind taken up with what he was doing, he seemed to hear Grace's voice, saying distinctly: If you persist in turning this performance into a personal debauch,—he lost the rest.

Going more carefully he found his place, saw what he wanted and turned his attention back upon the stage. Jeritza was sitting with her dying brother's head in her lap.

Evans began now to forget the stage and to think of Grace. He was surprised at her sudden ill nature, and yet.—Had he not himself felt several times far from in love with her to-day? To-day. That's it, to-day.

What kind of a woman is this? I have started her on a new track—where will she end? He felt mean, cowardly. She was just beginning while he was going back. Back! A shudder went over him. Back to work. To work. She probably did not love him. Already he was feeling the cost of her loss. He had been inundated. What am I? She will go on. Then he began in his mind to cling to her again.

Brüder! Schwester! he had the libretto in his hand.

Before the third act he was ready to say again, You must come back to America with me.

She replied, Shall I not ask you rather to remain here?

Wotan was giving way to his wife. Brünhilde must be punished for her interference on behalf of the lovers. The orchestra was perfect. After the fire music with its flickering, eternal rising and falling of the magic flame, they started home.

Come fully out of her mood, once the music was behind, Graze seized Evans' arm again in the old impulsive fashion, hurrying him along on the half dark Ring by the trees and empty benches—and all his depression went off like cigarette smoke disappearing—

Only, for God's sake, sweetheart, don't ask me to go to America. Don't act so tragic, she continued, we are young, dear, yes, we are young. That's what the machines have done for us—you especially, you'll live fifty years yet, maybe. Forgive me, dear, you'll go hurrying back to your sweet sister. Forgive me, I'm a jealous fool, I could murder the little cat. I wish I could see her. I'd strangle her, I know.

Come, said Dev, dancing with the spell she could cast about him now at will.

No, not yet. I will later, as long as you like. Let us go over to see the Johann Strauss monument. There is nothing more fantastic in the world.

They walked and talked for two hours as happy as they had ever been in their lives.

Chapter XXXII

Prater

IN THE morning, two days before his departure, Dev went to the steamship office to secure his tickets for America. Then lectures, a snack of lunch—and, impatient, he awaited Grace —who came eagerly, direct to him, looking happily into his eyes with such unabashed delight that he felt a fresh pang of misery at the thought of losing her. I shall lose her in only two days.—He caressed her cheeks, kissing his own hand by mistake in his unseeing earnestness, which made him laugh and her also when he told her of it.

No, she said, not now, it is too wonderful a day, come out with me for a walk first.

Will you come back?

Yes, and stay all night.—Come on.

They went by tram to the Prater, the great holiday promenade of the Viennese: There they walked all the afternoon for three and a half hours strolling along always in a straight line southward on the great central promenade to the end near the river by the willows—talking, resting. It was most beautiful weather. The violets were thick under the trees and many were picking them. They lay on the grass in the hot sun listening to birds, the frogs, and seeing boys playing by the reedy shore of a little inlet. Toward evening they returned up the drive stopping at dusk in a summer garden where to good music they had good beer and an ausschintz.

Lights, sundown: an evening forever memorable coming at the end of a day full of their love together when every speck of the meadow grass was felt equally between them and their talk was too trivial, not to mar its weight, to bear repeating.

Returning home to the room, their legs tingling with fatigue, they lay in each other's arms a long time talking, Dev not daring to mention his alarms at their approaching separation, which stabbed him so that he had forcibly to push it away, burying his face in her breast to drive it from him.

They slept for a long time, Evans dreamlessly but Grace troubled, crying into her pillow. When they wakened it was nearly two a.m. Both wakened at the same time at some loud noise in the street. They turned to each other instinctively in the dark a while without a word, and then began to talk. The dark was hard like a crystal, faceted and shiny to them now.

I want you to marry me. I want you to be my wife—and come back with me to New York.

I don't want to and I will not do it.

Grace, dear—

No, I will get up and go out into the street if you continue.

Grace, dear—

She got up from the bed and stood in the dark room.

Come back, he pleaded. I will not speak of it again. He was on his feet beside her, wrapping her in a blanket against the chill.

Now she lay beside him once more, she was crying. He kissed her tears away.

After a time they were quiet again and began once more to talk. She was now again as he had always known her, self-possessed and inflexible.

Your sister will satisfy you. You are that kind. Forgive me. This is not romance, Dev. This is reality, wake up! We are caught. Cannot even we keep one thing clean? What are our lives made up of, tell me: bitterness, disappointment—not with each other, nothing to do with any of us—it is inevitable. But not one thing clean. I hate America simply because it is my own slough—but we have found something clean, one small clean spot. And so it must remain: clean, a place to rest our heads on. We are leaving each other. Face it. There is no other way. Marriage is sordid, it is nothing that either of us wants.

That's all right, dear, but I don't give a damn about your reasons.

Neither do I. The fact is much harder and more certain. Go to sleep. We both need it. Kiss me and go to sleep.

But he was desperate and continued to plead.

No, dear, it's no good, she answered him. Let me talk to you then if you won't sleep. You are a curious mixture, Dev. There are two parts: that hard clearness which is your inner core and makes you go, and the tenderness of a woman. Dearest, I love you sometimes when I am alone so that I don't know what to do with myself. I am rock. I know myself. I am cold save when the sun is on me. But you are alive, a thing of the earth. Can you feel it in yourself? I want to tell you how I admire you, how I debase myself before you. How I understand your difficulties, how I want to liberate you—to fling you in the face of the world. But I can't do that, Dev, and besides you don't need me. That's the terrible thing to a woman, you don't need me. You will go on just the same. You are alive, you are a part of the earth. But not as a peasant. There's a good deal of peasant in you, as in all true aristocrats who are attached to the land. But back of that, what a peasant does not have is your mind, your spirit, that true hardness which sparkles like a diamond and which you—part of you— dreads to trust. You are right, too. I don't want you to be like me. You know better than I, down inside you, what is right. But, Dev, it doesn't come up in you—pardon me, dear, it is jealousy of your powers in part—it doesn't come up in you save by moments and with dread; you are afraid. Your tenderness makes you so. You are you. You must be as you are. But it maddens me; do not mistake me. No two human beings can live together. Your softness maddens me. I despise it. I am hard inside, that's why I can never do anything with music. I know all these things. I am hard and I like it. It lets me go about Europe this way. I am hard—and I have been madly in love. Even I. I tell you I was never so surprised in my life. No one but you could do it and no one will do it again. I am married to you, dearest, as few people are married. But I cannot live with you nor you with me. Get some one else. I tell you—your sister. I cannot tell you—I never want to see that woman. She is good for you—Oh, I don't know. It doesn't make any difference. I wanted just to tell you that I see how you are. There is moss and green stuff on your rocks, you are warm, too, all alone. I am cold. You are alive—You belong to the earth, you are hopeful. I am hopeless—I would kill you, make a senseless infatuated lover of you if I wanted to. And suppose some day I should take it into my head to deceive you. I'd do it; do not doubt. I love you, dearest, but I would do it, if—oh to keep you, to torment you, to make myself feel again what I should know I was not feeling. You are you. I am I till the end of time but there is no end to anything. Maybe we shall meet again.—

Dev was lit with excitement by this speech and the strict attention he gave to it, his mind picking up each word as a magnet picks up needles. Now he was overcome with admiration. Still.

A while they slept, close in each other's arms. When they waked it was just before dawn. There was a faint light. The sparrows had not even begun to twitter. They were not tired. They could just see each other as they smiled.

The conversation began of itself nearly where they had left it.

You like America, thoughtless Polacks, Italians, Wops, not too much of them—because they do not matter to you, they do not cause you any serious concern. But fine people should not cause you any strain; they do though, they make you irritable—wanting to run. You are not at ease with them as an aristocrat should be. Forgive me. That is why you want to run now to America, to America where there are no really fine people—or they are buried, voiceless, lost—which amounts to the same thing, lost to sense, to understanding—and cut off from the ground; stemless unless stupid stock like some Marylanders—or worse—silent, ashamed. They are neither aware like the best of continentals nor even the English with that temporal effectiveness, neither fish nor flesh.—

It is not even so much the place but that such a place exists at all—the terrible, unattackable, sphinxlike stupidity, so hard a riddle. It must be somewhere in our first principles, that error—with which we are surrounded—that our best efforts —intensities are lost; the confusion must have arisen by failure at the beginning, somewhere near the start. A false premise which the further we go by it, do our best works, the further we go astray. So that the utmost we can do is to stand still, to keep something clean. You see, I, too, am tainted with a fatal altruism—but something clean, it is the maximum.

No, he said seriously, answering what she had said before, I do not run from fineness, but small doses of it suffice. I soon tire. I feel a real need for the vulgar. I have been accused before of running away. Well, I want to plant it, IT; to see if it grows. Fineness, too much of it, narcotizes me. It drives me wild. I do not want that.

Yes, Dev, you are right. You really *do* thrive on the ground. You are alive. It amazes me. You are growing—like anything —like a burdock. I remember burdocks by the old barn because they grew there back of the house where we lived once when I was about five years old.

When it was seven o'clock they got up and began to wash and dress in the little room. Grace found a few things to make up for breakfast. Dressed and the daylight come, Evans began to speak to her of his writing—perforce, not knowing what else to say.

Yes, I have suspected something of the sort, of course.

Once before she had mentioned it! You are not just a doctor, Dev, what else do you do? Probably you write, since I see no evidence of paint—it would be impossible to be a bachelor of your age, not morose, theoretical, not stupid, lazy, opinionated, defensive, not unbridled, not inanely sensuous, not rich, not a gentleman, not an inheritor, not spoiled—but alive. What is it, writing?—But he had not told her more than that he kept a careful diary—as an excuse for the typewriter, the constant secret application.

I publish nothing of any value, he said now, very little, at any rate. I'm not interested in money or getting known. I write, that's almost all. I do try to get things published. It's all I can say. Meanwhile, infants, he added.

Why infants?

Because I don't have to hear them talk, I guess.

But they do talk, they cry. But that's not it, of course. They do not tax your mature wit; that's why you like them.

He gave her for a keepsake a copy of a book he had once published upon some characters from the American History. She was delighted.—Free from the collegiate taste, she wagered, pressing it with a real pleasure.

After breakfast she asked to be let go alone as usual.

When shall I see you again?

When do you leave?

To-morrow at six a.m.

To-morrow. I'll come here late. Good-by, dear.—She kissed him and went out.

Chapter XXXIII

Good-by Vienna

THE day of turning homeward, back once more! Raining
again. Good-by Vienna. What a difference now, grown a part
of me. Every stick familiar. Must go back and see it all again,
a quick rush around. Fool. All that was familiar is grown
already strange. Like going back to old familiar haunts. Wonder if she has really left the city. Grace. My God, what a fool!
Grace! dearest, where are you? *Wo bist Du?* Where art thou?
Unreal. Did she really love me? Here? He looked but saw no
trace. A dog could scent it. Helpless. Did she veritably say it?
The room is a strange room, a going away room. The room
looked sleepy, he felt burning, the legs shaky, unlocked at the
knees. He could see Switzerland stretching out behind the
west wall of the room. There, too! no dream. If someone
should say, stay here! If God should poke his head through the
ceiling and say, I will bring you Grace back again, stay.
Would you stay? No. Never. Under no circumstances; she
knew that. Must go, must get on my way. What for? I don't
know. Get on your way, it says, *Mene, mene, tekel, upharsin.*
Maybe not, though. Worse things than to get what you want.
No sense in it, just go. Go BACK. Oh you blackguardly,
snivelling craven. Back. Back and for no reason at all except

that it is back, just to go back. Glad of it just the same.
Good-by Vienna. Clothes pressed neatly. Tip her. Here, Elsa.
Good luck. *Ganz gebügelt*—what in hell's she laughing at?

All the preceding day closing his affairs he had had a little
relief in the detail, selling the tail ends of his courses of lectures, etc., clearing up his elastic mind—thinking even of
Switzerland which he had not really seen since boyhood days
at school when he used to collect birds' eggs there, finches',
black-birds', swallows'; even a magpie's egg from some im-
possibly high twig in the school grounds, pursued the while
by Madame Harson aided though and abetted by Pont the
stealthy, so that often they outwitted the old lady. But then
the sense of anguish and of loss closed down again "vice-like"
upon him. How shall I leave it? Home? Vienna is my home
now, forever. Come back! He smiled at his own simplicity.
For what?

Having settled his affairs at the Medical Society headquar-
ters he went back to his deserted, desolate room—where she
had often come. And she was there! Tears came into his eyes
in the amazement of his delight. He kneeled and buried his
face in her lap. Baby, she crooned and stroked his head. Then
he looked up into her face, into her eyes to see if she had
relented. She had not. What then?

You are kind, he said, getting to his feet.

She did not answer, but he felt he had spoken like a fool,
and said no more.

When are you leaving?

In two hours.

I had to come again,—I could not bear it.

Dearest! He kissed her with an empty tenderness.

She stayed an hour. Asked about his sister. Wished him a
pleasant trip through Switzerland. Hoped he would find his
sister well. Told him to take care of himself, not to be foolish
(what does she mean?). Kissed him again in tender fashion
and departed. He opened the door and let her go.

Rushing to say good-by to her aunt, he was told that she had left Vienna.—She left Vienna three days ago. Did she not tell you?

Toward noon he phoned for a taxi and in a heavy rain got to the West Bahnhof not looking out, but looking down at the dirty floor of the carriage, counting his pieces of luggage, fifth time I've counted them. Fool. Grace! Dearest—Oh, you fool, you fool, you eternal, everlasting, god-damned slobbering fool. Why else did she refuse to stay with you than that? A weak-kneed, diffuse, aimless, senseless, instinctive, slippery fool—running away from what? to what? to save your dirty hide. From what?

God, but it *is* raining. It was pouring down in plenteous rivers. He ducked for the shelter of the station portico, umbrellaless. Then suddenly he remembered the letter, Elizabeth Evans, Hotel du Lac, Genève, Suisse. Leaving his luggage with the porter (Dull excitement of going away, people not all so overwrought, indifferent smokers, ticket agent frowning behind his wicket, looking out at the rain, tapping fingers) he ran across in the rain to drop the letter in the slot in the wall of the Post Office, *Hotel du Lac,* he read it again. Stamp first. Last Austrian stamp I'll buy in my life, maybe. New money too, soon.

Back in the station in the middle of the waiting room there was a bird in a large wire cage wrapped in paper, the bird inside piping shrilly; couldn't see what kind. In the rush, when the gate was opened, he had been able to be in the lead. He got a good forward-facing seat next to a window.

The train jerked and started.—First move in many movements that will end only when I am in my consulting chair in my office at home. The first move. The train slipped and with effort got under way. Good-by, Vienna. What a fool, what a—If I could go back and have her now again. If I could go back. Go BACK! What a fool—

A Jew of the usual objectionable type made himself objectionable by closing the door to the compartment and smoking copiously, a vile smell. Dev by the window opened the ventilator, froze out the other, who took to the corridor. Fresh air! For this relief much thanks. He felt irritable and sick. Vienna was going by in the rain.

Heavy eastward clouds were to the north filling the sky in painters' masses, low and heavy (glowering) lowering. Rain was still falling mightily. Vienna was passing, rapidly now, a dull curtain hanging under the clouds, a dull curtain of wet roofs and window-gaps.

West, westward. Just the same it was a relief. Gone. The city was left behind. At the same time the sun shone through a cloud loop making the wet grass gleam before a back drop of smoke-gray hills. In a cut, the embankment rattled by; in the open again the ground was puddled with the brown wet; still it dripped and ran in the gully beside the track. But in the country lay the Danube. It is the Danube? The river was even with the fields, ovals of sheet water with grass sticking through and shrubs and trees. But steadily the sun came forth with ever a steadier shine, and so for hours the train marched, or rolled or rattled or flew or crept through the smiling dripping farmland, and pastures and low hills, the streams everywhere flooding their banks. The fields were sometimes in flower; God has sent all the colors there. Yellow bunches of cowslips Evans saw with his mind, deep orange buttercups, purple stems that seemed hyacinths, and a blue of gentians, intense cobalt as if instructing a recalcitrant sky. He saw heavy woods where some logging was going on, the red spruce logs lay numbered systematically on the butt ends, in even piles. And in the evening, having eaten well on the diner, he came to Salzburg, Mozart's cradle, gateway to the Tyrol, feudal castle, playground of the emperors—in a heavy rain, which lulling him, he walked to the nearest hotel and had baked carp for supper—a great hotel almost empty by reason of the too early season.

From his room he could see the *Festung* and the snow mountains to the west behind it, west—and behind them Switzerland, and beyond that—what?

In the evening after supper he went to his room. Music, he heard. Down he ran again to the salon. A few were dancing. An old titled Austrian lady, very old, smiling, sat on the sidelines, brittle, holding herself firmly together, a hat balanced upon her head, a shawl about her shoulders, "Baroness," wattled and alert. Her fixed smile did not relax before an old man, dozing by her side, his head drooping. To waken him, she ventured: *Sie haben nicht ihr buch, sonst lesen sie?* An old pleasantry, so old Dev shuddered. He did not waken.

Evans slept that night thinking of—another place, another place in which to be.

Waking next morning it was May day! The chestnut trees by the station were in blossom but the cobbled streets were still. He went out and began to walk toward the *Festung*. From the town came a slow procession, working women and men, with signs—Bread! Red flags but no music, no sound— they came on over the bridge, walking. Whither and for what? Women and men and children. Dev, walking, went on, stumbling by chance, among April showers, into the Dom where someone was about to perform upon the gigantic organ high up in the gloom, in the cold, in the hushed spicy air. He sat upon one of the cold oak seats and looked around at the vacant spaces of the medieval edifice. Very few had come to hear the organ in the cold damp church—far off from the world. The organist was playing a confused *Fugue*. The air shook before a sound was heard, so low were the heavy tones. The notes seemed blurred but never had Dev heard so powerful a roar, so deep toned. He looked, absolutely cold, and heard and went away.

He climbed the *Festung*, winding up the leaning causeway, past the portcullis, now eternally raised, by the weedy ramparts, wet with rain and lack of sun where the weed stems were loaded with snails large and small. But entering the fortress, the sun shone in the little court. There were the archbishops' rooms, handsomely ornate; the ancient stove of tiles,——1509 (was it Huntington wanted it for $150,000?

Thank God they wouldn't sell), yellow tiles, built by one man
who knew the art, five years it took him. He saw the two-man
organ on the open east porch under the eaves, the spiked
drum that plays nine tunes. At an open window at Vespers
it plays its hymns over the town. He saw the decorated door-
ways and the cruel dungeon, a deep pit, and the implements
of torture, made of wood; the well they drank of in a siege;
the twisted colums strong enough to have deflected a cannon
ball without deep injury—and from the topmost tower he saw
the view!

Returning slowly to the town, at Peter's Keller in the rocks,
he drank his beer and had two shirred eggs with a slice of
toast. He looked at a tart; a fat stolid thing she was who should
be working in a factory somewhere in New York, he said to
himself. She made him ill, so still she was, to look at her. He
came then into the Peter's Kirche whose columns had been
raised and raised into the narrow nave, up and up until they
seemed three times as thin and long as actually they should
have been, holding up the roof, taller than any other columns
he had ever seen—much the same as those of the double nave
at Toulouse—save that these seemed monoliths. So tall and
gray they were it was one of the most beautiful things that he
came upon in Salzburg, these slender columns with their
square capitals so plainly cut.

Chapter XXXIV

The Mountains

THE train next morning was at five. He got to the station in
the half dark. This compartment. Two men were in it; the
midnight train from Vienna. Two men were in it sleeping
under overcoats, windows closed; the place was stinking,
smoke filled. They were much peeved at the American who
walked in and flung open the window. *"Furchtbar kalt."* Hell,
it stinks in here.—Mr. and Mrs. Aleck Johnson of Virginia,
Pinky Pank River, 1627 on his mother's side, it was who had
come in just before Evans. They were charming, talking all
morning: told him all about their farm, the pangs they felt at
selling it. At six the sun came out, a superb day. The country
was half green, half forested, now. Chalets on high hills, isolated; a few people. At one station stood a woman with glitter-
ing head dress, gold or brass, stiff lacy frills, medals and metal
earrings. The Smiths got out at Innsbruck. Must visit Innsbruck some day.

Now indeed, after leaving Innsbruck, the real mountains
began, the train was winding and laboring to avoid them and
slip in. Now on the right Evans saw the jagged edge of the
great cliffs. As if coming from a shell he saw the cold, with-
ered mountains cut out on the blue sky, snowcapped and with

wind making a play of the snow on the high glissades.

He saw slanting ledges where his mind walked at ease aloof from the crawling world; V-shaped gorges he saw and inverted fans of fallen rock and sand by the cliff's face. Into his spirit he drew, along with his breaths, the stillness and the cold which his body could not have reached. Or he saw a great knob of even granite, shaped like a rock to hold smoothly in the hand and to stroke. Rocks precipitous, perpendicular, measured only by a few thousand feet but straight up, to man most difficult. Now he saw the pine, the evergreen woods starting up the slopes and stopping, or from the recent rains, finger-like spouts of water fell from the tops of the visible mountain walls, speaking of cliffs higher and melting snow. Or on flat rocks, black stains of running water spread out lacquerlike on the rock's face. To the north with the sun on them were great pinnacles, sparkling, snapping, cut out with its sharp knife on the lakes of hard blue. The minute features of the rock drew Dev from point to point, the particular conformation of some slowly turning pinnacle. Eagerly he watched it turn revealing its person. So arose the personalities of the gods, aloof, particular, visible, deathlike, near but far, nothing between us and them but air, space—frozen. Or from behind a running wall of rocks he saw a thing emerging, rising, growing in dimensions and he thought: taking his breath!— If these cliffs were *He*, what of that? The *Doner slag!* a great saddle, ten, twenty, thirty miles away, a bay of whiteness, inhospitable, but soft as feathers.—But there is an agony. One might pass through it if one were strong and skillful enough. Something MUST live there, that's imperative. Then what? The *Saeter girls* are nearest.

So he sat for an hour, two hours, his face pressed upon the windowpane absorbed in the mountains, while the train labored, and wound and stopped and started again at the little hamlet stations. To the south side of the car he shifted and saw a more gradual rise across pastures, green and flowery. But to the north a stream ran by the railway, tributary to the Rhine,

—Its headwaters; I don't know. Rhine and Danube, headwaters hereabouts, about the same parentage. One goes to Budapest; the other to Holland. Parting of the ways.

He went back to the mountains, once more rock ledges where no snow clings, a great snow field, then up, up to the forbidding summit, sunlight painting it orange, purple, black —A hawk there, a hawk!

Fish, trout—chamois too and ibex there must be up there. On the railroad folder there was a scene, an Alpine hunter with an ibex over the nape of his neck. In the center of culture there is a wild park—Switzerland.—He looked to see if he could see any wild life on the crags. No. Almost all shot off for meat during the war. Fish gone too, mostly; fished out while the game laws were in abeyance.—I'd like to see a chamois, said Dev.—There used to be a pair at Interlaken in the park.—I'm going there.

The gods began to appear to him again, as mountains and small flowers. Both he could see from his isolation in the shell of the moving train and he knew the details of the flowers, from within the train, the minute perfection of spot and fibril, the cold details of the mountains; though he could see but the gross contours—yet the details came to him. In the bark crevices of the trees, he could detect with his mind ants running, their slight antennae working nervously in and out— running perpendicularly.

Far off he recognized the aching sense of a woman, far off, a woman whom he had known, outside, far outside, going, not inside anywhere any more. A memory. Memory is the affirmation of genius; a fast-fading memory. Once he thought he saw her in the car, a pair of green satin slippers, and back he came with a start out of memory. She is in this train! Who? Should I know her if I saw her now?—He tried to remember her features and remembering he had been trying, he found himself looking at the ridge of a frost-cold, distant peak— having forgotten what he was trying to recall.

What have I forgotten? Just to recall it would slaughter me

certainly. I have learned painfully to forget: from the first moment, remember and forget. The weight of the stabs, one on the other—forgotten. Every painful wound carries away, forgotten, a share of memory. To forget the pain, we lose memory itself until there is nothing more. Nothing should be forgotten, yet we must forget.—He tried to remember hours of agony and moments of pain—I have felt too quickly and too much. The hooks of memory are worn smooth with the weight of pain that has slipped from them. I remember nothing. I see and it is forgotten. Only that is brilliant which is there, there. Everything else, good and bad, is slipping away, taught by the anguish. But that which is there—it is without memory and without pain. My life is an effort to avoid memory; an escape. Fasten I will upon the thing, there outside the window, that lives without pain and without memory. It were idle now to remember. She is gone. Only two days since I had her in these arms.

Dev grew sleepy and slept. All day long they were in the train, going. It took a solidity away from them all, train goers. They became fluid from the excess of their passage and flowed together—the lines between them as individuals melting, only to be redefined later.

Those that got out at noon were not of the same cast with those going on. The panorama of the day. More than half Switzerland, east to west, they saw.

All day, since five in the morning, the struggling and rolling train had moved with the sun through valley after valley, in mountainous passes until the mountains had seemed to enter the train possessing it so that it became a mountain train, a thing belonging to the rocks and snows. All, nearly all day, the window had been pelted with these sights. Evans felt almost a mountaineer; he grew used to the melting winter of the Alps and their implications: Thus the world is and I am part of it.

Into a meadowy valley now the train swung, in a great curve, north then south, then over the river and, This is Switzerland! The train drew up at the silly station of Buchs and it was a new country!

Evans stepped down and got some new money. For several million Kronen he received a hundred francs or so. Now the passengers had paid their tolls and now the train was backing out—I thought they would go straight on—backing out and turning.

South turned the train, seeking to sense the way. No good striking in there. Then in the valley he saw a castle from a book, moated and turreted. All around, the country was a field of checkered green. The castle, once a fortress, spoke with an accent romantic and sad. Long Dev looked at the castle, trying to remember. Romance lived so long as he could see the pointed towers, he strained to see.

The castle spoke to him from the center of the valley, but the words were missing, just a sound; he saw—and could not recall. With an insistent drag the train wrestled with the castle. Gone, said Dev, still looking at the handful of deserted stones. Gone! It shot a pang into him, a bolt from Wartau—the ruined castle of Wartau. Well, we are the inheritors. They are better than the mountains anyway.—The long Rhine valley holding its story among the fields had succeeded the savage promontories of the uninhabitable Tyrol. Here we soften, the shell weakens.

So this is Switzerland. We have been riding for a thousand years. The evening is coming on.—They were ascending a stream that broadened in the reddening day into a still, long lake, quiet with evening. This is the *Walleen See.* Westward along the bank the train, lately out of Vienna, ran by rowboats while the mountains stole close—close to the water so that they could look down into it: it was clear. There were small houses by the banks and skiffs on the water. Dev saw a man rowing a boat, bending over and rowing. Whither? Why? Evening asks unimportant questions. The evening was entering the train as the lake was fading into the red light. Now it began to grow dark and the lake drew its banks together at the western end and dropped behind.

The trainmen switched the lights on in the car. Everyone was stirring now. Another lake had come up to the train purring along its side, a great broad lake—On this lake is Zurich, at the farther end. An excitement of the evening, of the lake, of pear trees, in blossoms here and there in the fading light, kept Dev on his feet, standing in the corridor with the rest. They were passing evening towns. Once they stopped, twice—close by the water. The trees and the houses became more and more huddled as the night grew quickly murkier. But a new feeling came into the train, a city. And there, out over the water at last they could see it, lights, seeming to move out over the water. Sparks of light they seemed, gathering, foregathering, spreading out over the quiet sheet of lake water. It had grown warmer, much warmer as the train circled, circled behind the city. Then, Here we are! cried someone.—For to-night I shall stay here, perhaps for two days, said Evans.

Alighting, he stood upon the ground and felt it solid under his feet. His legs felt as might a bird's after a flight. He carried his own bags. He hailed a taxi. He found his hotel by the rushing outlet of the lake. He found his fresh smelling room. He spoke French. Later he found the main street of Zurich and walked down it to the lake. He saw the lake, quiet and warm. He looked at the faces on the streets. He went to the hotel again. He undressed. He washed himself. He drew the window jalousies. He lay in the bed. Rising again, he opened the window. He turned out the light. Thinking of many things, finally he went to sleep.

Chapter XXXV

Lucerne and Interlaken

THE little morning train from Zurich to Lucerne was so clean, so modestly patronized, so bevarnished, cane backed and seated, the windowpanes so shone, it seemed unfair to sit in it at all after this dirty world.

It was a dairy country: there were fruit trees and fields of hay uncut and full of flowers. Then in a little while they came into Lucerne.—I'll stay here a while, he said and found a hotel by the cathedral towers which, it being Saturday, began to toll their heavy bells.

All around to the south, Dev saw, beyond the quiet lake on which a white excursion boat was moving pleasantly, a ring of distant mountains while before him to the right across the water shot up a dark peak, Pilatus, by itself. I'll take that in, he thought. A horizontal cloud was spread across it near the top from which the peak itself rose into the sky as if cast off and floating. It was a still noon. Miniature Lucerne amused Evans, it was a place to patronize. An amazing little chambermaid with cheeks flaming red and round had brought him the water at his ring. She spoke French of a gutteral peasant accent. Her smile was fixed, but so bewildering, bewildered, frightened, Dev laughed heartily to himself once she had

227

gone outside and closed the door.—Good God, he said.

By the lake, on the broad graveled promenade by the Casino, he began to see the English, sitting about and walking up and down. He looked down into the warm lake in the warm sun under the blossoming horse-chestnut trees and saw the bottom. He walked in the sun, as the others also were doing and from there up to the *Drei Linden*. Then he went back and walked into the town. He read the names of the various hotels on the water front, the great and the lesser; there were greater and there were lesser. He saw the balconied restaurants.

Next day he rowed for two hours on the lake; he rowed out to the junction of the four lakes, a long row and he rowed back. But the best day was when he went up Pilatus—or rode up it with the others on the rack-and-pinion railroad.

In the valley at the foot the fields were butter yellow with the growth of buttercups. As the sloping train set out, an open car climbing through the woods, spruce branches came close to his hand. The ground was full of flowers; violets, clumps of them, anemones, purple hyacinths and low clusters of flowers, pink and white, with small waxy green leaves, of which he did not know the name. Up they went and as they went the flowers changed, and now the trees were left behind and they came out into a mountain pasture where great slabs of snow still lay white over the ground. Sticking through the snow were white and purple crocuses, masses—or clustered stars of them. Below a tiny trestle as the train crept over it, he could see them, on every side. But these gone, too near the top, nothing remained but snow or in one place, where the rock was split on a south wall a sprig of blossoming heather.

The top was wet with a great cap of slushy snow—sometimes it was ten feet thick—through which tunnels had been cut. The girls at the hostelry were out waving at the approaching train. No one had been to see them since the day before.

The next jump was to Interlaken. But here Spring had not yet come fully in. No one was there. There Dev rested—in the rain and mist. Interlaken pleased him. And here, he said I'll stay a few days anyhow. To the south; mist and rain. The streets were still, the great hotels were closed. It was higher here than at Lucerne; but grass in the yards and fields was rank.

He found a small hotel, the Hotel des Alpes, with only one other guest in it. So he got a fine room, and a nice girl to wait on him. This was better. The season is late, she said. Shall we see the Jungfrau? I hope so. When? Oh that depends on the weather.

I am a traveler, he said. So tucking his traveling things away, he walked down into the street and went up to see the town. The Casino was to open for the first time this season that same night. Standing by the municipal barometer, Evans read the weather news. Variable. The clouds were low, the Jungfrau was invisible in mist. Well—we'll wait for it.

Then he remembered that he had wished to see a chamois. That night he slept. There is seclusion here. I've been up Pilatus, I won't do the Jungfrau trip. No, not the Lauterbrünnen either.—I like this place at this season. He strolled—in the rain. It rained. He walked. The grass was dripping wet by the road and in the fields, wet and long and filled with masses of forget-me-nots and cornflowers, dandelions and daisies. There were other flowers, white and purple, and he came to the ruin of Malmfred's tower. He climbed about it in the rain. Romance. But at the bottom of the ruined keep it stunk, for a good reason.

Back he turned and on his way he came upon a modest brewery smelling sweetly-sourly of beer. All about it were the fields of long grass filled with flowers. It boiled up in his mind —America! The kind of visitors that come here are that sort —Switzerland is sickening—a strong prohibition party has sprung up: disease spreads.

But up a path he made his way hunting, solitary for a sight of a live chamois. He went up the hill, the Kleine Rüggen, and walked about under the trees in the rain looking for the cham-

ois in the enclosure there. He went through deep woods. It
was dripping wet. At his feet he saw the small white and
yellow flower he had wondered over on Pilatus but could not
descend from the car to pick. He picked some now from
among their laurel-stiff tiny leaves. They were sweet as of
strawberries, deliciously sweet. But the deer enclosure he
found at the peak was empty—nothing in it. He sat in a
broken shelter there and dug his cane down dismally into the
piney ground. There he sat, dismally, in the rain.

At the hotel, he spoke with the girl, a fine, intelligent,
self-possessed, comely girl.—In the winter I work at St. Moritz, she said. In the spring and summer here. Oh, the chamois
have been moved to a safer place on the other side of town.
The flowers? they call them *eiblumen*, for their color, egg
flowers, orange and yellow.—They should have named them
by their smell, said he.

In the evening he went back to the Barometer on the public
square to see if he could see the Jungfrau. Still the rain fell.
The amphitheater of the hills stretched before him, just the
abutments of the mountains showing; all the tops were hid in
cloud, a heavy cloud. Nothing of the Jungfrau could he see.
Sein de neige!

For supper alone in the silly dining-room he was pleasantly
served with talk and pretty smiles along with a good meal so
that he felt at ease and said he would return to Interlaken
some day. Why return? Are you not here now?—So he asked
if he could have rhubarb for breakfast next day since he could
see it growing in the yard.

That evening he went to the newly opening Casino, a broad
balconied chalet, before which against the blue green side of
a mountain in a park stood the greatest spruces he had ever
known, dripping with the rain, and pansies as large as a man's
palm. Evans played at the machines and lost ten francs or so.

The second day he went again to look for the chamois, in
the new park, on the eastern side of the town. Rain was still
falling. He found the park and saw ibex peacefully at their

hay. Some were on the roof of their shelter. But there were no chamois. So back he went, crossing the canal on a bridge and saw the rushing water of the lake outlet. But at the Barometer, though the rain had stopped—the Jungfrau was as heretofore totally invisible. I'll leave to-morrow. That night he spent reading a book the girl had found for him. Five days more to Bess. He didn't care at all. As long as the cash holds out, let it run on.

And so he slept to the sound of a hard rain.

Where art thou?

In the morning, he was leaving at nine, the Jungfrau showed its white breast. O swan of rock and snow—new fallen, blizzard white. A mountain of snow he saw, the snow white mountain breast, the sun upon it.

Sein de neige! He woke as from a lethargy. The stupid lethargy into which he was falling, to some kind of feeling at that sight. Snow breast, white and icy: a pang of anguish.

Then he wanted to go. Damn Switzerland, it lulls you to sleep.—So that he fled now with a purpose to the next step. Eagerly now he felt the end of this slow journey.

Chapter XXXVI

Geneva and Dijon

It was Geneva, where as a boy of thirteen he had gone to school. His heart beat wildly seeing Geneva once more through those half-forgotten eyes.

And Bess cannot be far off now. Bess is here.

She had picked a quiet, decent-looking place. Wants to make that sort of impression on me. All right. But his heart was racing with the pleasure of it all.

He went in. Yes, there is a room reserved. Mademoiselle had left word. She would return at five.

At last.

Bess! he could feel her everywhere.

That and a boy, himself, just out of sight around the corner, upon the lake steamer that time; swimming under the raft at the old swimming place in the crystal blue water; on the train that afternoon when he had made the first team, when they told him they would pass the ball to him, left forward, at the kick-off. The violets back of L'Horloge by the *ruisseau;* the very branches from which he and Pont had stolen the goldfinch eggs.

Bess would not be back till five. He dropped his things in his room, ran out, down the street, over the Rhone bridge to the old Lancy steam-tram station. It was an electric car now.

He smiled to himself remembering the day he had run away from school and how M. Rommel had raised Cain with him on his return, speaking a blistering stream of French at him of which he had understood not one word.

And there was the old gateway with the enormous horse-chestnut trees over the entrance. But the school had ceased to exist, the town had taken it for a City Hall. He wandered about the grounds and lived again those old torments and delights—until he could endure it no longer,—it had worn so thin. He had to retreat at a run. Back he must run to Bess! She was there, she was there *real* once more. And so wildly as he had run to see the old haunts, so wildly he fled from them again—to find Bess, actual, living, going on with it. Bess! He could not wait.

But suppose the spell will not work.

He walked more and more slowly the nearer he drew to the Hôtel du Lac. Only four o'clock.

Now he was no longer in a foreign country. The hotel was redolent of Bess. He had come definitely under a new influence which unconsciously he had been waiting now to test, to see what there was, as he had never done before, to see if it would do. For what? Now at least he realized fully what he had been looking forward to. He had come to Bess. Now he should see in, to ask of her—What have you found? and to be asked and to live again in the telling—maybe.

And Bess on her part. What would be her condition? Would she too be asking? Many things must have happened. He grew excited as he laid away his few things in his room, then smoking, he threw open the window—more rain! to look across a court, over a graveled roof below, upon which three pigeons were preening themselves in the light drizzle. He leaned on the window sill and smoked. He looked at himself in the mirror over the chiffonier to see what Bess would see. He brushed back his graying hair. How much should he tell her?

His first impression of his sister was from the back as she was mounting the stairs having missed him in the lobby when he had gone down to look for her at half past five. My God, she is young, she is exquisite. Bess! he cried. She turned. Exquisite, severe—My own beautiful sister!

Bess came down again with a quick run and—in the lobby —with a flashing smile, kissed him quickly, squeezed his hand and saying, You dear boy, led him to the stairs and took him at once into her room across the hall from his own. There she threw her arms about him and kissed him twenty or thirty times—with the strong show of affection that had always marked the relationship of the two when they had been apart for any length of time.

After that, however, and almost at once an embarrassment came up between them which it was to take many days to resolve. Both were reticent. Each stood back, watched the other intently—and was content to wait a while.

A sudden realization of what he had passed through since he had seen her last—and of all he would have to tell her if he told her anything—disconcerted the brother, and on her part, the sister presented an appearance very little different from his own. But they were glad to be near each other again, both of them.

Chase yourself, Dev, she said, I must change my dress. Let's have an early supper and get out of this. It is divine by the lake. It has stopped raining.

And so for the greater part of a week they spent these beautiful spring days together, buying a watch for "Sis," taking a trip to Ferney, old home of the divine philosopher. But the house was closed and the gates were bolted.

They explored once again the Salève where they literally bathed themselves in flowers on the short, sweet grass of the plateau. Such flowers! the blue columbine, acres of sky-blue gentians, yellow cowslips, and purple hyacinths, buttercups, until they gasped at it in bewilderment—nothing in their lives to give a word that they might understand it by. Nothing but the Greek could support such a wonder as this. Yet they had each other and it drew them somewhat nearer together to be thus employed.

They walked, they watched, they saw the men fishing at night from the lake bridges, they wandered in the old city and the new, they visited the Triano and fed the swans. They drank, they ate *patisserie* as he used to do when there at school. They had the same strawberry tartlets he had enjoyed thirty years before. They talked of the Riviera, of Italy, of Lake Constance where Bess had been for a time. But of their intimate lives for the past three months they said nothing at all. Geneva they both loved and resolving to come back to it SOON, presently the week had passed and they decided they must be going on. It was mid-May. Back to Paris! and then —Dev shut his eyes—home.

Of the trip to the great city the most striking incident was the halt at Dijon where they stopped at the famous Hotel de la Cloche, rendezvous of hiding lovers. All day, again, they had traveled; servants of the god-like train. Geneva, at the foot of the lake, though in the open, was still closer than Dev had remembered to the Juras, still bleak and snow-covered. But now they had gone through a gap in these, past flowery banks, poppies and fox-gloves, out into the great southern plain of France, the Dauphinée. It turned very hot.

France! blessed home of all wanderers. France! They looked hard at each other at the love they recognized each had for this haven of clean thought. Now indeed it was nearly summer, as out over the hot plain the train bore them past the grain fields, the slow streams with the yellow *fleurs de lys* of France growing on their banks. What a blessed relief! Both loved France as they loved the secrets of their own souls, to be revealed to no one. France understood these without being told, it kept secrets and it offered its understanding—austere or abandoned, in return. A feeling of warmth, of release, of deep maturity came over the two children, for so they were, beside this old traveled, beaten country. Burgundy!

South they had gone at first until the Mediterranean seemed to be again near, then north with a château far off on some river bank. For an hour Dev had been glancing through a book he found in the rack, at the end of the train, a commercial guide to the region, interspersed with informative paragraphs on the various industries and business features of each place they would pass. Particularly he had read of the wine industry, Dijon, noting the difference between *gourmand* and *gourmet*—how to hold a glass expert-taster-style, sipping the wine, thumb and finger holding the base between them, puckering the mouth, *cul de poule* and gently sucking in air to make the beverage bubble over the tongue.

And there at length from the train window they saw the low hill, the famous barren plain of the Côte d'Or, home of those great wines, the Burgundies, the blood of this land, of which he had been reading. One passage particularly he pointed out to his sister handing the book to her that she might see:

Les grands vins joueront toujours un rôle prépondérant dans les relations sociales, ils seront toujours un trait d'union entre gens de bonne compagnie. Que d'heures enchanteresse nous leurs devons? Sous leur magnétique influence, l'âme s'ouvre aux sentiments généreux, l'ésprit devient plus subtil, la parole plus éloquente. Ils ont le bon de développer les délicatesses du goût et de spiritualiser les plaisirs de la table.

At Dijon he was overjoyed to find old Bill Jessup, his Parisian publisher friend. For one thing it broke up the alignment of the talk between brother and sister. Nelly, his wife, was with Bill and as a matter of fact the two men soon formed an alliance as did the ladies also, thus relieving the brother and sister at once of the false situation they had fallen into.

One of Bill's hobbies was wine. He knew wines, collected them and enjoyed the subtleties of their characters. Unlike us Americans who do not know that one half of an orange is sweet and the other sour, the genius of these people is to pay attention. They have discovered here the grape, said Bill. The

Romans knew it. They have even found the imprint of the leaves fossilized in the rock of the place. It is a special soil for grapes, for wine—nothing like it has been discovered else-where in the world.

Marvelous, said Dev, the quintessence of the local virtue.

Oh shut up, said Bill. Are you interested in this?

Can't you see my eyes popping out?

I'm going to take you for supper to-night to a good *re-staurateur* here in Dijon, an old master of the *gourmets.* He'll show us something worth looking at. And to-morrow we'll make a wine-tasting trip to Baune.

Great.

Poor Ernest, they made him chief of the commissariat to provide for the Americans stationed here during the war. It broke his heart. All they wanted was whisky, whisky. They had no taste whatever for his rare vintages.

Damned good thing, I'll say, replied Dev.

Yes, but Ernest felt insulted, for the country's sake. He couldn't interest anyone.

All that day the four Americans wandered in the summer heat about Dijon, resting now over their drinks at some café or again seeing the curious façades of the twelfth century houses, built fortress strong, on what is to-day some back street; or again perusing, to shamefaced looks on the ladies' parts, some particularly gross praises in word and line to the perfections of one "Louise" scrawled in crayon on the wall of a house on the rue de la Jouissance.

That evening they had cocktails in their rooms and then betook them as promised, to Ernest's place, found only after a sharp appetite-enkindling walk of half an hour, round and about beyond the cathedral in the old city.

There was but one other party in the room, a strange party, as if at a family dinner a whore familiar with the *père de famille* should be invited to partake of it. The man himself was past middle age, but hearty. Their meal was nearly over when the Americans arrived. Bill asked Ernest about it. He said the

gentleman was a doctor of the place and the little bright lady
was his particular friend, to keep him going; the family knew
it was she who kept him going and so she was permitted to
be there.

And so the four Americans began to eat, and to drink
Richebourg, 1915, *Chambertin* the same, *Musigny, Montrachet,*
for two hours—until they could no more. Wow!

The science is exact. The grapes are not palatable; I told
you that. Small and bitter. The soil must be poor, of a certain
chemistry. They have tried them many places on earth but
nowhere do they grow as here.

There was a map on the wall of the H. de la Poste at Beaune
showing the famous vineyards. Here too the food was beyond
compare: *Chablis, Corton.*

To Dijon, to Beaune must one go, said Dev to himself, from
among all places "in the world," to eat and to drink well.

Chapter XXXVII

Paris Once More

Dev, said Bess one day after they had been in Paris a week, I'm married. Don't be alarmed. It means nothing: What are we going to do now?

I'm going back home in ten days.

Without even a word?

Well, not now at any rate. Come on!

It was the night of Cocteau's *Romeo and Juliet* at the *Cigale*. Everyone would be there.

At the theater all seemed far, far off to Dev.—I should be quarreling with the rest around the bar or else leave in the middle of the performance.—He was interested; not in the play, however. The cult was strong, it was club night among the more heavily financed geniuses of Paris—and the most controversial. The orchestra had struck just before the show. The *Chambre* was represented there, in that little hall. For charity. Picasso, Dérain—and many more; all the lights.

Wearying of the play, which started well but grew tiresome later, the brother and sister went into the small salon which adjoined the auditorium, on one side.

To-morrow, Sis, we'll spend the day in the country, a canoe trip, the Seine, Ardennes.

Great!

How much has it cost you over here? How much have we got left? I've spent about five bucks a day, he said. I'm about at the end. Got to go back and get more. You've got the interest on Mother's bit. You can stay on.

No, dear, I'm going home, too; unless you—

Europe is poison to us Americans—delicious—distressing.

Dev, I want a baby.

Stupid. My God, what next?

I don't care.

You, with your chaste ability to—do what you please.

I'm not chaste.

I said your ability to be chaste, civilly. You're no American. Stay here. You don't want a baby.

A baby and never to be far from you.

This frightened Dev.—God help me.

Oh no, I do not want to censor you, or protect you.—Dev sensed that she was getting ready to question him—but it passed. That's better.

I can never be at home here, said Evans, there is a deep loss in me that comes of my inheritance. Years ago I was lost— I am not of this club. That is what I am, a great zero.

You are a great fool to talk that way.

I belong to the sea, Evans continued.

Oh Dev, you are ridiculous. You can't even swim, can you?

Suppose we should go home?

Lets get a place somewhere up in Jersey—with a sassafras tree on it—at least twenty years old—that's old enough in our country. If I share the interest with you, you can quit your job, said the Sister.

No, you keep it. Stay here.

I will not—not for long anyway. I insist that you quit work. I insist.

Dev was disturbed. Sis, what in hell is the matter with you? We came out here—

Well? Speak, or I shall—

—He would not.

Then you must listen to your silly sister. Live here with me, we have two thousand a year certain. Live here with me. Oh Dev, you've got to stop idling. You've got to work. We can do everything together, everything there is to do in this world. You need me—and you are mine, blessed man. Is it saddening to you to hear me say nobody knows you but I? You are my—secret.

Explain me, advertise me—will you?

Don't be a silly baby. We can come out in you.—Dev was amazed. I can't do it—and, Dev, you'll never do it going back there to that desert. Stay here. Listen. You don't know anything of yourself. Do you know you have five times the ability of these people, these great men you admire over here? But you are going nowhere; they *are*. That's just it, Dev. Their very slenderness is where they beat you. They have made a virtue of their poverty—and that is what it all is. Your silly profusion—our silly profusion defeats us. Dev, you've got to quit fooling—quit your cash job and study it out.

Like Eliot?

Who is Eliot? Like nobody. You've got to sit down to it. Somebody must and few will get anything even if they do. But I know that you can. It is their devices with their poverty that you are admiring—not refinement in the sense of slenderness, but shelling away, shelling away to the core. You've never done that. You are spoiled; you are a baby. You've always got to hit something.

What has been telling you all this?

But they are poor and they work at it and work at it until it shines like a poverty-stricken door knob or a peasant's lamp —if he be industrious.

I can do that in America.

Nonsense, Dev, no one can. You've written a lot of stuff, dear, to break all our hearts that love you. You don't care about success. No, because you don't even know what success is—the place has tainted you so. No one does there. It is too blocked off out of embarrassment to be appreciated. No one would recognize it if it were before him and so you are pouting and indifferent but—it's making you sick. Dev, you've never let yourself go: Down inside you—

For God's sake, Bess, quit it. Down inside me is a small piece of slime full of worm's eggs.

Oh shut up, said his sister gently. She thought a moment then went on, All right, then, America, but where? We can't live in New York.

I've told you. Let's go up into Sussex.

And starve like proper martyrs, among the copperheads and rattle-snakes—we two Parisians—how entertaining.

Well, you insist on rescuing me. We can get fifty acres for a song and grow our own vegetables. Live on five hundred a year. There I'll write.

You mean you'll actually give up twiddling with money; you'll quit your practice?

We'll see.

Dev, you're not serious. You never are. And you think you can be an artist that way. The only decent thing about art here is that they begin with poverty and work and work seriously at it until—Look at the post-impressionists—three silly tricks and yet they made everything anybody has ever made out of them until it's given up a bounty. Answer what that is. America doesn't need that. You are just deceived. You want to, Dev, but you're not doing it.

Well, Bess—as I said before, where in hell has this come from?

You, you lover, and—my own misery. It's our baby, a pure American.

Siegfried—

Live with me here, Dev.

I won't be your cathedral—

You are—

A nun, are you?

A Parisian patroness. I think I shall organize a coterie.

Oh, come on, let's get out of this.

No, you shan't. Listen to me. You must. Out of their poverty they have made something. I don't know anything about your technique—but I love you and you've got to do it because I can't. Out of their onions, their potatoes, their dandelion leaves, their snails and sparrows. I've spent my months, most of them, thinking, while you have been gadding around. But I've come to my limit.

Would you prefer a concrete road or just macadam—and what if someone should show up and take me away?

I'd kill her, that's all.

Within the auditorium there burst out a great handclapping. All the doors to the salon were opened, through them the throng from the theater poured in among the refreshment tables and found seats. The brother and sister watched them in silence. All kinds of celebrities were there, most of whom neither of them knew, painters, international women, and many lesser fry.

An orchestra began to play. The crowd danced.

There were many Americans, many South Americans, people from all over the world. Bess turned her back, her brother stared.

There is no way. There is no way.

When Bess suggested it he went willingly by her side for their wraps and out into the lights of the Boulevard de Rochechouart.

Where shall we go from here? asked Dev of his sister.

Home, we are getting up at six to-morrow, aren't we?

The first taxi refused them a ride. No, he didn't care to cross the river. He was looking for a fare going to his own part of town.

Across the street were posters of the famous Fratellini Brothers, the international clowns.

Nobody is interested in them any more, said Bess.

Chapter XXXVIII

Seine Sister

SOFTLY the motion of the skiff—Spring. As though it had been spring forever—now again.

America, said Evans musingly, There are some things there —still some things there I want to gather—

Your aesthetic duty to the Stars and Stripes?

Where in the world have you stolen all this new smartness?

Dear brother, from you. I have done as you have preached —I am a woman of shame, she laughed.

You are happy?

Who can be unhappy?

Dev did not answer. She was shrewd—this sister, when she wanted something.

Where have *you* been these months? he countered.

Not out of Paris, save a week or so after you left—when I wrote you.

Hm, have you been so quickly successful?

I have discovered that I do not need it—with your success as my example.

What do you want?

You.

After a year in Europe, Kitten, kidding?

I don't want you to go back to America.

Look out, you'll dump us into the river.

The river and again the yellow *fleurs de lys.* Dev picked one and marveled at the color. A yellow lily, a wild yellow lily. At home it's blue. The blue flag, yellow-striped.

How I hate to think of leaving it, said Evans.

The flowers or your peers, old dear? Do you like them?

Come on, Bess, what have you been up to?

Oh, I have had a lover, Dev. You would know him if I told you. One of the ones you admire.—She smiled.

Of course, you can't blame me if you picked some damned fool, but the best of them do know their onions.

My dear, of course they know. You are a barbarian beside them: you know nothing.

Stop kidding me.

They know everything, and they—are all Americans, they imagine.

Why did you bring me out here?

To get away from Paris. And to tell you about my baby.

Dev grew angry.—You want a baby, hell. You want to make me keep you here, that's the kind of a baby you want. I'm not it. You're a beauty, I see that now. I never did at home. But don't come any of your clever schemes with me. Stay here if you want to. I'm not sold to you.

Bess was taken aback.

Brother, *dear!*

Oh hell, Bess, I'm unhappy. That's nothing, I'm not so unhappy, nothing that's happened has made me so, but I'm not selling out to anybody, not even to you.

You need a wife.

Do you want the job?

If you'll stay over here.

Um. If I could quit work.

You can.

Oh, Bess, you're a downright idiot.

Don't be rude, brother, it doesn't become you and besides,

you're broken-hearted, dear: anyone can see it but you.

What do you mean?

I mean what I say. Don't look at me as if I were a fool. I am, that's why I see so well. I've broken twenty walls down from around Saint Sulpice since I saw you last, said Bess.

It hasn't taught you much.

All right, but you've got to tell me what it is I should see then or I'll tell you what I *do* see and you'll have to accept my statement.

Dev was not pleased.—Stop trying to buck me up. I don't want to be saved.

It's not what you want, old dear, in this case, but what you are going to git, she laughed.

Some damn fool has been trying to get at you.

All right, I am that she of whom A. wrote the poem that you admire.

But did you—?

Yes, he tried—

And so now?

She laughed. How wonderful it is to be a writer. Oh, I wish I were you. The marvel of writing! Pick up a bit of paper— and find a message upon it—a communication from a distance: nothing so delightfully simple and exalting: but the art lies in what is being communicated, doesn't it? the difficulty and the art—

Most forget what it is, though, said Evans, interested, most forget what it is in the first place.—

Somehow, here in this small boat, lolling in this morning sunshine, alone on the quiet foreign river, Evans—for the first time in his life—had a feeling of real fear before his sister which he could not understand. Or was it admiration? It was fear, mixed with an admiration that was fast overpowering him and against which he fought a quickly failing battle.

But most of all he wondered at this strange woman before him out of whose mouth such unaccustomed words were falling. And inside his heart, somehow, he was being moved, *he* was being moved, that chronic sleeper, himself. It was this that frightened him. He was curiously elated.

There were things about Bess, Dev felt, that he had never felt about anyone in his life before. From this beginning, peace finally reigned between the brother and sister and Evans began to tell her much of his last two months. She listened intently. Speaking only to make herself clear on certain details. When he had finished, it was noon.

Bess gave a sigh of relief when it was done. Then she began to sing the first bars of the Aria from Manon. She trailed her right hand in the cold water, made a face at its coldness but kept the hand there grimly nevertheless.

Evans was steering for the shore. If the water was cold the day was growing sultry—his brow was sweaty from paddling. Bess had not made a single comment upon his story save to sing aloud.—I wonder what she's thinking, he said to himself.

Mine. Mine. Mine!

What's that?

No sooner had he stepped on the grassy bank and begun to pull the canoe up behind him than she cried, Oh Dev, you old darling, and pretended, laughing, to pull him up also by the hair on top of his head. As she did so, it had flashed through his mind, looking down: Leaves of grass. As a symbol how tasteless, but as a fact how delightful.

There on the bank they spread newspapers and commenced to set out the things they had brought.

I am a sensual savage, Dev, do you know it? said his sister, I could,—do anything. I want to bite.

Go ahead.

Ugh—no, I couldn't, not now.

He joshed her.—I came out here for a holiday with my little sister before sailing for Vinland, the famous—and not to be eaten—but to enjoy this voluminous, voluptuous spring season.

Well, dear, I want to sell you your little Sis—in spite of all that.

Suppose then, now that I have bared my soul, he said, suppose that *you* tell *me* how you have spent *your* time *really*.

So she told him of her week-long unhappy journey to San Moritz with her poet lover.—Winter sports, Dev, that's what they were, but now it's spring again; thank God, that's over.

But, is it?

Sweetheart, laws are made to be broken—by and for the proper person. I have done that. There are other things to be done now. Isn't that enough told for one sunny afternoon?

Dev said nothing but he fondled his sister's slender hand for a moment while his love and loyalty came quickly forward to support her.

So that's what you were up to?

Crying and gnashing my teeth.

Bess, you are a cathedral in which all the pagan gods have come to hide to live secure there forever. I never had such an excited feeling about anyone in my life as I have had about you to-day.

Very pretty, Mister, but what does it mean? Wind up your affairs. Get out of it. We'll go it together. I don't want anything. There'll be enough, just enough. A small place there and the rest of the time here. You'll earn something in time with your writing.

But what about—?

We'll adopt a baby, a war orphan. I will domesticate myself. —He laughed uproariously.

I love you, brother. She embraced him in play. I've had a queer time. Let's spend a winter telling each other of it. I've had enough.

Dev did not answer. Meanwhile she was going on with preparations for lunch—rather elaborate they were. They picnicked on the grassy bank with the violets.—Imagine brother, violets and trees and a river and a grassy bank just like Ophelia's.—She had brought a delicious lunch, with wine, brandy and liqueurs.

To celebrate the ceremony, she said.

What ceremony?

The marriage of spring and the river! Booby!

You are very sure of yourself.

I've waited for this, after the first week, two months, and two months in sackcloth and ashes is too much. It is finished.

As the meal went on Bess made coffee at a little fire with three stones and a green stick as she had learned to do at a camp in the woods of New Jersey. Then she began to drink cognac. More, more!

You're going to get pickled, little girl, if you're not careful, said her brother.

Of course I am, that was one of the things I wanted you around for, I'm an awful baby.

And so she drank and talked, trying to win him.

Proteus, he squirmed, he twisted, he tried to browbeat her, he ridiculed her—My dear, I am not an artist—but shall I not possess even my own appendages—

But she would not let go.—I am a woman. No, dear brother, you are all I have left and—I will not release you, not yet at any rate.

Down with the damned country, she said at last, let's unite on that anyway.—He cared for her until she fell asleep, then covered her and went down and washed his face in the river and smoked—thinking.—Always, a woman tricks you—and it's always the one you don't think is going to do it.

She woke when it was already late in the afternoon—or he woke her for coffee which he himself had brewed.

She was surprisingly fresh. Dearest boy! She was up at once, rubbed her eyes and shook out her hair. Marvelous! A hundred years have passed from me. Dearest brother, you must never leave me again, never have I lived till now. But, if you go—I am finished. Tell me, dear, you will not return to America. You must promise me that.

Here it was out in the open once more. Evans felt it had come. Bess was staring at him now unsmiling, her hair hanging down. She was leaning forward, her hands on the grass, her mouth half-open—waiting for his answer.

His voice caught when he went to speak. Now or never. What should he do?

Don't say that, Dev. Don't say what's in your mind. I tell you you're killing me.

Why don't you come back to America with me then?—He knew he was hedging.

She shuddered a little and bit her teeth hard together. When she looked up she was smiling but it was not the smile Evans was familiar with in his little sister. This is a desperate woman, he said to himself, and prepared to combat her. But she was too quick for him.

You want to be a great writer, don't you, dear? she began. I sympathize with your instinct for writing.

Keep your dirty fingers off that—a wave of anger swept over him.

Oh, it isn't that—fight me as you will, I'm going to see you do it.

How to find a way to do it and not be beaten off, driven off or beaten or dirtied. Yes, that's my life, he replied.

They have learned a great secret of life here in France, she continued. Oh, the damned historical fools who only see the reverse of it in the abandon of this country, as if abandonment and devotion were not of the same fabric—She did not finish.

Oh, come on, let's paddle back.

No, Dev, I refuse to be put off. It's not that, that's just one of the things. It's your way and so I'm on it—but that's not it. There's something here in France any damned fool can learn and you haven't learned it. It's deep. It's moral—

Morality! I knew you'd get back to that sooner or later. Is there any cognac left?

It's in everything they do, right through the scale—You have no sense for it. It's not to make you out a success, Dev. But something's got to be done for all of us. I won't have you laugh. I refuse to become what I will become if you don't help me—without first a struggle. France has taught me. You and I have got to do something with ourselves. Americans. I want to do some good with myself. Oh *good*, Dev, in the French sense, the moral sense. To use well what we have, that's all. We are incurably Americans, you and I, but we can help each other—if we will. That offers us our only hope; to make a beginning, to make something useful out of that country where there's no honor left but a starved, thin, lying one— along the rocks. We've got to live with honor—not the way we treated your precious Indians, Dev, but like a Frenchman to whom France means something. It means something to them, Dev. They get a sense out of it whereas America means nothing to us at all—nothing but "patriotism" and cash. What a meaning! But with honor, the ground, France, can be used. They can retain a connection with purity—with sources we have muddied away, just as our sorrow is that our purity— without morality—cannot be used.

Bess, you don't know what you are talking about. Art is a country by itself—A matter of learning how—

Without a moral core, it is as empty as—hell. You are unaware of this sense that I have, that we have got to make something moral out of what we have or we shall be just nothing. That's *la belle France*—fakers and all—but there it is. We are Americans and we've got to make something of it or we are just *nothing*. You don't see that. You think I'm a fool. I am. But I can see. You have got to find the words. I can't so I want you—or—I'm done. Can you see that?

And you want me to live here with you—

And let me teach you what morality means. Dev, you've got to listen—

Go on, then, I said I'd do it if you wouldn't—

What!

Finish what you were saying. Literature has nothing to do with life.

With truth? She was laughing like an *it*—damned fool. What the hell does she know? Yet, somehow he admired her crudity.

Dev, dear, listen to me. This means something to you, all this talk—you, I've got you, dear. I'm in love, dearest, with my brother—love, dear.

You've lived in Europe a whole year, Bess, quit that.

I tell you, it delights me. Criticize me, you fool, or I will and disgust you. You can or you can't—Fie, brother, or you won't. You must!

Bess was drinking steadily again now.

To hell with it. I love you all right, Bess, but god damn it, I'm not going to stay over in this country if I don't want to, not for anybody. But I'll be damned if I see why I should fight with you about it. Give me some brandy.

She handed him the bottle.

Here's to love, he said.

Bess drank another, quickly, then leaned across her brother's lap and threw her arms about his neck where she hung desperately.

You're not going, dear; you're going, of course, you're going. I'm not such a fool, Dev. I knew you weren't for me. But I had to try for you. I feel as if they were closing me alive into a tomb. But, I won't, Dev, and you can't make me.

He didn't know what it was he couldn't make her do, but he, too, was drinking—and it didn't matter.

Thus at forty gayly I celebrate *le printemps suzerain—à l'Américaine*—he said kissing his sister lightly.

But she, having drunk heavily, would not have it his way. She clasped him ever more tightly round the neck and pulled him down on the grass beside her.

She would not let him go, but burying her face in his coat, over his breast she sobbed wildly, holding him tighter, tighter.

He could not move her. She merely shook her head and refused to budge. So he ended by letting her lie there while he cuddled her tenderly.

At last, when it was quite dark, he got her into the canoe and managed to feel his way back to the landing whence they had embarked in the morning.

Clinging tight to him Bess insisted that they stay that night at the small inn of the place.

They were too weary for supper. There he put her to bed, kissed her and went down to the bar.

Chapter XXXIX

Cherbourg

SHE insisted a week later on going with him to Cherbourg—
Do you deny me my privilege as a mother to watch over my
family at its advents and departures? Off to the New World!
—She was with him at the Gare St. Lazare. It was cold, foggy,
drizzling as the train slid almost noiselessly out of the station.
They had not lit the lights; it remained pre-dawn inside the
compartment.

So over the low dairy country of Normandie they rode, by
the curious cathedral tower of Bayeux in the distance, the
endless meadowlands, foxgloves on the railroad embankment. Going away! and toward noon they saw the slab roofs
of the cottages near Cherbourg.

They had little to say to each other but sat and looked out
of the windows.—I am glad you came. It was the least he
could say.—Yes, I wanted to come.

At Cherbourg, they had several hours to wait before ship
time. The tender was ready but the *Zeeland* had not come in.
They were having difficulty to find conversation. They tried
the binoculars Dev had bought for the trip in Vienna, praised
them, spoke of the ones they had lent to the Navy during the
war. They could see a fishing boat rising and falling, far out.

Let's take a walk in the town.

Before them lay the great bare plaza on the wharf, with the

253

statue of Napoleon, mounted and pointing toward England in the center of it. This was to have been one of the great ports of the world. Trafalgar spoiled it. Two lines of children, girls and boys, were coming from Confirmation, steadily streaming black and white out of the cathedral.

From the wharf, in a heavy wind, Bess took the binoculars, scanned the horizon for the ship, restless. She walked at his side. He was anxious to get away. She maliciously began teasing him about America. The land of promise! she called it.

At the fish market they saw two peasants, man and woman, kissing each other absorbedly, a farewell.—Perhaps he is going as far as Paris, who knows, said Bess, but she looked covertly at them several times.

A fellow went by with a handcartload of leathery, shining sand sharks.—I suppose they eat that stuff.

They passed by the barbed-wire enclosure of the naval air station; great hangars inside, power wires going in, radio aerials flaunted.

Then they walked aimlessly till they came to a little tea place with a few tables in the back room. Quite necessary. There a British naval non-com was sitting with two French women, one young, pretty and crying. The other had some English. The man was looking at the table top, making figures on it with his finger nail.—You can't do that. You can't treat us like that, said the older woman. You must do something for her.—The girl was crying in stifled sobs.—You come here and then you go away and leave us. No. You can't do that.

The brother and sister did not look at each other but listened intently.

A whistle was blowing. The ship! They jumped. Outside they started to walk swiftly down the street. Nothing in the windows worth buying for Bess. Can't offer her cash. Here, buy yourself something to remember me by. No? The bridge across the inlet was open. A fellow with a bicycle was on the draw.

Wait again, damn it. Dev felt Bess looking at him; he did not turn. At last he was on the tender. Bess seemed to waver.

Guess I'll get on too, she said laughing. Show your tickets, please. All right. The gods are against me. Good-by, brother dear. Give my love to the New World.

Dev was feeling ill. But he couldn't help this miserable scene. Good-by, Bess. . . . He held her close and kissed her, not knowing why he felt so down. He kissed her hands.

She beamed with pleasure. Good-by, dearest, you're all I have left in the world. No, you are all there is. See you soon. Go on, and she pushed him toward the gangway.

Not over yet. He stood in the stern of the tender waving his handkerchief to her. She stood there unmoving until the head of the jetty cut her off.

Now he was on the ship—The sea! He felt better at once, but something was still there pulling him down.

It was a quiet day. The sea was oily, with a long ground swell. He was desperately tired and took a long nap on his bunk. He wakened, bewildered, gasping, a catch at his throat. Looking from the porthole he saw land not far off—One of the channel islands, I suppose. All that night he slept like a dead man.

Next day, now well at sea at last, he began to look around the ship. Few on board attracted him. But there was one man he delighted in talking to, a Scotchman with an Italian name, the son of an old time sailing master—himself a retired captain—who was returning from a leisurely knocking about in his old haunts round the world. An oldish man he was, powerful, straightbacked, red-faced and soft-spoken. He had a strong whisky breath to him in the early morning when Dev would meet him—waiting for breakfast.

—The country has gone to hell now for sure.—He seemed like one stunned.—But look at the English Navy and the German Army—two bodies of men not equaled on earth for hardihood and ability to give and take it—bred on beer; and the peasantry the world over on wine. When I was a young man on one of our trips, we made a stop at the Easter Islands —one of those small islands in the south seas where there'd be one or two men with the sheep during the growing season. Whisky doesn't touch those fellows. They take one of those cans they used to get kerosene in and put a couple of pounds of chewing tobacco in it. Then they'd fill the can with whisky and bury it in the ground for a month or two. I don't know what else they do with it after that. We were three men in our party, good strapping fellows used to an outdoor life and heavy drink. They offered us some of that stuff. I took one sup of mine and put up my hands but the other two downed theirs. It near killed them. But those fellows on the island drink it every day as a regular thing. Seems to make them strong. What are we coming to?

Approaching the Grand Banks, Captain Thomas had news of much ice ahead. Into the fog they plunged which, softly, silently lifting from time to time, Evans saw one, two, five, six sailless fishing schooners anchored in it, softened again now and disappearing. Twenty miles south they had had to steer in the night to avoid the ice. The foghorn had been going steadily. Toward noon the next day land again, Vinland! It was the long low shore of Newfoundland along which they coasted for several hours, ten miles out.

As they were approaching Halifax, Evans, on the side of the ship farthest from shore observed a humming bird, paralleling the vessel's course flying over the water.

At Halifax those in the ship bade some few of their companions adieu, then down the coast, now almost home. For the last night, Evans slept on the ship. In the morning they were in the waters off Maine, going south, south. The shoal water was oily smooth in the half-sun, half-mist—and schools of fish, leaping by schools, ruffled the water in patches on all sides—a still sea seeming not more than just enough to float the ship —and a shore mist—seventy-eight miles away. A ship he saw, the Nantucket Lightship, anchored, rocking lightly in the smooth sea and men out upon it painting it a metallic red. What a life!

So this is the beginning.

Appendix

The Venus

Wʜᴀᴛ ᴛʜᴇɴ is it like, America?

It was Fräulein von J. talking.

They were on their way to take the train to Frascati, the three of them—she, her companion, and Evans.

In reply, he shook his head, laughing—and they hurried on to catch the car.

She could speak English well enough, her companion could not, Dev's German was spasmodic coming in spurts for a moment or two but disappearing as suddenly leaving him tongue-tied. So they spoke English and carried their lunch. A picnic. He was delighted.

This day it was hot. Fräulein von J. seemed very simple, very direct, and to his Roman mood miraculously beautiful. In her unstylish long-sleeved German clothes, her rough stockings and heavy walking-shoes, Evans found her, nevertheless, ethereally graceful. But the clear features, the high forehead, the brilliant perfect lips, the well-shaped nose, and best of all the shining mistlike palegold hair unaffectedly drawn back—frightened him. For himself he did not know where to begin. But she looked at him so steadily, for some strange reason, as if she recognized him, that he was forced at last to answer her.

The tram was packed to the doors with passengers. Just before starting three tree-like Englishwomen had come rushing up calling out distractedly in English that the tram must not go, that somebody was coming—Do you see her? Oh,

Note: This chapter was deleted from the novel and published separately as a short story. Please see the introduction to this edition for details.

what can have happened? She had the correct information, et cetera—until finally Clara arrived just in the moment of the tram's departure and clambered aboard desperately, not a minute too soon. So that now they stood in the aisles, the four of them, sweating and glowering at the Italian men, who oblivious to such violence had long since comfortably settled themselves in their seats.

Fräulein von J. was placed immediately before Evans looking at him absorbedly like a child. Not knowing what else to do or to say, he too looked (as the tram went through some bare vineyards) straight back into her clear blue eyes with his evasive dark ones. She lifted her head a little as if startled, flushed (he thought) just a trifle but did not change her gaze. So they continued to look fixedly among the backs and across the coats of the Englishwomen in the aisle, who were jabbering away disturbedly about the threatening weather. She did not stir to look away but seemed to rest upon his look with mild curiosity and no nervousness at all. It was, as usual, his look which faltered.

Hearing the talk of the Villa this and the Villa that, about to be visited, Evans felt that he wished he could lose this crowd and was more than pleased when Fräulein von J. suggested that as soon as they should get to Frascati they head for the open country, delighted to find that her mood suited his own as well.

At the market place of Frascati, where a swarm of guides and carriages swooped down upon them, the three picnickers moved off at right angles to the direction taken by the rest, up a road that led between two walls around behind the town. They did not know where they were or indeed anything about the place or its beauties—they didn't care. Fräulein wanted to see the Italian springtime, that was the most definite of their spoken desires and Dev, sick of antiquities and architectural beauties, was more than willing to follow. The companion disliked Italian gardens anyway, lacking as they do the green profusion of the northern trees. With this they started, beginning at once to see violets along inside the fences, violets they could not reach. Following a brook which ran beside them, contrariwise down the hill, they trampled on, heading for open country.

What is it like, America? And so Dev began to tell her— Not like this—and all the time somehow he was thinking of his sister. Where is Bess? I wish she were here! till walking and talking, leaving the town behind them, they came quite out into the fields with a hill on the left and a little village off in the distance across the valley before them. They were in a worn dirt gully high hedged on both sides with banks cut into narrow paths by goats' hoofs. Before them four absorbed children gathering violets rushed forward in the path by ones and twos rivalling each other in their efforts to pounce upon the finer groups of flowers.

The children paid no attention whatever to the three hikers, not even by so much as one glance. Running ahead with cries of delight, each racing to exceed the others, they soon disappeared through gaps in the hedge. Evans was over and over startled by the German girl's delicate coloration and hair and eyes. Also, her hands were lovely, her ankles firm—like the Venus, thicker than the stage or dance-hall type, but active too—just suggestive enough of the peasant to be like a god's.

You have not told me yet, what it is like, America.

It is like. Dev began, something muffled—like a badly trained voice. It is a world where no man dare learn anything that concerns him intimately—but sorrow—for should we learn pleasure, it is instantly and violently torn from us as by a pack of hungry wolves so starved for it are we and so jealous of each of us is our world.

I think I know what you mean, she replied, it is that we are all good citizens on top and very much better than that inside. It makes me think of the *Johannisfeuer*. You know Sudermann's play?

America is a pathetic place where something stupefying must always happen for fear we wake up. Yes, I have read the play.

By this time they had come quite around behind Frascati hill. Here they had lunch in a diminutive, triangular grove of oaks where there was a grassy bank with a few daisies on it, and the tall trees bending overhead. Then climbing through a fence they took the road again up to the right around the hill climbing steeply now on a stony path. It was a hard walk this part of the way and before long they were tired, especially Frau M. who was glad to stop near the top and rest.

But after a few words in German which Dev missed, Fräulein von J. cried, Come on! and they two went on alone about two hundred yards ahead up to the woody summit, to a place from which they could see Frau M. below them lying under an ash-tree. Here there were a few stones of some ancient construction almost gone under the wood soil and rotted chestnut leaves. It was a chestnut grove cut and counter cut by innumerable paths which led north over the brow of the hill—to Frascati, no doubt. But now at this early season, the place was deserted. The random, long, dart-shaped dry leaves covered the ground all about them, two foreigners resting on the old stones. Elsa waved to Frau M. from where she sat, then she turned again to Evans, Tell me what you are. You do not mind? I want to know everything. What is America? It is perhaps you?

No, Dev shook his head.

Is it something to study? What will it do? Shall we go there to learn? She asked in rapid succession.

Dev shook his head.

But you will return to it?

Yes.

Habit?

No, it is something.

It is that I may the better hide everything that is secretly valuable in myself, or have it defiled. So safety in crowds—

But that is nothing. That is the same as in Europe.

America seems less encumbered with its dead. I can see nothing else there. It gives less than Europe, far less of everything of value save more paper to write upon—nothing else.

Why do you look at me so? Dev asked her.

Because I have seen no one like you in my life, few Americans, I have talked to none. I ask myself, are you an American?

And if I am—

Then it is interesting.

He said, To me it is a hard, barren life, where I am "alone" and unmolested (work as I do in the thick of it) though in constant danger lest some slip send me to perdition but which, being covetous not at all, I enjoy for the seclusion and primitive air of it. But that is all—unless I must add an attraction in all the inanimate associations of my youth, shapes, foliage, trees to which I am used—and a love of place and the characteristics of place—good or bad, rich or poor.

No, she continued, it is not that.

Evans felt at that moment, that there was very little in America. He wanted to be facetious but the girl's seriousness was not a thing to be fooled. It made him pensive and serious himself.

He could say that it was just a place.

But you must not tell me that America is nothing, she anticipated him, for I see it is something, and she looked at him again with her little smile. You seem to me a man like I have not seen before. This is America?

I am a refugee, Dev continued, America is or was a beginning, to clean out the—

Then, she replied, it is as in Germany. I did not think so when I saw you.

And I, Dev answered, did not think so when I saw you.

Why am I in Rome, do you think? she queried next.

He did not know.

To become a nun.

And with a shock he remembered the German youths in their crimson gowns whom he had seen filing down the Quirinal, down the long steps; the Scotch youths playing soccer in the Borghese gardens Sunday afternoon with their gowns tucked up, or doffed, garters showing and running like college athletes for the ball. He remembered too, the Americans with the blue edge to their gowns, the Spanish, the French.

Yes, she continued, that is it. I am in Rome to feel if the church will not offer me an answer. I was fourteen years old when the war ended. I have seen the two things—to throw myself away or to take hold again. I have seen the women running in the stadiums, I have seen them together. If we were peasants, we could be nearer—but we must lose it all, all that is good. I am a German, an East Prussian. My mother is dead. My father is a general—of course. What shall I do? I do not want anything—Tell me what is America. You must say. Is it just a place to work?

Dev nodded.

You see that I am young—I am young, of course. You come to me carrying a message. I do not know what to do. I believe you will tell me. I am not a fool—and I am not gifted either. There is nothing for me. Is there? I cannot walk about letting my hair loose to surprise men because it is so yellow. You perhaps, yes, if you please—and she smiled—but not those whom I do not want. I cannot marry. It makes me sick to marry. But I want, I want. I do not care that I am virgin or not. No. No. That is childish. I cannot remain as I am—but I must—until this (and she tapped her forehead) is satisfied. You have said something to me. What do I say to you?

Dev thought "running wild" that if they should do as he wished they would both end that night in the jail at Frascati hungry and very much disturbed—possibly—but no more than that. Fool.

They speak to me of my body. It is beautiful. For what? Of what use to me?

She talked quite coolly.

Within a few years I must lose this. Why not? and I have nothing else unless it is a mind to have, to have and nothing that I want. Not painting, not music, philosophy, tennis—for old men, young men, for women? No. America, that seems something new.

You would find nothing in America, Evans quickly interposed. The girls there cannot go half a mile out of town for fear a Negro might rape them, or their complexions be spoiled by the weather, or the Japanese come too close or they be buried in snow or baked in summer; or they marry business managers or become secretaries and live together two or three in apartments. Their thoughts are like white grass so heavily have they been covered by their skins—and so heavily covered are they to protect them from the weather that when they are uncovered they do not exist. One must snatch another up quickly from the general supply, from a patent container.—Evans was ashamed of this speech of which as a fact Fräulein von J. understood not one word. But the few women he had admired were not pretty and the pretty ones he did not admire.—Never think of America, he concluded. The men are worse than the women.

Are you then one?

Evans had no reply.

When I saw you, I saw something unusual, I am never mistaken. I saw something different from what I see every day, neither throwing away nor taking hold to the old horrible handle, all filthy—Is it America? I asked, but you tell me nothing. It is because you will not do so.

America, he began again haltingly, is hard to know.

Yes, she answered, because she had made him serious so that he must speak his mind or say nothing.

I think it is useful to us, he continued, because it is near savagery. In Europe, you are so far from it that maybe you will have to die first before you will live again.—But Dev was not such a fool.—Europe, I do not know, he corrected himself, I am seeing a few superficial moments only.

But he had a quick pupil.—That is enough, replied Fräulein von J. I see now what I saw at the beginning. You are a savage, not quite civilized—you have America and we have not. You have that, yes, it is something.

It is very difficult, said Dev. I am not a typical American. We have a few natives left but they would not know me—

You are holding on to something, she said.

It is very difficult, Dev went on—something very likely to be lost, this is what—So he took out the flint arrowhead he had in his pocket and showed it to her.

She was impressed. She held it hard in her hand as if to keep its impression there, felt the point, the edge, tried it, turned it over.

Yes, she said, I have seen the same thing from our own fields, more finished work—but it is very far, very far. No one believes it is real. But this you carry in your coat? It is very strange. Where did you find it?

In a corn-field in Virginia, there are many of them there.

Are there many Americans who know this that you are saving?

Dev shook his head. I have seen but a few. There are pictures pressed into my mind, which have a great power of argument. Summer pictures mostly, of my part of the country, one of the old pioneer houses fast to the ground. There is nothing like them in Europe. They were not peasants, the people who built them, they were tragic men who wasted their wits on the ground—but made a hard history for me—not for me only, I think; they were like all earlier peoples but it has been so quick and misplaced in America, this early phase, that it is lost or misinterpreted—its special significance.

You think then it might be useful to—me? Yes, that was what I saw in your eyes—She looked again. Yes, it is so.

She shook her head gently from side to side in marveling realization. Come, she said, I was right. What an America is that! Why then did you not look at me all this week? I was troubled. I wondered what was the matter with me.

Dev said he had been excited studying something he wanted among the antiquities.

But a feeling almost of terror, Dev thought, mixed with compassion perhaps, came now into her eyes as she continued to look at him.

It must be even more lonesome and frightening in America

than in Germany, she said. She shook her head. She seemed
as if looking off into a new country and to be feeling the
lonesomeness of it.

America is marvelous, replied Dev, grossly prosperous—
She shuddered, No. So were we. So will we be soon again.
—She was frightened.—How can you stay where you are?
Why do you stay there? You make the church impossible—
but you are alone. I will pray for you.

They started to get up quietly from their serious mood and
were rather startled to find themselves still in the surround-
ings of the pagan grove. Not too sure were they that they
knew each other as well as they had been feeling they did for
the few moments of hard sympathetic understanding just
past, projecting themselves out; each feeling, each trying
hard, to get at the other's mood. They laughed, and Dev gave
her his hand but she did not move away.

It is very difficult, she said, for us to support ourselves after
we have passed the semi-consciousness of the peasant, and his
instincts. We fall back, do we not? You are brave, she said, to
want to find some other way—and one that is American. It
seems curious to me.

Moving to rejoin Frau M. they saw that it was getting on
into the afternoon and that they must be stepping along if
they would be back in Rome by nightfall.

You believe in America like a church, mused Fräulein von
J. almost to herself.

Dev did not think so.

Do you believe then that the church is an enemy to your
belief?

Yes.

She looked away.

Oh come on, said Dev, let's get out of this.